LADY *of the* NIGHT

Richard B. Hayman

iUniverse, Inc.
Bloomington

Lady of the Night

Copyright © 1996, 2012 Richard B. Hayman

iUniverse books may be ordered through booksellers or by contacting:

iUniverse
1663 Liberty Drive
Bloomington, IN 47403
www.iuniverse.com
1-800-Authors (1-800-288-4677)

ISBN: 978-1-4697-9576-8 (sc)
ISBN: 978-1-4697-9578-2 (hc)
ISBN: 978-1-4697-9577-5 (e)

Printed in the United States of America

iUniverse rev. date: 4/5/2012

Cover photograph of a painting by artist Gary Sheahan was
provided courtesy of the Winnetka Historical Society.

To my son Rik, a fellow reader and a fellow writer.

The poem "Pond in the Wood" by Elizabeth A. Hayman printed with permission of the author. The author's photograph appears courtesy of the photographer, Brenna D. Hayman.

Preface

My wife and I retired from teaching the same year. My son, Rik, said to me, "Dad, you need a project to keep you out of Mom's hair. Why not write a book?" When I asked if he had any suggestions, Rik, at that time a reporter for the *Milwaukee Sentinel*, pointed to the *Lady Elgin* disaster. That was all I needed. As I pursued the story, I found it tragic, fascinating, and far-reaching. Credit is due to Rik for giving me the idea and for his prodigious editing of the final manuscript.

Thanks to my wife, Elizabeth, for allowing me to use her poem, "Pond in the Wood." Elizabeth's maiden name is Flynn, the first name of a character in my novel. Any resemblance is purely intentional.

Acknowledgment is due to my grandchildren, Ryan and Chris Westa, who form the basis of the characters of Brian and Liam. If any of my other friends or relatives think they find themselves in my book, who am I to say that they are not?

Daniel Flynn was helpful in providing electronic assistance. Thanks to Deborah, Joel, Katelyn, Meaghan, Brenna, Bridget, Kevin, Kathleen, and Erica for moral support. The memory of my mother Dorothy, a writer and a poet, contributed to the success of this project.

I appreciate the research assistance provided by Mrs. James Maher and the Irish Cultural and Heritage Center of Milwaukee. I am also grateful to the Winnetka Historical Society, Executive Director Patti Van Cleave, and Curator Katie Macica.

Finally, I would like to thank the Irish. As Elizabeth likes to say, "There are two types of people in the world: those who are Irish and those who wish they were Irish."

Prologue

Caw! Caw! Caw! A black cloud of angry crows ascended from the clearing with wing-thumping cacophony as thirty riders on horseback emerged from deep within a remote forest in Milwaukee. They rode hard and fast, dazzling the crows with yelping and hollering and shooting their rifles into the air. Dust filled the late Saturday sky, obliterating the April sun. The men were young, faces painted with Celtic symbols, likenesses of tribal warriors in the ancient days of the High Kings of Ireland. They converged in the center of the meadow, shouting, "Cuchulain! Cuchulain!"

Out of the pines on a handsome black horse came the hero Cuchulain, a band of gold around his head and a fierce wolfhound embroidered into his long green-and-orange robe. Beneath the robe he wore a white ruffled shirt, black leggings, and boots. Instead of a rifle, he carried a spear. As he charged into the midst of cheering men, he waved the spear and screamed "Aaayee!"

The men dismounted and led the horses to nearby trees for tethering and then returned to the center of the meadow to stand in formation for muster. Cuchulain took roll.

"Lugh."

"Here."

"Conor."

"Here."

"Conmael."

"Here."

So it went on, each man responding proudly to his chosen name, each name that of a Celtic hero. The man called Cuchulain spoke, his deep voice filling the meadow.

"Horsemen, well done. This is not the Union Guard. This is more than a game. We must prepare for war. You know the enemy, and the enemy is real. We will break into groups. If you are hurt, you must deal with it. There are no doctors here to mend you. If you need something to hate, think of a man with a face like a horse and the nancy voice of a British lord. Fall out."

Groups formed in various parts of the meadow in clusters of three or four. Soon the dust that had settled from the horses clouded the area again, causing much coughing and cursing as the young god-heroes went at each other in mock battle. Fists crunched against flesh. Kicking and biting were followed by moaning and grunting. Blood flowed from orifices and the colors of the day were black and blue. Rifles discharged and men lay still in a pose of death.

Cuchulain flew from cluster to cluster, shouting encouragement and taking part in the fray. Several bruisers attacked Cuchulain and landed in the dust. One did manage to get him down, only to find his own arms pinned to the ground.

The ballet began to slow down. A cannon on wheels appeared from behind a bush guarded by three cannoneers who were making a combined effort to load and fire the weapon. The effort failed because the cannon brigade was besieged by other groups. There was a loud boom. The cannon exploded in a puff of smoke. The ball hurtled across the meadow into a clump of pines, disturbing a flock of furious crows and sending the tethered horses into a frenzy.

The success of the cannoneers in firing the weapon signaled the end of the activity. They returned the cannon to its place of concealment. The men stopped struggling and returned to the center of the meadow, some flushed with pride while others looked sheepish. Cuchulain remounted his black horse and waited for all the men to return.

Together again, the men stood in military formation. Cuchulain surveyed them critically. "Were there any fatalities?" There was an outburst of laughter. He smiled. "You're a spirited tribe of lads, but you are badly in need of direction. Order must proceed from chaos. In the weeks to come you will learn strategies. Each of you will plan an entire battle. There is no substitute for guts, provided you use your brains."

The men began to chant, "Cuchulain! Cuchulain!" He raised his spear for silence. "The sun is setting. We must return to our other ways of life. I caution you to breathe no word of our brotherhood to a soul, not even wives or parents. Our safety and theirs depends upon absolute secrecy. Before we part, here are words of inspiration." Speaking in Gaelic, he recited words from the epic Celtic poem "The Cattle Raid of Coolie." Interpretation was unnecessary. One of the rules of the brotherhood was that each member should learn Gaelic. He raised his spear again.

"Before we part company, let us part the leaves with a hearty Celtic yell." Thirty voices joined in a prolonged war cry that would have deafened the enemy, had the enemy been nearby. Then the men headed for their horses and were gone, leaving alone the man they called Cuchulain.

He dismounted the stallion and stripped, folding the robe, leggings, and shirt into a cloth sack on the saddle. As he stood naked by his horse, he imagined himself a true Celtic chief. Many times warriors of old fought in the nude. Then Cuchulain donned his everyday apparel and became Jack O'Mara, son of a Milwaukee grocer. The year was 1860. Jack was one of Feeney's Boys.

Part One

The Bloody Third

Chapter One

"Stay out of trouble, Blevins."

"Yes, Ma."

"You know how I worry when you're down there."

"No need to worry, Ma."

Blevins mounted the old steed and waved to his mother, who stood at the entrance of the family home in a residential district of Milwaukee. "And stay away from O'Mara's grocery store." Blevins grinned and said nothing. His mother's eyes twinkled. Dorothy Morgan, younger in spirit than her seventy years, had a Gaelic wit, a mixture of Welsh and Irish.

"But if you must visit O'Mara, Blevins Morgan, do give my regards to his pretty young daughter Flynn and tell her she's not to be stealin' away my son."

Blevins chuckled. "Bye, Ma." He nudged the old steed, who headed reluctantly down Wisconsin toward the center. He didn't plan to go to O'Mara's today. Today he had work to do. He would have to forego the pleasure of being with Flynn. He directed the old steed past various business establishments that constituted downtown Milwaukee. There were the usual fancy carriages and stylish dressers associated with any downtown area, but this was not London, New York, or Boston. Even Chicago was staid compared with the frontier town of Milwaukee in the mid-nineteenth century.

Milwaukee had a rough-hewn atmosphere in which success was measured by hard work. The affluent had gained their wealth by earning it or stealing it. There was no scarcity of fortune dishonestly gained. The law was treated casually even by its enforcers. People were safe enough during the daylight, but trouble was never far beneath the surface.

Blevins's old man, "Wild Bill" Morgan, was a blustery, two-fisted Welshman who owned a print shop, the success of which enabled the Morgans to own a home in a middle-class neighborhood. In the shop, Blevins printed a weekly newspaper he hoped to expand into a daily.

He arrived in the heart of the roughest section of town, a neighborhood of Irish immigrants, most of whom were first generation. The monthly arrival of Irish fleeing from famine and workhouses made this the fastest-growing section of Milwaukee. Politically, the section was designated the Third Ward. People called it the "Bloody Third."

Although Blevins lived in another part of town, his newspaper, the *Third Gazette*, focused on the people and events of the ward. There was never a scarcity of news. It was Blevins's hope to gain the support of the politicians in the predominantly Democratic district. To get ahead nowadays, a small newspaper had to be partisan. Even most large newspapers were committed. Of course, the fact that Blevins was courting Flynn O'Mara, daughter of an influential Democrat, didn't hurt. Blevins wished that grocer Dan O'Mara was more enthusiastic about the alliance.

Blevins waved to Father Delaney, who was on his way from St. Patrick's parish hall to the church to hear confessions. St. Patrick's was the social hub of the ward. Dinners, picnics, and other gatherings were well attended. Father Delaney himself was an immigrant from the county of Knock. Young and personable, he was the object of wistful sighing among the ladies, who considered it a shame that such a catch should be wasted on the priesthood.

Dances were held Saturday nights at the parish hall, frequently attended by the young bucks of Barry's Irish Brigade, the local division of Wisconsin's Union Guard. On such nights, traditional Irish jigs and reels were played. The melodic sounds of tin whistles, bagpipes, and drums filled the air. The old Celtic ways were hard to set aside. After years of Christianity, the church had been unable to completely eradicate ancient pagan influence.

Blevins was not Catholic. He considered it ironic that the only cathedral in Ireland named after the patron saint was Protestant. St. Patrick's in Dublin was Church of England. Its dean had been Jonathan Swift, author of *Gulliver's Travels*. Many Protestants despised

England's policies toward Ireland. Dean Swift wrote a scathing tome condemning England's inhumanity. The issue of Irish independence was not religious. Wolfe Tone, martyred leader of the United Irishmen in the Rising of 1798, had himself been Protestant. Blevins made his sympathies known and was welcome everywhere in the Third Ward.

A banner waved over Feeney's Pub declaring: WARD THREE FOR THE LITTLE GIANT. It was an election year. It was Lincoln vs. Douglas, as the issue of slavery raged across the land. Stephen Douglas held overwhelming support from the staunchly Democratic Irish.

It was too early in the day for a pint, so Feeney's would have to wait. The pub was a good place to pick up gossip. Feeney himself was an odd duck who had arrived from the old country carrying nothing but a tattered leather satchel. In no time at all, Feeney had established the most frequented watering hole in the Bloody Third, patronized by an assortment of unsavory characters. How Feeney had raised the money in the first place was a dark secret.

"Blevins, you auld Welshman," shouted Sergeant Flaherty. Blevins dismounted in front of the police precinct. "When are you going to get yourself a decent horse?"

"I have one," Blevins laughed and patted the rump of the old steed.

"At least get yourself a sweeter rump to pat. I know where you can get one."

"Have you no shame, Officer, have you no shame?"

They entered the building. Lieutenant Hogan sat behind his desk, chewing on a fat cigar. "Flaherty! Where the hell have you been? You're supposed to be out protectin' the good people of the ward. Here you are, strollin' in one hour late."

"In the line of duty, Lieutenant. I had to stop a catfight between two colleens at Mrs. Murphy's boarding house. Good thing for them I happened along." Flaherty winked.

"In the line of duty, is it? Knowing you, I'd guess you started the fight. I hear you're on intimate terms with the widow Murphy."

"Oh no, sir, not at all."

Hogan sighed, releasing a billow of cigar smoke that drifted to the ceiling, forming an ugly black cloud. "Head to the waterfront, Sergeant. Coupla' ships due in from Chicago. May be trouble." Flaherty shrugged and sauntered out of the room. Blevins's ears perked up.

"Expecting trouble?"

"Not really. Say, you're not going to report that crap about Mrs. Murphy, are you?"

"That depends. Can you give me a better story? What's going on?"

"Just the usual, Morgan. A domestic quarrel or two. The brawls at Feeney's. Oh, and someone tried to deface the Little Giant poster in front of the pub. Probably a German from the other side of town. Say, there's a story for you."

"Doesn't sound like much of a story to me. Isn't this the Bloody Third? Have the lawbreakers moved to another ward, or are you lads just not doing your jobs?"

"We always do our jobs." Hogan puffed on the cigar, flicking hot ash into a standing ashtray next to his desk. "Nasty habit," he grinned, "but it won't hurt if you don't inhale. Did you know about the fire?" There was no window to ventilate the room. Blevins wondered how Hogan could avoid inhaling.

"Fire?"

"The Buckley residence burned to the ground. Did you know them? No? Terrible loss. Thank God no one was killed. The thing is, it didn't need to happen. The conflagration was avoidable." Hogan didn't have many fifty-dollar words in his vocabulary. Blevins supposed "conflagration" was one of them. If Hogan wasn't careful with his glowing cigar, there would be a conflagration in the police station.

"Aren't most fires caused by carelessness?"

"Ah, me boyo, you haven't heard the half of it. Who knows what caused the fire? At first, it was a small blaze. It was the firemen themselves let things get out of control. Donnelly and O'Farrell. It was their fault, really."

There were two volunteer fire departments in the Third Ward, and they were fiercely competitive. Blevins had an inkling of what Hogan was about to say. "Tell me, Lieutenant, which of the two groups arrived first?"

"Well, that's the thing, you see. Both volunteer gangs arrived at the same time. They got into a hell of a brawl, threw buckets at each other, stamped and cursed, and while the donnybrook was raging the house burned to the ground."

"Talk of too much of a good thing. The Buckley family, what became of them?"

"They're holed up in the parish hall until a suitable replacement home can be found. That should be soon. Father Delaney held the volunteers responsible. You should have heard Father at church. He said that Donnelly and O'Farrell better call a truce or they'll be dealing with eternal fire, if you know what I mean."

"It might be worthwhile to visit St. Patrick's, if I have time."

"While you're there, maybe Father will hear your confession."

"He'd have to beat it out of me. If that's all you have, I guess I'll be going. I was hoping for a murder or two."

"Come back tomorrow. Maybe you'll get lucky, you bloodthirsty prod." Hogan pulled a huge sandwich out of the desk drawer.

"Are you going to eat that whole sandwich right now?"

"What of it?"

"Maybe I'll stay and watch. It may be the big story of the day. Police lieutenant chokes on sandwich after inhaling foul-smelling cigar."

"I don't inhale. Get out of here, Morgan. Go peddle your papers."

Hogan had mentioned that there were ships due today, so Blevins headed down to the waterfront. He liked to watch the bustle of activity when the Great Lakes ships arrived. Several dock workers acknowledged Blevins, who was a familiar face. He ignored Sergeant Flaherty, who leaned on a mooring post and gabbed with two women who were always around when a ship arrived.

"Hey, Mick!" Blevins shouted. Several Irish dockers turned to glare at him. When they realized that he was addressing a coworker and not hurling an ethnic insult, they returned to their work. Mick, a burly, bare-chested youth with an anchor tattooed on his left bicep, nodded. "What's on the schedule this morning?"

"The *Lady*," Mick pointed. Sure enough, a speck appeared on the Lake Michigan horizon. The *Lady* was what the dock workers called the *Lady Elgin*, the most popular passenger ship in the Midwest. Owned by the Gordon S. Hubbard Company of Chicago and named after the wife of Lord Elgin of Canada. The *Lady Elgin* was a three-hundred-foot luxury paddlewheel steamer, a floating hotel that made pleasure cruises along Lake Michigan.

"Stick around and watch her dock," said Mick. "It'll only be a half hour, and she's a magnificent sight."

"I wish I could, but I have to go." The morning had been a waste, but the afternoon held promise. Hogan had given him a lead. There had been an outbreak of fires in the ward. Maybe there was a story in that. He nudged the old steed into a reluctant trot and headed for St. Patrick's.

Chapter Two

"WHEN YOU WORK, WORK. WHEN you play, play," Dan O'Mara advised a customer, who had heard it many times. "But when you play, stay away from John Barleycorn. Liquor, thank God I never touched it."

Flynn tried to imagine her temperate, seventy-year-old da at play. A man of immense energy, he had dedicated his life to hard work as a grocer. Like many men of Ireland, he had married late and had been in his forties when Flynn was born.

"Would you hand me a bag for that candy, darlin'?"

Flynn watched him fill the bag and hand it to a little girl with blonde curls and a radiant smile. Flynn helped the girl's mother take the groceries to a wagon outside the store. This was her brother's job, but Jack was at a Union Guard drill.

"'Tis a fine girl you are, and the apple of my eye."

Flynn was indeed the apple of her da's eye. The O'Maras had been childless the first few years of marriage. Just as they were about to give up hope, along came a baby girl. Mother Marion named her Flynn after her maiden name. (Flynn and her beau Blevins thought it hilarious that they both had "last-name first names.") The proud father had doted on Flynn. Nothing was too good for her. If it had been his to give, he would have given her the world. She was tiny, an attribute inherited from both parents. She had long, blonde hair.

Jack was born two years later, followed by Maggie. Growing up, they complained that Flynn was the favorite child, which was true. If Flynn had wished it to be otherwise, she couldn't have made it so. The truth was that she had no wish to change her favored status.

"Where's that big lummox?"

"Blevins? He's working."

"Working? Is that what you call what he does?"

"Now, Da—"

"I do hope, darlin', that things aren't getting too serious."

"Blevins and I—"

"He'll never have a pot to piss in."

Flynn was silent. They had been over this before. She always backed down. Eventually there would have to be a major confrontation. She loved Blevins, and if he proposed she would say yes in a minute, in spite of the certain disapproval of friends and family. Blevins was Protestant, not a member of the Irish-Catholic community. He was ambitious and would someday move away, taking her with him. Flynn was an adult, not resigned to wasting her life in the confines of the Bloody Third. If she did not leave with Blevins, she would leave with someone else.

"Tall, dark, and not so handsome," Da joked about Blevins, who towered over Flynn. Maggie, in one of her spiteful moods, asked if Flynn used a stepladder when she kissed him. "Or do you lie down for him?" Flynn ignored Maggie, which was the only way to deal with her jealous younger sister.

A large, overweight man, balding and wearing red suspenders, entered the store. Da beamed. Councilman Garrity was an old friend, a crony. He was ward boss of the Democratic Party. Flynn sighed. She knew she'd be in for a talk marathon. Da loved politics and was highly regarded among the young partisans, who often sought his opinion. Councilman "Garrulous" Garrity, not much younger than Da, visited frequently, sometimes leaving the store without purchasing the groceries his wife had sent him to get.

"So, Councilman, how does it look for Douglas?"

Garrity lit his pipe and puffed on it before responding. "Wisconsin is divided. Douglas wants the states to decide on slavery. Well, you know, he spearheaded the Kansas-Nebraska Act. Lincoln, he wants it all one way under the federal government. The Democrats are split, and the South is putting up its own candidates. It doesn't look good for Douglas. I only say this to you, Dan. As you know, the ward is solidly behind the Little Giant."

"Doesn't personality count for anything? Douglas is the most eloquent orator in the nation."

"There are those who think Lincoln to be a man of the people. Not eloquent, perhaps, but down-to-earth and in touch with the common man."

"You wouldn't be thinking about switching sides?"

"Bite your tongue," Garrity laughed. "Say, Dan, I understand that Douglas is planning to speak in Chicago sometime down the line. What do you think of a group of us going? We could sail on the *Lady Elgin*. Make a day of it. Even take the ladies."

"I'd have to think about it. I don't know if I could leave the store."

Flynn sat behind the candy counter, half listening and half dreaming. She imagined herself cruising on the *Lady Elgin,* wind blowing through her hair, dampened by the cool fresh water spray of Lake Michigan. Flynn had never been anywhere. Oh, when she was a child she had come across the sea with the family, but she barely remembered that. She yearned to go to Chicago, but she knew Da would never let her go alone.

Garrity was still at it. "Did you know, Dan, that Governor Randall recently defied the law and refused to return fugitive slaves to their rightful owners?"

"Alexander Randall did that?"

"The governor is in constant battle with Washington. In Wisconsin, though, he's a hero. The federal government is deputizing marshals to come out here and track the slaves. It's a power struggle. Randall insists that it is up to the state."

"That damned Fugitive Slave Act." Da rested his backside on a pickle barrel. As he warmed into the subject, his nose reddened. Da had a bulbous nose, the result of a skin disorder and not, as some folks thought, the result of drinking. *"A slave cannot become free by escaping to a free state. The slave must be apprehended and returned to slavery.* I equate it with the idea of returning immigrant Irish to live under the oppressive yoke of English tyranny."

"I wish you'd return to politics, Dan. At one time you were a real force. You could be that force again."

Da laughed. His nose had become bright red. "I've had my day, Garrity. Let the young carry the torch. You know where I stand. God bless you, councilor."

Two customers entered. Flynn waited on them while Da and Garrity continued talking. After a while, Garrity left without remembering to buy anything. Other customers came and went. Her brother Jack burst into the store, colliding with a customer who dropped a sack of potatoes. The sack split. Potatoes rolled merrily to the far corner of the store. Jack scurried to retrieve them and put them in a new sack. Then he helped the customer take the potatoes and other groceries to a wagon outside.

Da was angry. He scolded Jack for driving away customers. Jack began to get hot under the collar, and Flynn sensed a storm brewing. It was always this way. Jack deserved to be scolded, but Da would go too far until Jack exploded. It was a tempest in a teapot and neither of them was able to stop.

"Da, it was an accident. For heaven's sake, be more careful, Jack."

Jack grinned sheepishly, and Da mumbled under his breath. That was that. Jack, home from a Union Guard drill, was late relieving Flynn in the store. Jack had been late too many times during the last few months. Flynn was sure there was something going on with him, but she hadn't made an issue of it so far.

"Can you two get along without killing each other?"

"Don't worry about it," Da said, and winked.

"Thanks," replied Flynn, not at all reassured. Flynn was exhausted. She wanted to bathe and go to bed. Mother had fallen asleep crocheting in the rocker. Maggie was playing with a doll on the plaid divan.

"For the love of God, Maggie, you're too old to be playing with dolls. You're sixteen and should be taking your turn in the store."

"Oh, Jesus. Jesus, Mary, and Joseph."

"Don't be blasphemous. You're hanging around too much with that slut down the road. What's her name? Look at Mother, asleep with no blanket. Wouldn't you think that you—"

"You're such a boss."

Flynn took a blanket from the divan, crossed to the rocker, and covered her mother's shoulders and legs. "I'm going to bed. Jack's in the store with Da."

"Do what you want. You always do."

"Good night, Maggie." Maggie pouted. Flynn headed upstairs. Was this the fate of eldest children, to be envied by their siblings? She tried not to let it bother her. She had earned it. She'd helped her parents more than Maggie and Jack combined, and she was more responsible than either of them.

Flynn undressed and took a sponge bath, using the large ceramic bowl on the dresser. She slipped on a robe and sat on the edge of the bed brushing her long, blonde hair. The brush strokes soothed her. Warm thoughts of Blevins lulled her into a pleasant trance.

Feeney had spent his early childhood on a farm in County Mayo, born and raised a country boy in Ireland. The memory of his father's voice was evoked from deep within himself.

"It was a fine race, my boy, the race of Castlebar. The British army led by Cornwallis himself marched into town and were met by simple farmers like your da, using only pikes and pitchforks."

"Why did they call it a race, Da?" Young Feeney knew why. He'd heard the story many times, but he never tired hearing it. Da guffawed, a merry twinkle appearing in his deep, blue eyes.

"It was the summer of 1798, you know. Wolfe Tone's United Irishmen invited the French to help drive the cursed English from our land."

"Yes, I know." The boy was eager for his da to get to the good part. "Why a race, Da? Who raced in Castlebar?"

"Why, the British, to be sure, or didn't you know? They marched into Castlebar with loaded guns and raced out with us in hot pursuit— we with our pikes and pitchforks, no guns, your auld man leadin' the parade."

Da boasted of having been a personal friend of Wolfe Tone, the martyred leader of the Rising of '98. The astonishing Irish victory at Castlebar was followed by tragic defeat. In the long run, the ragtag rebels were no match for the massive British army, Lord Cornwallis still stinging from losing the colonies. The support of a small fleet of ships from France, recruited by Wolfe Tone, hadn't been enough. The uprising failed, the French went home, and Tone cheated the executioner by taking his own life.

Da had returned to Mayo to tell the story again and again to an appreciative son and anyone else who would listen. The dream of nationhood faded. The British exacted reprisal, scouring the countryside, imprisoning people at random. No thought was given to due process or the right to trial. One afternoon the soldiers came to the farm, arriving at dusk with a force much larger than needed to subdue an aging, unarmed farmer with a small family.

"Leave my da alone, you nancy English cowards!" He spit at them as they tied his father's arms and legs. Three soldiers dragged the tethered old man onto an open wagon. The boy attacked them and was flung to the ground. "Cowards! Cowards of Castlebar! You can't lock up my da. He didn't do anything." Rising, he was flung down again. Ma was shaking her head and staring. His sister Mary was sobbing.

"You'll regret it. I won't rest until my father is free. I won't rest until Ireland is free."

"So that's the way it is," smirked the leader, winking at the other men. "Torch the farm. Burn it to the ground."

The order was executed. Amid flames and billows of black smoke, the soldiers departed with old Feeney thrashing on the wagon. In stunned silence, young Feeney, his sister, and his mother sat on the lawn and watched the flames consume their home and belongings. If he closed his eyes, he could see the flames as if it had been yesterday. If he had kept his mouth shut, it might never have happened. The flames burned guilt into his brain. He had become a Fenian and had come to America with an agenda.

So here he was on a fine Sunday morning strolling along the lake instead of attending Mass. The pub was closed on Sunday. It was the law, this being a holy day. He wasn't a churchgoing man. Because of the church, Ireland had become a matriarch. The men had become emasculated, first by the British, then by the church. Ireland would never be entirely free until it also got out from under the yoke of the church.

That meant returning to the past. Young lads needed role models who could be found in the heroes of old—before the English—before St. Patrick. He had found the young men, spirited Irish Americans, here in Milwaukee. They would become Gaelic-speaking warriors. With the help of the Brotherhood, they would return to the old country with a thirst for English blood.

Soon the world would know of Feeney's Boys.

Chapter Three

Near the town of Sligo in County Donegal, the flat top of Ben Bulben commands a view of Drumcliff and the sea beyond. Maeve O'Neill dreamed of Ben Bulben as her fingers stroked the harp. It was on Ben Bulben that her namesake Maeve, Celtic Queen of Connaught, was buried. A mound marked her burial site where visitors came, climbing the mountain to see the grave, which was called the Mound of Maeve. Village *garsúns* winked and made snide remarks about what the mound might signify.

The faces of the crowd gathered in St. Patrick's hall blurred in Maeve's vision as her thoughts returned to Donegal. Her hands and fingers coaxed cascades of celestial chords from the bardic instrument, moving without instruction from her mind. Her mind was in Bundoran, where she was born, and in the Irish village of Killibegs, where she had one day awaited her fisherman husband, who had never returned. Drowned in a storm, his bloated body had floated in with the tide and was identified by the pattern woven into his woolen sweater.

Maeve paused to allow waves of applause to wash over her. She spotted her two young sons in the hall. Brian was eleven and Liam was ten. The concert was the only weekly social event they were allowed to attend. The lads were sometimes bored, but other children were there competing in the high-step supervised by Father Delaney, who did a mean high-step of his own. Brian and Liam were good dancers, performing with wild abandon, cheered on by the less daring youths. Maeve encouraged them in music. Brian had no interest. Liam tried the tin whistle, producing what could only be described as a shrill squeak.

Maeve began a livelier number attributed to Carrilan, the last of the great Celtic harpists. Caught in the spirit, people clapped to the music. Brian and Liam danced. They had been the reason that Maeve had decided to journey to America. Had the boys remained in Killibegs, they would have become fishermen. Maeve had loved their father and mourned his death. She vowed that she would not lose her sons to the sea.

Maeve, Brian, and Liam had crossed the Atlantic on a sturdy passenger ship, using part of Maeve's savings to avoid the perils of a coffin ship. Her harp playing and weaving enabled her to put money aside, and she had a small inheritance. She was a descendent of Hugh O'Neill, a seventeenth-century earl who had fled Ireland after England crushed the Gaelic nobility.

Her plan had been to avoid the seacoast of America, with its reliance upon the fishing industry. In Ireland, no place was far from the sea. She chose Milwaukee because it was an inland city with an Irish population, even though the Third Ward did not have a strong reputation. The size of Lake Michigan had flabbergasted her. To Maeve, a large lake was Lough Gil, near Sligo, or Lough Corrib, in Connemara. As a child, she had vacationed with her family on the lakes of Killarney, serene and placid. Men rarely drowned in the lakes of Ireland.

Her first thought on seeing Lake Michigan was, "Dear God, I've come this far only to find another ocean." But she liked Milwaukee and concluded that the lake, large as it was, was not as threatening as the roiling Atlantic.

Carrilan's song ended, but the audience wanted more. When the applause diminished, the hall became quiet, as the encore began. To the harp Maeve added a second instrument, her voice. Her voice was clear and soft, as it lilted o'er the hall.

> 'Twas early, early in the spring,
> The birds did whistle and sweetly sing
> Changing their notes from tree to tree,
> And the song they sang was old Ireland free.

Jack was transfixed by Maeve's stunning rendition of "The Croppy Boy." The performance filled him not with sadness for the doomed boy, but with desire for the dark-haired Maeve. In his life, he had not imagined such beauty. Willowy and graceful, with swanlike hands that floated over harp strings creating ripples of harmonious sound, Maeve had deep-blue eyes and an enigmatic smile with an aura that was haunting and regal.

In a past life, she might have been a queen. The concept was in conflict with his Catholic rearing. Many of Jack's recent thoughts and actions were in conflict with the teachings of the church. Right now, Jack wanted Maeve. He would have her, any way he could.

Maeve was near perfection. One blemish marred an otherwise classic beauty. On her left cheek was a soft, brown mole. The tiny mound fueled Jack's imagination, and he began to think of it perversely as the Mound of Maeve. In ancient times, Queen Maeve of Connaught had warred against the hero Cuchulain of Ulster in the Cattle Raid of Coolie, rendered in verse by the bardic epic narrative, "The Tain." Cuchulain had conquered Maeve and kidnapped a legendary bull with unusual propagation abilities. Jack fancied himself to be Cuchulain. Cuchulain had conquered Queen Maeve just as Jack would conquer Maeve-with-Mole. Propagation was no small part of his fantasy.

Maeve was on the last stanza of "The Croppy Boy."

> 'Twas in old Ireland this young man died,
> And in old Ireland his body laid;
> All the good people that do pass by,
> Pray the Lord have mercy on the croppy boy.

A tear trickled from Flynn's eye as Maeve finished the encore. Ireland had a sad history. Although there was no sadness in her own family, she was moved by stories she had heard. She had grown up in the parish and attended the parish school under Sister Katherine and Sister Marie. Flynn had not traveled beyond the ward, other than a few trips to the fair in Madison. Flynn knew there had been sadness in Maeve's life.

When Maeve had arrived in the ward, she had been met with a cool reception. A beautiful young widow with two boys and independent ways was a threat to the matrons of the community. To make matters worse, she didn't care. She set up housekeeping in a small home with a plot of land and a garden, and she kept to herself. In time, she grew on folks. The boys attended Mass. Maeve helped at picnics, played the harp, hated the British, contributed to the church, and kept a low sexual profile. Once the other women knew that she had no designs on their husbands, they gradually accepted her.

The one drawback was that she was not a devout Catholic. She befriended Father Delaney, who tried to bring her into the fold, but she would have none of it. The boys, however, took instructions in the faith.

Flynn had been watching Jack watching Maeve. Although Flynn was inexperienced, she recognized the nature of Jack's gaze. Alarm bells clanged in her head. Jack liked to brag about his exploits, but Flynn knew it was all bluster. Jack was romantic, but naïve. She wondered if he was taking on more than he could handle. She supposed he was a man now, no longer her baby brother.

"Oh!" Flynn exclaimed, feeling a hand on her shoulder. She turned. Blevins grinned apologetically.

"I didn't mean to startle you. You seemed deep in thought. A penny for your thoughts."

"My thoughts are worth more than a penny."

"How much?"

"You couldn't afford it."

"Were you thinking of me?"

"No."

Maeve had been replaced by a traditional Irish band, which burst into a loud, foot-stomping reel featuring tin whistles, bagpipes, and bohdran.

"Let's get out of here."

"What? I can't hear you."

"Let's go for a ride."

"Where are we going and how will we get there?"

"Come on. I have a cab waiting."

Flynn resisted, but not much, as Blevins led her toward the door. Her sister Maggie, who was doing a flagrant high-step with Brian, caught Flynn's eyes and smirked wickedly. "I'll be in trouble with Da when I get home," Flynn mumbled, "but it'll be worth it." Blevins led her to the horse-drawn cab and climbed in beside her.

"Lookout Hill," he ordered the coachman.

"Look out, Flynn," she quipped, and they both laughed. She snuggled close to him. "We can't be gone too long. I have a curfew. I was supposed to stay at the parish hall. My snotty sister saw us leave together."

"You're a big girl now. You don't need your parents' permission."

"Mostly my father. Oh, I know, I know. They worry about me. I do live there, and I feel obligated to follow their rules."

"When we live together, there will be no rules."

"Shush," said Flynn, wishing to avoid that issue. "Let's just be quiet."

The horses' hooves went clip-clop in hypnotic rhythm. The moon beamed through the cab window illuminating the lovers as they kissed, drawn into a world of self where no one else existed.

Lookout Hill was one of the scenic attractions of Milwaukee. Adjacent to North Point Lighthouse, it was located within acreage owned by Gustav Lueddemann, who opened up the grounds as a public park known as Lueddemann's-on-the-Lake. There was a picnic area and benches, usually crowded on Sundays and holidays. The location offered a view of the city and a wide expanse of Lake Michigan. It was not crowded now. No one else was there. Blevins signaled the coachman to pull over, asking him to wait. Blevins and Flynn strolled to the benches and sat on one of them.

"Some people would think we were daft, coming here at night to see a view in the dark."

"Oh Blevins, it's … it's enchanting."

"I doubt many have seen the view by moonlight."

The moon cast a fairyland atmosphere, bathing the woods and lake in magical light and creating mysterious shadows. The warm, flickering glow of candled windows from dimly seen houses in the distance suggested an elegant landscape.

"I discovered this place one moonlit night when I was nine," Blevins said.

"My, my. Were you courting at that age?"

"It wasn't like that. I ran away from home. I went off on an adventure. There was a rumor in the neighborhood that the British were invading Milwaukee with the help of Indians. The rumor was started by other children, not a grain of truth in it, of course."

"Of course."

"I decided to go to Lookout Hill, for the honor of my country. I don't know what I thought I would do. Fight an army with my toy knife? I had no plan, but I was full of patriotism."

"My brave Blevins. Maybe it was the story. You were going to see what was going on and report it back to the neighborhood. This may have foreshadowed your becoming a reporter."

"Could be. Anyway, it wasn't dark when I left the house. A neighbor asked me where I was going. I told him it was none of his business. I got into trouble for that remark later."

"It was a rude thing to say. Your parents never cured you of it. Of saying rude things, I mean."

"True, true, and don't think that you'll cure me, either. Shall I go on?"

"I'm all ears."

"By the time I reached the hill it was dark, and not a soul stirring. The moon was full, as it is now, creating this stunning visual effect. I forgot about my mission and surveyed the view, awestruck. Then I realized that it was night. I was alone and scared. I ran all the way home, where the entire neighborhood was searching for me. My parents were frantic. My father took me into the print shop and whaled me within an inch of my life."

"Blevins, how many girls have you brought up here on a moonlit night?"

"Only you. This is my secret place. No one else knows about it. No one."

She took his hand and moved closer. They sat quietly. She broke the silence. "I have a secret place, too. At least I did. When I was a child there was a place I liked to go to meditate and write."

"Write, you?"

"You needn't think you're the only one who can write, Blevins Morgan. Don't take that male patronizing attitude with me."

"I'm not, really. I'm just surprised. You never mentioned being a writer."

"Women aren't supposed to be intellectual. It may also surprise you to know that I love to read. I have a good head on my shoulders. If I could, I would run my father's grocery store. That will never be. It's a man's world. I say that with no bitterness. It's a fact."

"I thought you wanted to be a teacher."

"Yes. Teaching is a door that is open for me. The point is there are so many doors that are closed. I'm sorry, Blevins. I didn't mean to spoil a lovely moment. I was about to tell you of my secret place."

"Please do."

"When I was a child, there was a wooded area in my neighborhood. In the middle was a quiet pond. When I wanted to escape, I would go to the pond in the woods and never be disturbed."

"I'd like to see the pond."

"It's gone. There are houses there now. I wrote a poem about it, which I will share with you someday."

"I'd like that."

"Do you know what I think, Blevins?"

"What?"

"I think this cab is going to cost you a fortune. We've been here a while."

"Flynn."

They kissed, a long soulful kiss. He wanted more, but she gently pushed him away. "We have to get home or I'll be in trouble. Besides, it's getting cloudy." The moon had disappeared into a field of clouds. They boarded the cab, and Blevins directed the coachman to proceed to O'Mara's. Rain began to fall.

"I love the rain," whispered Flynn. "Sometimes I lie in my bed for hours, listening to the pitter-pat of raindrops on the rooftop. It's so peaceful."

"That's where I'd like to be. In your bed, listening to raindrops."

"It's not listening to raindrops we'd likely be."

The horse sloshed through increasing rain. The cab stopped in front of the O'Mara residence. Blevins started to disembark, but Flynn held his arm. He tried to kiss her, but she held him back. "It's been a lovely evening. Thank you for sharing the view. Don't help me out. You'll just get soaked." Before there was time to argue, she jumped out and ran to the house through the rain she dearly loved.

The cat sat on the bureau, staring at the bed. Maggie huddled under the blankets, trying to ignore the cat, hoping Tiger would leave and let her sleep. She closed her eyes. A small object fell off the bureau, bounced, and rolled across the floor. She peeked over the covers as the cat swatted another pearl, which bounced and rolled across the floor.

"Jesus. Jesus, Mary, and Joseph," she hissed. Tiger, who had heard Maggie's favorite expression many times, hissed back. The cat crouched and leaped off the bureau. The hairy ball of fur sailed across the bedroom, claws extended, landing with a grin on Maggie's chest. "That does it! You miserable, milk-slurping, bird-killing, pearl-whacking poor excuse for a cat! If you were my cat, and not my sister's, you would just have reached the end of your ninth life." She grabbed Tiger roughly by the scruff of the neck and dragged him yowling to the outside door. When she opened the door, she collided with Flynn and dropped the cat. In the road, a horse-drawn carriage was pulling away. Maggie glared at her older sister.

"Oh, are you in trouble. I saw you leave the dance. Da knows. I told him. Nighty-night. I wouldn't want to be in your shoes in the morning." Without waiting for a response, Maggie ran to her room, jumped into bed, and pulled the covers over her head. Flynn sighed. She felt something furry rubbing against her ankle.

"Oh, hello, Tiger. Come with me. I'll give you a nice, soft pillow." Flynn headed upstairs. Tiger had other plans. The cat slunk into Maggie's room with a glint in his eyes.

In Feeney's dream, the farm was burning and men in uniform were dragging his father away. Then darkness. He was searching for Da in a cold, empty room, and the wind was howling. "Da ... Da," he called. A person, not Da, stood behind him in the shadows. Feeney turned slowly, fear in his heart. It was his mother. Her eyes were strange, and she was shaking her head. A cold chill came over him. The flames of the farmhouse burned in her eyes as she stared at him with smoldering accusation. "I'm sorry, Ma," he choked, but she was gone.

He had buried his mother in Glasvenin Cemetery. There had been professional keeners and a black hat procession with hired pallbearers. Sister Mary and he rode to the Dublin graveyard in a red coach drawn by two white horses and driven by a coachman in livery. Mary and he had been the only people attending. It had been a grand send-off, and Mary had never asked how her brother had come up with the money. That night Feeney dreamed of fire.

Chapter Four

RAINDROPS RAN LIKE TEARS DOWN the pane of the attic window in the small apartment above the pub that Feeney called home. From the window he could see the waterfront. The windblown rain and swaying masts reminded him of his Atlantic crossing on a Galway coffin ship in 1848.

In his memory, salt spray had wet his face, a cold gust of wind penetrating his body and chilling his heart as he gripped the rail of the *Primrose*. A vision of recently departed Ireland haunted Feeney. There was a field. Men were crossing the field, pushing wheelbarrows piled with corpses of famine victims. Men, women, and children were shoveling. As each wheelbarrow was dumped, its pusher disappeared into the twilight for another grisly load. There had been many such fields, mass burial grounds for hundreds of starving Irish.

Now Feeney sailed on this dilapidated coffin ship heading due west. How many days had they been at sea? Tonight, like most nights, he remained on deck, preferring the violent weather to the teeming mass of humanity in the forward hold. Feeney longed for sleep. The skeleton of the old vessel creaked and groaned, protesting the onslaught of the high seas. The ship should never have been brought out of retirement. In her prime she had been unsatisfactory. Now she was downright dangerous.

The racket of her labored progress did not drown out the moaning of the emaciated passengers below. The *Primrose* was no wheelbarrow, but she had dumped her share of famine victims into a watery grave. Those who clung to life prayed for renewal in America. Feeney did not pray. If there were an afterlife, he would deal with that when it arose. Now he had other problems. He would not trust in God to solve them. God might not approve.

Feeney sighed, clutching a weather-beaten satchel, the only baggage he had. The piece was ordinary, made from leather and worn from use. Inside were a few articles of clothing and a partly filled pint of whiskey Feeney planned to finish before arriving at customs. The satchel contained a false bottom, under which was a secret compartment holding a fortune in American currency. The compartment also contained a pistol.

There was enough money to feed the bellies of every hungry person on board, but Feeney's plan reached beyond a mere boatload of poor Irish farmers. He was a man with an agenda. With grim satisfaction, he reviewed the plan—the plan to save Ireland from the hated English.

Two swarthy deckhands confronted the daydreaming Feeney. "What's in the bag, farmer boy?" one snarled. Feeney said nothing, hoping the moment would pass. "I asked you, croppy, what's in the bag?"

"Nothing you'd care about. A change of clothes."

"No grog, for instance?" The other deckhand smirked and wet his lips. Feeney cursed silently. They must have noticed him sneaking a pull from the half-empty pint.

"No. Anyway, it's my business."

He turned away, as if to end the matter. The larger of the two deckhands tried to grab the satchel. Feeney turned back with a clenched fist, which he drove square into the assailant's nose with a sickening crunch. Blood gushing from his face, the man screamed and went down. The other man started toward Feeney, who had a cold, menacing look on his face and a large, sharp knife in his hand. The man backed away. "Keep your damned bag and your grog," he muttered. "You ain't no bleedin' farmer boy."

"C'mon," said the other, recovered from Feeney's jab. The two headed aft to find an easier victim.

Feeney slipped the knife into a sheath beneath his shirt. Perhaps he should have taken the pistol out of the bag, but if anyone noticed, he would not remain inconspicuous. For several years now, he had been a dedicated Fenian. He had risen high in the secret organization sworn to overthrow England. He was driven by the flames in his dead mother's eyes and Da's tales of farmers with pitchforks battling an army. A new rising was coming. This time they would be ready, with trained, well-armed freedom fighters.

The money in the satchel was Fenian. Feeney was a recruiter, told that he would find what he sought not in Boston or New York but on the shores of an enormous lake in the town of Milwaukee. Now the satchel was locked in a safe, here in his attic room.

Part of the money had been used to establish the pub. The pub had prospered, enabling him to return the initial investment. He kept a strict accounting. The Brotherhood had not called him to task, but he knew one day they would. They had sent him to Milwaukee partly because of the growing Irish population of the Bloody Third, but there was another reason.

Captain Garrett Barry was in command of the Union Guard, a brigade of Wisconsin militia. The locals called it "Barry's Irish Brigade." Barry was a man of integrity, highly respected in military circles, and somewhat of a hero. It was said that he was incorruptible. Feeney had not tested that theory yet, but he had at least proven that Barry was not invincible.

Every recruit in the Union Guard was Irish American. A few of the older lads were first generation. All of the young men were proud of their heritage and hostile to England. This was a rich field for the plucking. It had been easy to recruit members into his secret army. The training they received from Barry, who was unaware of what went on, would prove invaluable to the cause. At the same time, they were being indoctrinated by Feeney and several individuals who formed the inner circle of Feeney's Boys.

What was needed now, he thought, was a real act of war involving the whole group, a crime that would bond them by making them equally guilty. There is no stronger cement. The boys, he knew, were tired of playing games. This act, whatever it might be, would make a strong statement. It would have to be in the open, but not so open that anyone would be caught. It would be sudden and unexpected. Disguises would be used.

Feeney paced the room. The rain had ended, so he opened the window to let in the air. There was movement on the docks. A schooner slid out of its berth and set out to the open lake, its sails billowing in the brisk breeze. An idea began to formulate. It would be ideal and could be actuated in just a few more days.

The Irish Republican Brotherhood had sent Feeney to recruit men and obtain arms for a rising to take place in the unspecified future. When the moment came, the Fenians would attack police barracks throughout Ireland, holding hostages and demanding that England leave the nation forever. This time they'd be prepared, with help from America. Feeney was just one of several agents in the country. The potato famine had forced many young patriots to come here. Exiles. The Brotherhood wanted to bring them back.

Feeney had his own agenda, a daring plot unknown to the Brotherhood, at least at this point. Feeney would stage his own uprising, using the most trusted of his boys. It would be timed to parallel the takeover of the police barracks in Ireland. Feeney planned nothing less than to seize the government of the Dominion of Canada. The boys would cross the border secretly. They would proceed to Ottawa, capture the government buildings, and hold the officials hostage. If the British didn't meet their terms, the officials would be shot and the capitol set on fire.

Some of his fellow Fenians would think him daft to even consider such a harebrained plot, which is why he hadn't broached it with them. The risk would be great, the chance of success slim. Surprise was the key. If the plan failed, the patriots would die martyrs. What glory if the plan succeeded! The glory would be his and his alone. Da had died in captivity. Feeney's invasion would erase the accusation in Ma's eyes. It would absolve him.

Keeping his plan from the Brotherhood was one thing, but he had to trust someone. So far, the only ones who knew were the members of the inner circle who were meeting here tonight. The purpose of the meeting was to plan an activity to keep the boys busy. He'd thought of it a moment ago, as he was looking out the window. Now he heard them on the staircase below.

Lugh and Jack were engaged in a heated argument as they came up the stairs. The dispute raged as they burst through the door, Flaherty close behind. A door slammed downstairs. That would be Kelly, late as usual.

"You're a damned fraud, Jack. The mighty Cuchulain, hah. You've never participated in a real battle, have you?"

"Fraud, is it? Here's a question for you, Lugh. *Cid na cotlai for colcaid?*"

"What?"

"*Cid na cotlai for colcaid?* Well, how about it?"

"I don't know what the bloody hell you're talkin' about."

Jack shot a sidelong glance at Feeney. Jack was a romantic. It was he who had introduced the concept of Celtic role-playing.

"See? Lugh doesn't even speak Irish."

"Of course I do."

"What did I say? Prove that you speak Irish."

"I don't have to prove anything to you."

"You said 'bloody hell.' That's British. Bloody, indeed. You must be a Brit. What do you think, Kelly? Do you think Lugh's a Brit?"

Kelly, who was never inclined to get involved, shrugged. Flaherty, the instigator, rose and looked at Jack. "There's only one way to settle this. Settle it with your fists. I, for one, would enjoy a spirited round of fisticuffs, only as a spectator, of course."

"As an officer of the law," said Kelly, "how can you suggest such a thing?"

"Are you not one of us, Kelly? We're all in the same boat, boyo. If you want to be a good boy, join a choir." In fact, Kelly was a member of a choir and sang a lilting tenor. Flaherty's barb stung him. He was about to respond when Feeney's voice stilled the room.

"Lads! Let's get to the business at hand. The boys are tired of playing games. What are we going to do about it?" Feeney's voice rang with authority, so it was a surprise when Lugh spoke up.

"Before we get into that, there's something that needs to be addressed. It's about this Canadian scheme of yours."

"Of ours, Lugh."

"Of ours, then. How is it to be financed? An invasion of Canada, even on a small scale, costs money. Are we all to chip in, or do you propose to rob a bank?"

"Lugh, Lugh, I have a fund. Your own da in Dublin contributed to it, as you must know."

"That was a few years ago, Feeney. How much is left?"

This was a direct challenge to Feeney's leadership. He wouldn't have tolerated it from anyone but Lugh, who had Dublin connections. Feeney went to the safe, knelt, and unlocked it while the others watched.

Removing the old leather satchel, he took it to the table and opened it.

"An empty satchel!" exclaimed Kelly.

"Not empty," corrected Feeney, as he removed the false bottom and pulled out the pistol. Kelly gasped and Jack's eyes widened. Lugh stared with a cold, unflinching gaze and said nothing. "When you see what else is here, you'll understand why I keep you at gunpoint. I am an excellent marksman, by the way."

No one doubted that. Feeney tipped the satchel upside down. A mountain of US currency tumbled onto the table. Flaherty whistled appreciatively and moved toward the table. Feeney pointed the pistol directly at him, and he stopped in his tracks.

"What's the matter? Don't you trust me?"

"I don't trust anyone, especially you, 'Officer' Flaherty."

Lugh laughed softly, and Flaherty reddened. Feeney immediately regretted the insult. Flaherty, although not one of the boys, was useful because of his connection to the police. The man was corrupt and was in it for what he thought he might get out of it.

"Actually, Mike, I do trust you, as much as I trust anyone. If you would now, put the money back in the satchel and return it to the safe. I will keep my gun in hand until you have done that." Flaherty reluctantly complied, while the men waited. Jack broke the silence.

"The boys are raring to go, worked into a frenzy. They are conditioned to fight, primed for action, and cannot be contained much longer. If we don't come up with something, they'll go off on their own. That's a scenario none of us would like to contemplate. That's why we're here. Let's listen to Feeney's proposal. I assume that you do have a proposal."

"Yes." Feeney lowered the pistol and sat behind the table. "Flaherty, you hang around the docks. Is a British ship soon due to arrive in the port of Milwaukee?"

"Not directly from England, but a British-owned cargo ship, the *Lynne*, arrives Wednesday with a load of rum bound for Chicago."

"Hmm. Yes. Wouldn't it be a shame if that rum never got to Chicago?"

"Are you thinking another Boston Tea Party?"

"You do have a sense of humor, Jack, me boy, but you may have hit upon something. Hmm. Boston Tea Party. Yes. Indeed. That's just what I was thinking."

A long silence. Everyone had the same thought at once. Jack put it into words. "Sweet Jesus, what a waste of good booze that would be." They roared with laughter and all talked excitedly at once. The talks continued well into the night.

It was an idyllic day in the country, sunny and warm. A mild zephyr wafted the scent of wildflowers over the meadow. They sat in the grass under a chestnut tree near a stream—Maeve, Brian, Liam, and Jack. It had been Maeve's idea to have a picnic. She had insisted the boys come along. They feasted on bread and cold chicken. Maeve and Jack sat on a blanket drinking wine, while the boys searched for chestnuts.

"I can't find my nuts," giggled Brian, and Maeve ignored him. "Can I have some wine, Ma?"

"Yeah, can I have some, too?" echoed Liam.

"It's 'may' not 'can.' No, you may not."

"It'll stunt your growth, lads," growled Jack, beginning to think this outing had been a mistake.

"What are we going to do now?" asked Brian, while Liam threw chestnuts into the stream.

"Enjoy the trees and stream and relax."

"Nah. That's a bad idea. It's boring, Ma."

"Well, that's what I want you to do."

Jack poured himself another glass of wine, after offering some to Maeve, who declined. Liam hurled the last chestnut and came up from the bank.

"Say, Ma, can we go home? I mean Brian and I could get a head start. You walk too slow. We know the way. When we get home we can practice the high-step or play war. We'll be all right."

Maeve considered. She looked at Jack. "Go ahead, only go right home. Don't dilly-dally and don't get into any mischief. We'll be right along. You may as well take the picnic basket." Without another word, the boys took off, Liam swinging the basket as he ran.

There was an awkward silence. Jack felt a lump in his throat. They were alone, a moment about which he had fantasized, and he didn't know what to do.

"It must be hard raising two boys alone."

"The woman always raises the children alone, whether the father's around or not."

"I know fathers who would disagree."

"Fathers are never at home. They are at sea, in the field, or at war. When they are home, they are less than useless."

Another silence ensued. Jack's body raged with lust, debilitating him. He was on the verge of stammering. Maeve glanced at him dryly. He was a man of exceptional good looks, nicknamed "Handsome Jack" in the ward, with the reputation of being a ladies' man. The reputation was unearned, perpetuated by his own bragging. He had never had a woman. Aggressive in war games and sports, Jack froze when opportunities for sex presented themselves. His nervousness was apparent.

Seeking to put him at ease, Maeve rose and said, "C'mon, get up. Take the blanket and let's go down to the bank, near the water." His throat went dry, noting the invitation in her voice. He picked up the blanket, nearly tripping over it on the way to the water's edge. Together, they spread the blanket and sat on it.

"I love the gurgling sound of the stream. It's peaceful, unlike the sea, which is vast and violent. I feel protected, sitting here with you. You are so ... strong."

Jack self-consciously put his arm around Maeve's waist. She did not resist. She leaned her head on his shoulder. He whispered in her ear in a hoarse, dry voice.

"I love your mole."

"You love my what?"

"Your mole. The mole of Maeve."

Before she could respond, he kissed her cheek where the brown spot lay. This was meant to be an overture, but Jack was not prepared for what happened next. Suddenly, Maeve was all over him. She pushed him back on the blanket and climbed on him. Her blouse was unbuttoned, her breasts in his face, and her hands were playing him like the strings on a harp. Jack began to feel aroused, then out of control. This was not how it was supposed to go. He yelled and tried to get up. Maeve, skirt over hips, tumbled onto the blanket into a disheveled heap. Jack lost his balance. Jack's sexual fire was extinguished by the chilly water of the stream as he plunged into it, drenching himself from head to foot. When he managed to stand and achieve a firm footing, Maeve was laughing hysterically, tears of mirth streaming down her face. Jack waded ashore, nonplussed. Maeve extended her hand to help him up the bank.

They faced each other. Maeve, with a contrite look, said, "I'm sorry." She started laughing again. Jack was angry and humiliated. "I can't help laughing, but I said I was sorry. Let's fold the blanket and go. The boys must be all the way home. Oh, and you need dry clothes." She stifled another laugh. Carrying the blanket under one arm, Jack walked down the road beside Maeve.

"Look at it this way, Jack. That was a great icebreaker." She could suppress her merriment no longer and exploded. This time, Jack permitted himself a faint smile. By the time they were halfway down the road, they were holding hands.

———————————————

"Let's take this path." The path led from the road into a deep forest. Liam stopped swinging the empty picnic basket and stared at Brian, who was already heading down the path.

"Wait a minute, Brian. Ma said to go directly home."

"Let's see where this leads. It won't take long. Ma and Jack are still at the stream."

"Do you think they are in love?"

"Nah. Let's go. We have plenty of time."

"Oh, all right. Maybe we'll find an underground tunnel."

"You and your tunnels." Liam was always looking for underground tunnels, ever since he had read a book about a subterranean land inhabited by giants. Once he had tried to dig a tunnel in the backyard, leaving a deep hole. Ma had tripped over the hole on the way to the clothesline.

They strolled down the path dappled with spots of sunlight filtered through the leafy roof of spreading tree branches. Brian, staring up at the natural ceiling, fell over a stump.

"Ow! I skinned my knee."

Liam, eating a berry, ran over to help Brian. "Are you all right?"

"I'm all right. What's that you're eating?"

"A berry." Liam had read a book about a boy who had eaten a berry and developed superhuman powers. "Want one?"

"Nah. You shouldn't be eating strange berries. They might be poisonous."

Liam fell to the ground, writhing and moaning in a grand, theatrical display of feigned illness. Brian laughed in spite of himself. Brian hated to encourage his brother, but Liam was a born comic. Now he was pretending to puke into the picnic basket.

"That does it. Let's head back to the road."

"No. Look." Liam pointed to a break in the path ahead that appeared to be a clearing. "Let's see what's there."

"We'll go that far. Then we'll go home."

Liam picked up the picnic basket and they walked to the clearing, a field surrounded by the forest. The grass had been trampled by animals.

"This is it. Satisfied?"

"Caw!" came the cry of a crow. Liam ran across the field, flapping his arms, pretending to be a crow. "Caw!" Liam tripped over a stump and went down like a sack of potatoes. Brian shrugged. He'd had it.

"Brian! Brian, come over here. Come over here now!"

"What, is this another of your jokes?"

"Come. See what I found."

Brian wondered if his brother had found an animal hole, mistaking it for an underground tunnel. He sighed and walked over to where Liam had tripped. "Well, what is it?"

"Look. It's a cannon. A real cannon."

Brian followed Liam's gaze, and there, behind a bush, was the cannon. "Wow!" shouted Brian, running to it, with Liam close behind. They examined it, climbing all over it, taking turns aiming it, and making explosive noises with their mouths.

"I wonder if it's loaded," said Liam. Brian walked to the barrel. He peeked inside, hoping it wouldn't go off while he was looking into it. "It's dark in there."

"What's this string over here?"

Brian went behind the cannon and examined the string. He had seen cannons fired during holidays at Union Guard demonstrations. He knew that loading, aiming, and firing a cannon required several men. He also knew that if a cannon was in a state of readiness, it could be fired simply by lighting a fuse.

He was sure that the string was a fuse. The cannon was loaded. He informed Liam, who looked scared. Brian reached into his pocket, pulling out a flint. A friend of Brian's filched cigars from his da, and the two friends would sneak off and smoke. Brian kept the flint handy for such occasions.

Liam, momentarily distracted by the sight of a deer grazing on the other side of the meadow, turned just in time to see Brian light the fuse. "Get down!" shouted Brian triumphantly. There was a horrendous explosion that pierced Liam's ears, shook the ground, and created vast quantities of smoke and dust. The grazing deer was thrown into the air by the force of the cannonball's impact, and a black cloud of truculent crows cawed out of the trees in a flurry of flapping wings.

"Brian, Brian!" Liam peered through the smoke looking for his brother. Then he saw Brian on his hands and knees, coughing.

"Are you all right?" asked Liam.

"I think I shot a deer. We'd better get out of here as fast as we can."

The two boys ran all the way home, stopping occasionally to catch breath. It was only after they arrived home that Liam realized he had left the picnic basket on the ground near the cannon.

Chapter Five

THE MOON SMILED IN THE midsummer sky, reassuring the world that nothing could happen under its warm, happy glow. Blevins and Flynn were on Lookout Hill, where they had arrived after an evening of horseback riding. In the distance, they could see the masts of the ships down on the waterfront. Beyond was the placid water of Lake Michigan, which mirrored the sheen of the moon.

At the dock, the British-owned schooner *Lynne,* carrying rum bound for Chicago, lay peacefully at her moorings. A guard stood watch on the forecastle. Several crew members below sported with two hookers who frequented the docks and were on friendly terms with Sergeant Flaherty, who had put them up to this evening's debauch. Other crew members were in town, celebrating at Feeney's Pub or enjoying the dubious pleasures of Mrs. Murphy's boarding house. The captain of the *Lynne* was visiting a relative in Racine.

The whole scenario had been orchestrated by Feeney. The moment for the tea party was ripe. It was too bad about the moon. A darker night would have been preferable. On the other hand, too much secrecy would defeat the purpose of making a statement. Let the moon shed light. Stillness fell upon the dock, the calm before the storm.

The watchman was in a near comatose state, in the midst of a fuzzy dream involving soft mist and softer maidens. In the dream, he heard thunder. The thunder increased and seemed to come closer and closer. He awoke, but the thunder continued. He looked at the sky, but there were no clouds. The sound was coming from somewhere else. Looking down the docks and up the hill, he beheld a sight that astonished him.

Down the hill galloped a legion of horsemen, yelling and whooping. Like Indians on the warpath, the horsemen were painted, but the designs on their bodies were unlike any the watchman had seen. He recognized the words the riders shouted as Gaelic but didn't understand any of it. The men leaped from their horses and stormed the *Lynne,* charged up the gangplank, and swarmed the deck. The watchman didn't have a chance. He was bound and tied to a mast. The crew members below, caught in various states of undress, were too startled and embarrassed to fight, but the odds would have been against them if they had. Wide-eyed, they watched as the invaders lugged one barrel of rum after another to the upper deck. It took two men to get a barrel topside and heave it overboard. Countless barrels of rum floated across Lake Michigan.

The men fired rounds of ammunition into the drifting barrels, cheering as the bullets hit, causing fountains of rum to spurt from each punctured barrel. The barrels were on the way to the bottom before reaching the horizon. "Davy Jones will have a party tonight," laughed one of the warriors.

The noise of the gunshots attracted a crowd of onlookers gathering on the docks. No one thought to interfere or to go for the police. Why spoil the show? The watchman managed to wriggle out of bondage and tackled the nearest painted Celt, who happened to be Lugh. They struggled, but the watchman's heart wasn't in it. "Let's give this lackey a drink of rum," said Lugh. He and several others dragged the watchman to the side and threw him overboard. The onlookers applauded. The victim floundered in the water and started swimming toward the shore.

"You're swimmin' in the wrong direction, boyo," shouted Kelly. "The rum is out there."

"Let's sink him," cried a voice. Several shots hit the water, spurring the watchman to swim faster.

The crew and hookers were on the upper deck, racing for the gangplank. No one stopped them. The hookers dallied, but no one took the bait. One of them shouted, "Any of you fine lads want some fun, come to Mrs. Murphy's later."

The fine lads weren't listening. Several had bodhrans and started beating the ancient Celtic drums. Tin whistles came out and a fiddle. To the tune of a traditional reel, the crowd clapped and stomped. Couples danced.

From Lookout Hill, Blevins and Flynn could hear the gunshots and music. "Something's happening on the waterfront," said Blevins.

"Shall we?"

"I'll race you."

Hair flying, in gales of laughter, they raced their horses down the hill to the strains of bodhrans, fiddles and tin whistles. Just as they arrived at the dock, the music and dancing stopped. Exhilarated and breathless, they reined their horses.

A slow drumbeat started. The men on the ship began to chant "Cuchulain! Cuchulain!." The drumbeat and chant increased in intensity. Out of the darkness at the top of the hill appeared a figure on horseback. He charged down the hill into the crowd. His face was painted. He wore a robe with a wolfhound emblazoned on it and carried a spear. "Cuchulain!"

Cuchulain did not dismount. He rode the horse right up the gangplank to the roars of the men onboard and the cheers of the excited mob. Astride the horse, he faced the crowd and raised an arm, spear in hand. The crowd hushed.

"Irish of the Bloody Third. Pass my message along. May there be no peace for England until there is peace in Ireland. Hurrah for the bold Robert Emmett. Hurrah for the patriot Wolfe Tone. England, get the hell out of Ireland. Erin go bragh!"

Suddenly there was a lump in Flynn's throat. She'd had a premonition when she'd seen the man with the painted face, but as soon as he started speaking, she knew. It was Jack. My God, what had he gotten himself into? She glanced at Blevins, but Blevins was oblivious. Well, that was a relief.

Several unlit torches were unleashed from Cuchulain's saddle. Igniting one, he then lit each of the others with his own, distributing the torches among his men. He applied his torch to one of the sails, and the others followed. Cuchulain screamed, "Ayeeee!" Raising his spear, he spurred his horse down the gangplank and up the hill. The other men leaped off the burning ship, mounted their horses, and rode off into the night.

The police arrived, Hogan with the usual cigar. Blevins needled him. "Hey, Hogan, the party's over. Where the hell have you been?"

"Breakin' up a brawl on Third and Wells. Have you seen Sergeant Flaherty?"

"I don't frequent the places he likes to go."

Hogan couldn't hear Blevins above the roar of the fire. Smart-aleck reporter. That was all he needed. The policeman moved in on the crowd. He'd had an inkling something was going to happen down here tonight, so he'd deliberately stayed away. He was no Fenian, but he was Irish and nobody's fool. He knew the people who paid his salary. He also knew where Flaherty was, but unless the man was caught red-handed, Hogan would leave the man alone.

"All right, all right, move out. Go home. The bucket brigade will be here soon. You'll need to be out of the way."

The crowd dispersed. Hogan noticed that Blevins was questioning some of them. No doubt there'd be a comment in his paper about the inefficiency of the police. Hogan listened to the crackle of burning wood as he lit another cigar. He had told the crowd that the bucket brigade was on the way. They had been notified, but Hogan doubted any volunteers would arrive.

Feeney stood at the window of the attic apartment peering through a telescope at the raging fire and billowing smoke. In his mind, he saw his father's Mayo farm burning to the ground, and his mother's smoldering eyes. "I'm sorry, Ma," he choked. "I'm sorry." There was no answer.

Captain Garrett Barry, graduate of the US Military Academy at West Point, class of 1839, reached for the decanter and emptied its contents into his glass. A few more sips and he began to feel unsteady on his feet. Time to go home—nothing more to be accomplished here today. Taking his coat off the rack near the window, he was about to don it when someone pounded on the door. Barry consulted the calendar on his desk. No … nothing scheduled. Who in the hell would that be? Barry had a gnawing headache.

"Who is it?" he asked in a slurred voice. "Come in, damn it. Come in."

The door opened, and a tall, thin man entered. He was fortyish, with heavy-lidded eyes and dirty, straw-like hair. The clothes he wore appeared to have been slept in. A strong, gamey odor lingered in the air.

"Howdy," the man said amiably, and Barry noticed that he was gap-toothed. "You Barry?"

"That's what it says on the sign above my door."

"Ayeh. Cap'n Garrett Barry, Union Guard."

"And you are?"

"Joshua Doughty, federal deputy marshal." He produced identification, which Barry ignored. Nowadays anyone could get deputized. The government was not selective. This man was living proof.

"Hey listen, you c'n call me Josh."

"Mr. Doughty. I am about to leave for the day. What can I do for you that will only take five minutes?"

"Cap'n Barry, sir, I can see that you're indisposed. No doubt you are … tired," he implied, glancing at the empty decanter, "after a long day's …. ah … work, but I will not take much of your time."

Doughty scratched his crotch. Barry decided he would not shake hands. The man removed a drawing from his pocket, handing it to Barry. It was a crude drawing of a black man with white hair, a misshapen nose, and a scar on his upper lip. Barry studied the drawing. The face was vaguely familiar. The image blurred in his vision.

"Have you seen this man, Cap'n?"

"No."

"He's a runaway slave, hidin' somewhere in Milwaukee. Belongs to a South Carolina plantation owner named Clayton. Me and Clayton's trackin' him down. Clayton's stayin' at a nearby inn, along with another deputy. They sent me out here. They're workin' on other leads. I came to you."

"Why me?"

"I'm aware of your disagreement with Governor Randall and I know you're committed to obeyin' the law of the land, that law bein', says the Supreme Court, that you have to apprehend runaway slaves and return 'em to their rightful owners. I'm askin' for your help, and the help of the Union Guard. Say, you don't like me very much, do you?"

"You noticed that?"

"That ain't important. There's nothin' personal in this, Cap'n. We both know the law."

"Locating this slave may be difficult, Deputy. Do you know how many blacks are here in Milwaukee? Many are free or protected and hidden by abolitionists. You may be looking for a needle in a haystack."

"Don't think so. This black man has a few outstandin' features, as you can see. He also has a feature which you can't see, at least not in the picture. Owner beat the man on a regular basis. Lots of owners do that. Keeps 'em in line. Thing is, Clayton got carried away. Beat him so hard he walks with a permanent limp."

"Does this runaway have a name?"

"They call him Moses. Somethin' about deliverin' his people. He ain't the only one they call Moses. These bad slaves are gonna learn that the North ain't no promised land. You and me, Cap'n. It's our sworn duty to learn them that." Doughty winked.

"What's the man's real name?"

"Damned if I know."

"Doughty, I don't like you, and I don't like what you represent. Yes, I am sworn to uphold the law, in this case a questionable law. But you ... you take pleasure in what you do."

"Oh yes. I do. I do indeed." The marshal grinned, displaying the gap between his brown, tobacco-stained teeth.

"I am not obligated to help you search. You track him down. I am not a detective. If you find your man, I will do what I must."

"Of course you will. If you learn of his whereabouts, will you let me know?"

"Is there anything else?" Barry's headache was getting worse.

"We'll be in touch." Doughty extended his hand, but Barry just stared. Doughty shrugged and started to leave.

"Oh, one question, Doughty. Why does it take three men to track one slave—an old one with white hair? What makes Moses so important?"

The deputy scratched his crotch and considered. "That booze didn't dull your brain none, did it? Moses didn't escape by himself. He took twelve others with him. We tracked them to Racine, where they all disappeared."

"How do you account for that?"

"Underground Railroad. Underground's strong in Racine, but try to prove anything."

"The twelve slaves all owned by Clayton?"

"Lock, stock, and barrel."

"He must be a cruel master to lose so many."

"Ayeh. Clayton's one mean son-of-a-bitch. The slaves are his property. Don't forget that. And don't forget your sworn duty, Cap'n. Keep in touch, now. Adios. Until we meet again." Doughty executed a mock salute, clicked his heels, and slammed out the door.

Barry sighed. It had been a long day.

———————————

Mary Barry greeted her husband with a warm kiss. "Whew, you've been drinking. Must you, Garrett?"

"The situation's under control."

"What does that mean? Do you have to drink at work? Can't you at least wait until you get home?"

"I'm home." He grinned and headed for the liquor cabinet in the vestibule.

"Garrett!" The sharpness of her voice stopped him. "Dinner is ready and on the table."

Willie Barry, age twelve, came bounding down the stairs. "Hello, Da. Whew, you've been drinking. Must you, Da?"

Barry guffawed, and Mary put on a mock stern face. "You've been eavesdropping. Must you, my little copycat?" The three walked into the dining room. Young Willie took his place at the table with his four sisters. Johanna was sixteen and most resembled her mother. Mary Ann was thirteen. She had red hair and freckles and an Irish temperament. Elizabeth was ten and little Maria was six. Willie was the only boy.

"I told Old Ned to hold the food until you arrived. He's prepared a boiled dinner."

"Boiled dinner? That's one of your specialties. Why didn't you prepare it? Yours is the best."

"Ned used my recipe. You know how busy I've been."

"With the abolitionists."

Mary, who knew her husband disapproved of her antislavery activities, was silent. Garrett studied his wife. Mary was the eldest daughter of a wealthy Connecticut family. When she and Garrett had met, Garrett had been a promising young officer recently graduated from West Point. He came from a poor background, but he charmed Mary's family, who liked his conservative values. When the newlyweds settled in Milwaukee, her money had enabled them to live in a large house. Garrett considered himself a lucky man. Not only did Mary have money, she was an Irish beauty whose smile illuminated her whole face.

To her credit, she did not lord money over him. She'd literally meant what she'd whispered to him on their wedding night. "What's mine is yours."

Mary was a free spirit. Garrett could not keep her away from male political discussions at gatherings, especially if the social issue involved a woman's place in society. Garrett did not consider himself a chauvinist, although to some extent he was. He was aggravated by Mary's liberalism, which she expounded while her sister socialites talked about sewing and the latest gossip. Her attitude was surprising, considering her background.

Her stance on slavery was an issue between her and Garrett. Mary was an abolitionist and attended local meetings. In fact, she was a leader. When Lincoln had spoken at the Milwaukee Fairgrounds in 1859, she had been a member of the committee that had arranged his appearance. The event had not been a complete success. Eight hundred people had attended. There had been complaints that Lincoln was ineffectual and that "you could hardly hear him." Mary continued to support him. In a ward that was strongly pro-Douglas, this was an embarrassment to Garrett. Mary was disenfranchised, but if she could vote, her vote would cancel her husband's.

"I'm hungry, Ma." Willie was the Barrys' pride and joy. He would grow up to look just like his father.

"You poor thing," laughed Mary, ringing the dinner bell. "Ned, we're ready for dinner."

Plates of steaming meat and potatoes were served. "Thank you, Ned," said Garrett, looking up through the steam at Ned. The servant was black with white hair, a misshapen nose, and a scar over his upper lip.

"You're welcome, Mr. Barry. Will you be needing anything else?"

"That will be all."

The man called Ned returned to the kitchen. He walked with a limp.

Barry sat at his desk, sorting papers. The whiskey decanter had been refilled, but he avoided it. This was no time for fuzzy thinking. Too much was going on. Things were getting out of hand. There was the matter of Ned, or Moses, or whatever his name was. Of course, Barry had recognized him the moment Doughty had shown him the drawing. Mary had brought him home one day claiming he was a free man looking for work. She'd been devoted to him, so Barry hadn't said anything, although he suspected he'd come from the Underground Railroad.

Worse, he suspected that Mary was involved. Mary would not normally lie to him. Being an abolitionist was one thing. Being an active member of the subversive Underground Railroad was another. Barry was not in favor of slavery. He did not agree with the Fugitive Slave Act. However, he had served his country and always done his duty. He was fiercely loyal to the government and would not stand against the law of the land.

Barry didn't know what to do. He had a headache. He wondered about the fire last night. Who was Cuchulain, and what group did he represent? Feeney wanted to see him and was waiting outside in the hall. Barry didn't know Feeney very well but disliked him. The pub was a bad influence on the boys. He supposed, eyeing the whiskey decanter wistfully, he had no right to judge. He went to the hall and summoned Feeney. Feeney carried a satchel, which he placed on the desk. Barry stared at it, as if it were something evil.

"I'll come to the point, Captain. In that satchel is a sum of money. It's a large sum of money, a donation. It's all yours."

"Are you offering me a bribe?"

"That's such an indelicate word. Think of it as a contribution to Captain Garrett Barry's Irish Brigade, a windfall for the Union Guard."

"It's not just a contribution. You expect something in return."

"You don't have to kill anyone, Captain. You're an Irishman. All that is required is that you do what any loyal Irishman would do. Support the cause."

"The cause?"

"Join us. Join the Fenians. Help us throw England out of Ireland. Take the money. Use it however you will. It is yours. In return, your expertise. Prepare the lads for the great rising that is soon to come."

"You want me to become a Fenian."

"Yes, and to train and recruit your young Irish American guardsmen. There's no conflict of interest here. You will just continue doing what you are doing now. When the time is ripe, you will provide us with trained men and weapons."

"Go to hell."

"Do you have any idea how much money is in that satchel?"

"I don't want to know. And I don't want to know how you obtained it."

"Legally, I assure you."

"I don't care. I want no part of it."

"You are already a part of it."

"What do you mean? How am I a part of it?"

"You really don't know, do you? Captain Barry and his heroic brigade. Hmm. I overestimated you. You really are naïve. Captain, a large number of your boys are already Fenians."

"In an Irish American brigade, it stands to reason that many would be sympathetic to the cause of Irish freedom. I believe in it myself."

"Oh, really? I am not speaking of mere sympathy. The boys are not only with us in thought, they are with us in deed. You know the adage: actions speak louder than words."

"What actions? What deeds?"

"Can't you guess? You heard about the fire yesterday."

"The burning of the *Lynne*? A shameful act of vandalism. It's on the tip of every tongue in the ward."

There was a long silence. A flush of anger began to creep up Barry's neck as the implication dawned on him. Feeney nodded and said nothing.

"Our boys did that?"

"My boys did that. Feeney's Boys, and Fenians all. To a man, every one of them is a member of the Guard. By the way, you did a splendid job of training them. The man they call Cuchulain? One of your finest."

"They are criminals, and you are a criminal. Who are they, Feeney?

Give me a list. By God, they will be expelled, every one, including this Cuchulain, whoever he is. They'll rot in jail with you beside them, you miserable, skulking, poor excuse of an Irishman."

"So that's it, is it? Rot in jail? That's what you'd have them do?"

"Indeed."

"All of them?"

"How many are there?"

"More than a third of the entire Guard."

"I don't believe you."

"Do you really think I will give you a list? Name names? Now why on earth would I do that? Think about it, though. Think about the burning of the ship and the efficient manner in which the task was carried out. Who else around here would be so capable?"

Barry's hand started to shake. He went to the decanter and poured himself a stiff one. This was no time to control the habit. He only needed one. He didn't offer a drink to Feeney.

"That's it. Sure. A drink will calm you down. I'm not the enemy, boyo. It's the Brits. The Brits are the enemy, always have been. Together, you and I could turn the Guard into a juggernaut, an unstoppable force that would free Ireland forever. We'd have support in the ward, and with the money I offer—"

"Feeney, I am an American above everything else. This is my country, not Ireland. I feel a sadness for the Old Sod, but no loyalty. Yes, my ancestors, like yours, have been persecuted, but I have put that behind me. I am committed to the Guard and what it represents. What you ask would be a betrayal. I can only hope to undo the damage you have done, if what you say is true. Get out of here, you bastard."

"You're making a mistake."

"You're making the mistake, 'boyo.' There's a federal deputy marshal in town. I will report the matter to him. I could arrest you myself for trying to bribe an official."

"Oh, you won't do that. You won't carry our conversation beyond this room."

"Why won't I?"

"Suppose it came out that the Union Guard was infiltrated with Fenians engaged in illegal activities. Where would you be? What would happen to your own grand plans? You don't believe your men are involved, but you're not sure. If you open this can of Irish worms, it will blow the lid off everything, including your own precious career."

"Get out of here," Barry snarled. "Get out of here before I kill you."

Feeney grinned. "The incorruptible Captain Barry." He left the office, satchel in hand.

Chapter Six

FROM THE BRANCH OF THE large oak tree, the boys could see the open meadow and the commotion on it. It was hard to tell what was happening because dust was everywhere, and it was impossible to identify the faces of the men who were shouting, whacking, punching, and shooting. Three men at the cannon were angry that the weapon wasn't loaded and had been fired. They were shaking their fists. The boys couldn't hear what they were saying, but it was clear that each thought the other at fault for the cannon not being ready to fire. The boys exchanged guilty glances.

"Let's get out of here. I'm scared."

"We're at a safe distance."

"But they're killing each other. Look! Look at the bodies on the ground."

"Nah, they're not dead. It's a game." As if to prove Brian's point, the "dead" rose and went to the center of the field. The cannoneers joined the other participants. "See. Wait a while. We can't go now, because we have to get what we came for. Do you see the picnic basket?"

"It's where I dropped it, near the cannon. We can't go for it now. They'll see us. Never mind, let's go home."

"Shh! There's a man with a painted face in a funny costume. The others are shouting his name."

"Cuchulain!" the warriors chanted. A man riding a white horse waved a spear and addressed the throng. The boys were at too great a distance to identify the man or hear what he was saying.

"Now!" urged Brian.

Liam dropped to the ground, thinking his brother was close behind, and crept toward the picnic basket. The soldiers were far enough away. Even if they saw him, they'd never catch him. Just as he reached the basket, a crow, sitting on the cannon, screeched, "Caw!" Liam's heart leaped to his throat. He grabbed the basket and ran to the shelter of the oak tree. A quick glance behind assured Liam that no one had noticed.

"Whew!" Liam exclaimed, looking up into the tree. Brian wasn't there. "Brian!" Liam called in a low, urgent voice. There was no response. Liam paused to catch his breath and then climbed the tree to an overhanging branch. From there he surveyed the area but saw no sign of his brother.

Across the meadow, the men were disbanding. A few on horseback rode toward the oak tree. Liam lay still on the branch, praying silently that no one would look up. Brian had crept into a clump of bushes close to the proceedings. Cuchulain was addressing the men in a strange language. They all cheered, mounted, and started to leave. One came Brian's way. The dust provided cover.

After the dust cleared, Cuchulain was still there. He had removed the costume and stood naked beside his horse. He used a cloth to remove the painted Celtic circles from his face. Brian gasped. "Jack!" he cried, covering his mouth to prevent the sound from escaping.

Jack dressed, mounted the horse, and galloped away. Brian left his place of concealment and walked onto the field. On the ground where Jack had left it was the spear, the spear of Cuchulain. Brian took it and held it, which gave him a feeling of power. He raced across the meadow. With a mighty yell, he flung it into the air. The spear soared skyward, narrowly missing a crow in flight.

"Liam! Liam! Look what I found!"

Partway into town, Jack realized that he had left the spear. He turned back, urging the horse to full speed. Horse and rider were panting when they reached the meadow. The spear was gone. Did one of the men find it and take it for safekeeping? Jack hoped so. If it fell into the wrong hands, it would raise a lot of questions.

"I know who you are," Maeve told Jack, after the second cup of tea.

"I'm glad. It would be improper to invite a stranger to tea."

She glanced out the window and down the road at the disappearing shapes of Brian and Liam with fishing gear. It would be a while before they returned. "No, I know who you are— Cuchulain."

Jack was stricken. "You know nothing of me."

"I know all about you. I know you are the leader of a group of Irish patriots."

"Patriots?"

"If you are not the leader, you are an active member. You are the man who torched the *Lynne* and disappeared into the night. Everyone is talking about the incident."

"You think I am that man?"

"Where is your costume, my brave Celtic god? I would like to see you in it. Ah, yes, I would. I wish you had invited me to your tea party."

"I don't know what you mean."

"You know exactly what I mean. Wait—I want to show you something." She left the room. When she returned, she held the spear of Cuchulain. "Does this look familiar, Jack?"

"Where did you get that?" He reached for it, but she pulled back.

"That's my secret." She didn't want to implicate Brian and Liam. She'd caught them with it, and they'd spilled the whole adventure. She didn't think they'd associated the incident with the fire on the waterfront, if they even knew about it, but she had made the connection. She had taken the spear and told the boys not to say anything about it.

Etched into the head of the spear was a fierce wolfhound identical to the figure embroidered on the costume of the rider Cuchulain. Maeve, who was steeped in Celtic lore, knew the story of the wolfhound. A young boy in Ulster killed the wolfhound that guarded the gate of a castle owned by Cullen. The boy took the place of the animal and guarded the gate until Cullen could find another watchdog. The boy became known as Cuchulain, which in Gaelic means "the hound of Cullen."

"Give it to me. Give it to me now."

"No, not now. Jack. Jack, calm down. Easy now. Come with me. Come. I want to show you something else."

He followed her upstairs. The spear was in her hand as they entered the bedroom. "Excuse me for a moment," she said, and she left the room, taking the spear. There were two striking objects in the room. Near the lace-curtained window stood the harp, an elegant curved instrument with a sensual aura. A wisp of air blew the curtains inward, causing them to brush lightly against the harp strings.

On a table in a corner, a candle flickered—a thick stub of a candle—hot wax dripping down the sides. Beside the candle was a leather-bound book. Jack moved closer to read the title. It was a story he knew well. It was "The Tain," the ancient epic poetic saga, in Gaelic, of the legendary Cattle Raid of Coolie. Cuchulain, the "hound" of Ulster, raided Connaught and fought Queen Maeve's army singlehandedly by defeating each of her champions one at a time. The prize was a bull with supernatural propagation powers. Cuchulain and Maeve were lovers for a short time.

Behind him, he felt movement, and heavenly music floated across the room. Jack turned toward the angelic sound, and there was Maeve at the harp, wearing a flimsy white shift, and nothing else. The scent of burning peat clung in the air. Her eyes were glazed as she looked at Jack and sang "Fand's Farewell to Cuchulain" in a husky voice, all the while stroking the harp strings.

> *Celebrad dit, a Chu chain!*
> *Aso sind uait co sochraid.*
> *C'en co tisam duthracht lind;*
> *Is ard cech recht co h-imchim.*

Jack translated, reciting the words in English.

> Farewell, kind Cu, here abide!
> I go from thee in high pride.
> Parting wish is left undone;
> Good every rule till broken.

"You know 'The Tain,'" she said.
"In Gaelic, yes."
"Then you know that Cuchulain was beheaded."
"So it is written."
She stroked the harp gently and beckoned to him. "Come." He

approached her, and she let her shift drop to the floor. "Today," she whispered, "you are going to lose your head."

Afterward, while Jack was snoring, Maeve ruminated. She had found her magic bull. She dressed. She would allow him to sleep a while, but he'd have to leave before Brian and Liam returned. Maeve laid the spear beside Jack. "The shaft of the warrior," she laughed and took a long look before covering him with the linen sheet.

The train arrived at the LaCrosse and Milwaukee station as scheduled. When the passengers disembarked, there was no sign of O'Mahony. Lugh looked at the telegram.

ARRIVE TUESDAY THE FOURTH BY RAIL STOP WILL WEAR WHITE SHIRT WITH BLACK ARMBAND STOP SEND SOMEONE TO MEET TRAIN STOP O'MAHONY

No one fitting that description had arrived. Lugh would have recognized O'Mahony without the white shirt and black armband, which is why Feeney had selected him to meet the train. Lugh had met O'Mahony in Cork at a gathering of the Phoenix National and Literary Society, a Gaelic literary club that became the foundation of the Irish Republican Brotherhood. James Stephens, the hypnotic, charismatic leader of the IRB, had sent John O'Mahony and Michael Doheny to America to organize an American IRB. It was O'Mahony who had coined the word "Fenian" after the Fianna, the name of an ancient army of Celts. The word was now used to designate members of the Brotherhood on both sides of the Atlantic.

Feeney would be in a bad mood. The lads were eager to meet the man in charge of all the Fenians in America. One of the anticipated activities was the swearing-in of Feeney's Boys, because Feeney didn't have the authority to administer the oath. O'Mahony's delay would not sit well. Lugh was in no hurry to return with bad tidings.

Feeney sat at the bar with his back to the door, so he didn't hear the stranger enter.

"*Inno battar teglach Finn.*"

Feeney spun around, startled to hear an allusion in Gaelic to the Celtic hero, the giant Finn McCool. The stranger was tall, wore Donegal tweed, and smoked a long cheroot. He extended his hand.

"John O'Mahony, at your service."

"Glory be to God! O'Mahony, is it? The telegram said you'd be wearin' a white shirt with a black armband."

"The telegram also said I'd be arriving by train, and I a connoisseur of stagecoaches." A hint of a smile flirted at the corner of his mouth. "One can't be too careful nowadays. It was a hell of a ride on the new plank road between Chicago and Milwaukee."

"Would you be carryin' any luggage?"

"Not a bit of it. I travel light. I would appreciate a pint of your finest, if you would be so kind."

Feeney drew a jar and slid it across the bar. O'Mahony took a deep breath and drained the glass in one swig. "Ah," he said, stifling a belch. The door burst open. Lugh stormed into the pub.

"O'Mahony didn't come. He wasn't on the—"

"Train," said O'Mahony dryly.

"Why it's yourself, O'Mahony!"

"It's sorry I am for the ruse. I take it you were sent to meet me. Tell me, lad, how did you know it was I just now?"

"I'd know you anywhere. Remember the Phoenix National and Literary Society in Cork? I was introduced to you there. Shook your hand."

"Ah, did you, now? What's your name, lad?"

"This is Lugh Finnegan," Feeney volunteered. "Son of Fergus Finnegan of the Dublin IRB."

"Of course. Good man, Fergus. So you were at Cork? Did you meet James Stephens, then?"

"No, sir, but I met O'Donovan Rossa. Oh yes, and Michael Doheny."

"Doheny ... *bedad*, if you won't have a chance to meet him again, being that I brought him along. Michael will assist with the swearing-in. Is it set for tonight, then?"

"It is indeed," replied Feeney. "Meanwhile, you'll be needing a rest. Do you have accommodations?"

"Doheny and myself are situated in a fine establishment on River Street, to which I shall now repair."

"The meeting is at 7:00 pm."

"The divil himself couldn't keep me away." O'Mahony grinned and sauntered out the door.

"There goes a fine figure of a man."

"I hope the divil, as he put it, doesn't keep him away. The devil can be found easily on River Street in any of the fancy brothels for which the street is renowned."

If there had been fire laws in Milwaukee, the meeting at the pub would have been illegal. The boys were crammed elbow to elbow to hear O'Mahony and be sworn-in. Even the area behind the bar was crowded, and some lugs were stealing beer from a barrel. Feeney glared and made mental notes of who the lugs were so he could deal with them later. Michael Doheny was on a small stage that Feeney had built for the occasion. Heavy smoke made it difficult to see Doheny as he spoke.

"I travel with John, and we've gone many miles together. He is the embodiment of Fenianism. Think of Wolfe Tone, think of Robert Emmett, think of James Stevens, think of James Plunkett—think of John O'Mahony. John cofounded the IRB and organized the Fenian movement in America. You may not know that John invented the word 'Fenian.' Tonight you will take an oath, which will be absolutely binding. Once you are in it there is no going back. If you have doubts, now is the time. Leave now, before Mr. O'Mahony takes the stage. You're with us to a man? Fine, then, lads. Here's the gentleman you've all been awaiting, Mr. John O'Mahony!"

O'Mahony allowed the thunderous applause to abate before speaking. "Thank you, Michael. Michael fights by my side. It's a true patriot he is, and a fine man. Well, lads, at last we meet. The escapades of Feeney's Boys are becoming legendary. Praise be to yourselves, lads. By the way, I heard about your tea party. I regret that I could not attend."

Wild cheering and stamping went on for several minutes. O'Mahony stood there and grinned.

"You are a credit to your Celtic ancestors, the Fianna, the army that defended the castle of King Cormac MacArt on the sacred field of Tara, commanded by the giant Finn McCool. To become a member of the Fianna, a man had to memorize twelve books of poetry and be able to pull a thorn out of his foot without breaking stride. To be a Fenian there is only one qualification: total dedication to the removal of British rule by whatever means necessary.

"O'Donovan Rossa, founder of the Phoenix National and Literary Society, likens Ireland to the phoenix. In legend, the phoenix was a bird that rose from its own ashes, and Ireland will one day arise from the ashes of British conquest. No Fenian will rest until that has been accomplished. To quote the immortal words of the martyr Robert Emmett, spoken before his execution, 'When my country takes her place among the nations of the earth, then, and not till then, let my epitaph be written.' The time will be soon, and bold Robert Emmett will have his epitaph."

The cheering resumed, but O'Mahony signaled for silence. "Next," he shouted above the din, "will be the swearing-in." Doheny handed him a document, which he waved at the audience. "This is the oath, which Michael and I will circulate among you during the social hour following my speech. Your signature makes you an honest-to-God Fenian, bound to the rules of our organization. Michael will read the oath aloud, so you will understand what you are signing."

Doheny read the oath in a high-pitched, articulate voice, pronouncing each word slowly and carefully.

"I do solemnly swear, in the presence of almighty God, that I will do my utmost at every risk, while life lasts, to make Ireland an independent democratic republic; that I will yield implicit obedience, in all things not contrary to the laws of God, to the commands of my superior officers, and that I shall preserve inviolable secrecy regarding all transactions of this secret society that may be confided to me. So help me God! Amen!"

After the signings, the mood of the patrons relaxed and the meeting became festive with beer drinking and arm wrestling prevailing. O'Mahony fielded questions as he moved about the room.

"Mr. O'Mahony, as Fenians, what should our positions be on the Lincoln-Douglas election, and what should we think about slavery?"

"Ah, I wouldn't be telling you what to think about that. As to slavery, we Irish are no strangers to it. We have our own battle to fight.

The English landlord is no different from the Southern plantation owner. Douglas is a compromiser. Most of the Irish, being Democrats, favor him. Lincoln will bring war. If war does come, lads, learn your lessons well. Learn the strategies of war. Your experience will be useful when you come to Ireland for the rising of the phoenix."

The merriment continued. One lad did a high-step on a table and fell off with a terrible clatter. Jack O'Mara climbed on a chair and recited "Cuchulain's Death" in Gaelic, greatly impressing O'Mahony.

"Mr. O'Mahony," said Lugh, "I don't want to make a wrong impression, but what's the point of the Celtic role-playing? Isn't it a quare thing, this running about in costumes, speaking Gaelic, and invoking Celtic gods? Are these activities in which grown men should be involved?"

"A quare thing? Lugh, we do have a past that goes back before England even knew we existed. We have a mythology as ancient and rich as the Greeks. We honor our past. It helps us to know who we are, to affirm our separateness, that which makes us unique. So you're the son of Fergus. I remember Fergus, and you're like him, a hard-headed realist. Welcome, Lugh Finnegan. There's a place in the movement for realism."

O'Mahony lit a cheroot, the third in a row. "We were here before the English, we were here before the Christians, we were here before Christ. We are the Irish. We are the Celts. The world needs to know. We have our own culture, our own history, our own tongue. There are those who would turn away, blend into England and anonymity; assimilate, as it were. We Fenians would have none of that. Quare, is it? Oh, I think not."

The lads had been guzzling for some time, which would set Feeney back because it was on the house. They were singing a lusty rendition of "Rory of the Hills" when O'Mahony slapped Feeney on the back and said, "Doheny and I would like to see you upstairs."

"Did you sign them all, Michael?"

"That I did."

"'Tis a fine group, Feeney."

"It is," agreed Feeney, pleased at the compliment, but wary. Something lurked beneath the surface.

"James Stephens made me head of the Brotherhood in America. That's a heavy responsibility. Stephens is concerned that things are not under control. Some brothers are straying."

"Straying?"

"Going off on their own, acting independently. A faction has split the Fenians in America. There is a plot to invade Canada, to hold the government hostage." Feeney's mouth dropped. "Would you know anything about that?"

"For Jesus's sake, no."

"Be advised that the plot does not meet the approval of the IRB. One of the reasons I have been touring the country is to investigate the extent of the conspiracy."

"Why is the IRB against it?"

"It would never succeed, and it would create ill will. Our fight is against England, not Canada. Yes, Canada may be a dominion of England, but such a move would be an act of terrorism that would tarnish the Fenian image in North America," said O'Mahony.

"We also have to talk about your little tea party," said Doheny. "It may not have been a bad idea, but it did not have the Brotherhood's approval. Since your gang was not officially IRB then, we will overlook it. In the future, our approval is required. We must be informed of what is being carried out in our name."

"I let on to the boys that I was pleased with the activity," said O'Mahony, "and indeed I admire their spirit. I admire your spirit, too. The burning was a romantic gesture. But you put a lot at risk for a few barrels of rum and a charred ship that, by the way, is in the process of being repaired."

"The boys were restless and crying for action."

"You didn't have to set fire to a ship. Fire has a special meaning for you, Feeney, does it not? Wasn't your family's farm in Mayo burned to the ground, your da imprisoned?"

"You do know a lot about me."

"Yes. The fire explains a lot, and you the son of the farmer. We all want revenge, myself as well as anyone, but there is a danger when things become too personal. The movement takes precedence over the individual. You must think of the greater whole, and you must go through the chain of command."

"I will keep that in mind from now on."

"There is also the question of the money that was entrusted to you. We want an accounting. What have you done with it?"

Beads of perspiration formed on Feeney's brow. The room was silent. Feeney went to the safe, opened it, brought the satchel to the table, and dumped its contents, including the pistol. The door burst open and Flaherty charged into the room. O'Mahony and Doheny froze at the intrusion of a uniformed policeman.

"Relax, gentlemen, it's only Flaherty. He's one of us. Duty prevented him from attending the swearing-in. Flaherty, shake hands with O'Mahony and Doheny. I don't need to tell you who they are."

"It's an honor," he said, but his eyes were on the money. "I came to tell you that the lads are gone and the pub is secure."

"Thank you, Officer. I will lock the place myself after my guests depart, so you may go. You may want to double-check on your rounds later tonight."

"Yes, sir, I will." Flaherty left, again glancing at the money.

"I don't question your honesty, Feeney," said Doheny, "but the money's doing no good just sitting in your satchel. It's not earning interest. If you don't know what to do with it, give it back. I can think of a dozen good uses for it. For one thing, we need rifles."

"Let it rest, Michael," said O'Mahony. "If we need it, we know where to find it. Return it to the safe and note how you use it. You're a good fella, Feeney, and we're lucky to have a man like you. Keep us posted. We don't like surprises. Michael and I are out of here at dawn. 'Tis a long haul to New York, with endless stops along the way. Those stagecoach trails, you know."

"Are you certain you won't be takin' the train?"

"That remains to be seen," O'Mahoney winked, "but you can stop looking for a man with a white shirt and a black armband."

The two men left. Feeney collapsed wearily into his favorite chair facing the window. They knew about his plan to invade Canada. How did they know? Who was the informer within the inner circle?

Chapter Seven

CAPTAIN GARRETT BARRY SAT IN a hard-backed armchair behind a plain wooden desk. One look at him was to know that he spent little time behind the desk. Tall, lean, and muscular with graying hair and a walrus mustache, the captain fairly burst with energy, at least when he was not drinking. His eyes were piercing and his smile warmly determined. There was a light rap on the door.

"Come in," he said gruffly. An orderly entered, placing the mail on the desk. "Is that it? Only one letter?"

"Yes, sir."

"Very well. By the way, it's not necessary for you to knock when you bring in the mail."

"Yes, sir."

"It's not necessary at other times, either. You're my orderly, for God's sake."

"Yes, sir."

"We've discussed this before. Do not knock. Do I make myself clear?"

"Yes, sir."

The orderly saluted and hurriedly departed. Barry sighed. The young lad was terrified of him. He glanced at the letter. It was from Alexander Randall, governor of the state of Wisconsin. Before opening it, he crossed to the liquor cabinet and poured himself a stiff shot of Irish malt, which he sipped slowly, allowing the liquid to warm him inside.

He crossed to the window with a view of the open parade ground and the expanse of Lake Michigan beyond. The sky was overcast, a typical bleak Wisconsin afternoon. The weather was not what occupied his mind. At one time, Alexander Randall and Garrett Barry had been friends. Barry had received letters of commendation for what Randall termed "the crackerjack Union Guard."

Times had changed. During the past year, a rift had developed between them. It was more than a rift, Barry thought; it was a chasm. The letter on his desk could only be bad news. He was in no hurry to deal with bad news.

Barry was a soldier, and Randall was a politician. Ultimately, it came down to that. War and politics, oil and water. The Dred Scott Decision ruled that slaves did not have rights and could not become free by escaping to a free state. The Fugitive Slave Act required that runaways be returned to their owners.

The states were expected to enforce the law. During the past year, fugitive slaves had been pouring into Wisconsin. When pressed by the federal government, Randall flatly refused to go after slaves, declaring the Fugitive Slave Act unconstitutional. His defiance escalated the power struggle between Wisconsin and the United States.

How much control should the federal government have over the states? Randall was putting it to the test. To many, Randall was a hero, but the governor's stance put Barry and the Union Guard in the middle. Barry must make a choice: openly defy the federal government or disobey the governor of Wisconsin. The dilemma aggravated Barry, but he didn't doubt for a moment what his choice would be.

Barry, every inch a military man, put the corps above all. A West Point graduate and classmate of Ulysses S. Grant, he believed in the absolute authority of the federal government, regardless of his own opinion of this law or that law. On a personal level, he had reservations about slavery. The issue was creating conflict within his marriage. Mary's underground work and the harboring of Ned, if that was his name, jeopardized his career. If Ned were discovered, Barry's integrity would be compromised. He couldn't let it continue. He needed to talk sense into his stubborn wife.

Whatever might come of that, he wouldn't commit his brigade to subverting the law, to commit treason. The governor had asked him point-blank for support. Barry's own words came back to him now, as he gazed out the window and drained the last drop of whiskey from the glass.

"I will support the government of the United States."

He had no illusions that his statement would be the end of the matter. He'd been waiting for the ax to fall. He crossed to the desk and ripped open the letter.

Captain Barry:

With regret, I hereby terminate the Union Guard. Since you chose to disobey my directive, your brigade is no longer a concern of the state of Wisconsin. Return all arms, ammunition, and equipment belonging to Wisconsin. You do not need to return the uniforms, which you purchased on your own. My decision is effective immediately.

Alexander Randolph

Bastard! So much for commendations and the "crackerjack" Union Guard. He'd expected a reprimand but hoped Randolph would leave it at that. Now he saw his whole career go down the drain.

It might have been any routine drill, but for the men of Captain Barry's Irish Brigade it was special. Word spread quickly that the governor had disbanded the Guard. Everyone knew it had happened, and everyone knew why. The support was for Barry. Randolph would lose votes within the Bloody Third when the next election occurred. It was a hot, sunny afternoon, but the guardsmen were in full parade dress, as they stood in formation to hear their captain for the last time. Sitting before them on a white horse, he cleared his throat before he spoke.

"My brave lads. Our governor has seen fit to disband the brigade for reasons known by most of you. You have served Wisconsin well and may continue to do so by joining another unit. Our parting is not to your discredit. With my unqualified recommendation, you have a reference wherever you go. As of this moment, you are released from Captain Barry's Irish Brigade. Goodbye and God bless you all."

The men remained at attention. No one moved. It was an awkward moment. Barry stared at the men. The men stared back. He cleared his throat. "Union Guard, at ease. Fall out." The brigade stood rigidly at attention, disobeying the order. Jack O'Mara, leader of the platoon, stepped forward.

"With your permission, sir, I would like to speak for the brigade."

Barry nodded.

"Meaning no disrespect, sir, the men of Captain Barry's Irish Brigade refuse to be disbanded."

Barry smiled. "It's already been done. What's the alternative, Jack?"

"We'd like the brigade to become a volunteer unit for the United States, a federal militia, with you leading us. Would you consider it, sir?"

"A volunteer unit would need funding. We have our own uniforms, but we would need rifles and ammunition, and that's the least of it."

"We have some ideas about that, Captain."

Barry considered. The idea had occurred to him, but he had dismissed it. It was difficult to get financial backing. Backers always wanted something in return. He thought of Feeney. To accept money from the Fenians would be obligating the brigade to a foreign power. Irish independence was not the concern of a brigade of US volunteers. Barry would never agree to that.

"Do you speak for the entire brigade?"

"I do. A poll was taken. The result was unanimous."

"Then, by God. we'll do it. If there's a way, we'll do it. Let's find out what these ideas of yours are. We'll all keep in touch. For now, I've given an order. Men of the Union Guard, fall out."

Barry thought he'd never heard such whooping and hollering. He began to get excited himself. The Union Guard, guarding the Union. He had to admit that he liked the idea.

Jack had first heard of the disbanding of the brigade from Feeney, who had heard it, he said, from an undisclosed source. It had been Feeney's idea that the boys should become volunteers. Feeney knew that if Barry thought the idea came from him, he'd drop it like a hot potato. Barry would never accept Fenian money, but the money would have to come from somewhere. There was one person who could save the day. He summoned Jack O'Mara to his attic lair.

"Your da," said Feeney, "has been a political force in the ward for some time, has he not?" Jack admitted that this was true. "And your da is pals with the ward boss, Councilman Garrity." Jack nodded. "Jack, you consider yourself a hero, a modern Cuchulain. You are the bravest of our entire group. Now you can be a greater hero. You alone can save the Union Guard, and, in doing so, save Feeney's Boys."

"I thank you, Feeney, for your confidence, but what on earth can I do?"

"Go to your da. Convince him of our need. Persuade him to seek out Garrity. There's an election coming up. Saving the Union Guard would be a feather in his cap. It's my guess that the Democrats would cough up the resources, being that the ward is staunchly Democrat. Your da is a strong Democrat and an influence on Garrity.

"I don't know if my da would do it."

"It's worth a try, Jack. Would you at least give it a try?"

"I'll speak to him tonight."

"That's grand. By the way, don't even mention the word 'Fenian.'"

"To my da? Do you think I'm daft?"

"Sometimes I do. Just a wee bit."

They both laughed and went downstairs, Feeney to the pub and Jack to O'Mara's grocery store.

It was a rainy day. The faint, mysterious aroma of incense was subdued by musty dampness in the dark, shadowy interior of St. Patrick's, where Father Delaney meditated, sitting alone in a pew, absorbing the quiet atmosphere. He was not praying or thinking churchly thoughts. This was his favorite kind of day and his favorite place to be on such a day, in the solitude of an empty church, where he could allow his mind to wander.

That an Irish priest was in charge of an Irish parish in the city of Milwaukee was the result of a decision made by a German prelate. John Martin Henni, past bishop of Milwaukee, was now archbishop of Wisconsin. Parishioners had been upset that German Catholics had infiltrated the Wisconsin hierarchy and controlled the church. When Henni, a German, had become archbishop, things were in a state of upheaval.

Parishioners of other nationalities, especially the Irish, were on the verge of separating. Henni had come to the rescue by assigning priests of the same ethnic background to the parishes. Father Delaney, from Cork, Ireland, had been appointed parish priest of St. Patrick's. The wise prelate left Delaney alone and did not interfere with parish affairs.

In the parish, Father Delaney was more revered than the pope, coming, as it were, from the old country. Delaney had been a renegade in his native land, a gadfly expressing nationalistic views and anti-British sentiment, not hesitating to express them from the pulpit. When he was a child roaming the banks of the Lee and the mountains of Macroom, celebrating Mass was forbidden. He had grown up attending secret masses held in mountain caves. His youthful admiration of the priests who risked their lives and put God above England had led him to the vocation.

The faith of the priests and celebrants at the clandestine masses made a deep impression. On stormy Sundays people trudged miles in the rain and were soaked to the skin. (Delaney still liked rain. It was symbolic of sacrifice.) The bonding of the celebrants had been powerful. Delaney remembered tears streaming down the faces of grown men.

Delaney hated the British, who tried to force the Anglican Church down the throats of his countrymen, forcing simple, honest folk to sneak to Mass as if it were shameful. His open hatred of England was a sin for which he was often required to do penance. He'd been warned that as a priest he must overcome the hatred. He had not overcome it.

The contemporary church condoned England by silence. Masses were no longer held in caves, but the faithful were still oppressed. The English were the plunderers of the earth. It was their way or no way. What happened before would happen again. Irish children had to speak Gaelic secretly. In school, Gaelic was forbidden. Children were punished for speaking it. Whenever Father Delaney expressed concern, he was hushed or put off with frowns. "Where," he would ask himself, "are the cave priests, the heroes of my childhood?"

Because he would not remain quiet, he was sent to America. He assisted at small parishes in Green Bay and Kenosha before receiving his present assignment. In the ward lived kindred spirits. No one censured him for uttering anti-British sentiments. The parishioners liked and trusted him.

Because people trusted him and because he heard their confessions, he knew most of what went on in the ward. He knew about Feeney's Boys and the truth about the fire on the *Lynne*. He could do little with this knowledge because it was revealed in the confessional. The priest did not encourage Fenianism, condemning the paganism. He did not approve of Feeney.

Feeney did not attend church. Father Delaney had made overtures, but Feeney had mumbled something about the Church not saving his da. Delaney had no idea what private demons drove Feeney, but he was a driven man with personal motives and a hidden agenda. He was a dangerous and violent man out to avenge some secret wrong.

Then there was this Celtic thing with Jack O'Mara. Jack was a romantic, a boy not grown up. The Celts had been pagan sun worshipers before St. Patrick brought Christianity to Ireland. How deeply was Jack into this? How many others were in it with him? Jack had a wild imagination. Delaney worried that Jack believed himself to be a reincarnated Celtic hero. Where would all of this lead?

A loud voice behind him brought Father Delaney out of his reverie. It was old Garrity, wanting the key to the parish hall.

"If you recall, Father, Dan O'Mara, his son Jack, Captain Barry, and myself are scheduled for a meeting."

"Follow me, and I'll open the hall."

The others were waiting at the entrance to the hall. Delaney opened the door and let them inside. He produced another key and led them to the third door on the left, which he opened. The room was dark, so Delaney parted the curtains. The light was dim, but it would do.

"The room is yours. There is a table and chairs. It's no luxury, and dark on a dark day. There's no charge, and a donation is not expected."

"Thank you, Father."

"Leave everything when you're finished, and I'll return to lock the doors. Have a good meeting." Delaney smiled and left the building. It was raining.

The four men sat around the table. Introductions were made and small talk ensued, with much laughter centered around jokes told by twinkle-eyed Dan O'Mara. During a lull in the conversation, Garrity cleared his throat.

"Gentlemen," he began, the wattles on his neck quivering, "let us get to the matter at hand, the predicament of Captain Barry's brigade. There's no need to rehash all of it. Dan filled me in on the details, which his young son Jack, here, brought to him, and which I later verified with Captain Barry. I'm prepared to offer support on behalf of the Democratic Party."

Barry nodded. No one spoke. Attention was riveted on Garrity. Garrity removed a handkerchief from his pocket and wiped the sweat off his bald pate. "I had to call in a few markers, and my friend Dan was able to pull a string or two. We can give you a portion of what you need."

"How much is a portion?"

"The ward will underwrite your daily expenses."

"That's a generous offer," Barry responded, "and I'm grateful, but you must realize that it takes guns and ammunition to run a brigade."

"I'm coming to that. We have found a sponsor willing to donate whatever you need within reason."

"And who might that be?"

"The Little Giant himself. Stephen A. Douglas."

Garrity paused to let that sink in. Barry's face was impassive. Was his poker face a mark of innate coolness, or was the captain pie-eyed? Garrity detected barley on his breath.

"Go on."

"The money won't come directly from Douglas, but from the Douglas campaign fund."

Barry emitted a low whistle. "Stephen Douglas is well known as a philanthropist, but I cannot believe that he or his fund would donate so much without expecting something in return. What's the hitch?"

"The hitch, Captain, if you must call it that, is that the brigade show public support for the Little Giant."

Dan O'Mara exploded in a belly laugh. "Oh, hell, the lads are all voting for Douglas anyway. A piece of cake, my boy."

One of Garrity's suspender straps slid down his shoulder. He raised a flabby arm to make the adjustment, displaying a wet blotch of underarm sweat. For such a dark, cool day, "Garrulous" Garrity had a vast propensity for perspiration.

"You weren't paying attention. I said nothing about votes or voting. Voting is a private matter. 'Show public support' is what I said."

"How are we to do that?"

"Douglas wants you in Chicago."

"What!"

Garrity took a deep breath, pushing his ample belly against the table. "Douglas makes a campaign speech in Chicago on September 7. There will be a rally, which thousands are expected to attend. There will be a parade. The Union Guard will march in the parade, with you, Captain, leading your men."

"Is there anything else?"

"The entire brigade will also attend the rally, carrying banners proclaiming support for the Little Giant."

"Is that it?"

"That's the offer."

"I need to sort this out. My first reaction is to reject the proposal. I don't like mixing the military and politics."

"Be realistic. It's done all the time. Isn't your present status the result of a politically motivated decision?"

"What would be so wrong about it?" asked the red-nosed O'Mara. "Why did you agree to meet with an influential Democrat, if you had such misgivings? This is a good proposal, my boy. Consider it carefully."

"I am considering it. I see nothing wrong with declaring for Douglas, but the fate of the Union Guard mustn't be tied in with the results of an election. What happens to us if the Democrats lose? If attending a parade and rally is all Douglas expects, I see no problem."

"Good."

"If there are no other strings ..."

"There are no strings," said Jack, who'd been listening quietly up to this point. "The decision is yours. There's no pressure involved. These people are trying to help."

"How do we get to Chicago, Mr. Garrity?"

"The *Lady Elgin* is scheduled to make a run from Milwaukee to Chicago to arrive on time for the parade, returning later that evening." Garrity loosened his tie and unbuttoned his collar. By now, he was drenched. The exertion left him winded, and he paused to regain control. "Captain Wilson, the skipper, says he can accommodate the whole guard, including wives, sweethearts, relatives, and friends. The ship has a capacity of more than three hundred people, not including the crew."

"The *Lady Elgin,* is it? Now that's going in style."

"Indeed. The *Lady* is a pleasure craft, you know, the most luxurious steamer on the Great Lakes. Food, wine, and dancing will be provided, with music played by a German band."

"German," said O'Mara. "There's the worst of it."

"Now, Dan, we all know there's no love lost between the Irish and the Germans in this town, but in the election the Germans are on our side."

Jack nodded. "It's not so much that they favor Douglas as that they fear Lincoln. Freeing the slaves could mean war. Many Germans came to this country to escape conscription."

"And many Irish came to this country to escape impressment into the British Navy," retorted Garrity. "Forget that. This excursion will be great fun and the parade itself a lark."

"What is the date, did you say?"

"September 6. The ship leaves the dock Thursday, the sixth, at 7:00 pm and arrives Friday morning. The lads will march in the parade and demonstrate before and after the speech. There should be a few hours for free time in Chicago before the return voyage late Friday night. During this interval, arrangements will be made to get the rifles and load them on the ship. The ship will arrive back in Milwaukee Saturday morning."

"That would be September 8."

"By God, you have it all worked out, all but one thing. How can we afford such a grand voyage?"

"There's one thing Garrity left out," said O'Mara. "Captain Wilson's an old friend of mine. He's offering a special rate. The fare will be one dollar round trip. Of course food and other amenities will be up to the individual."

"Gentlemen, are we all agreed?" Garrity shot a questioning glance at Barry, who nodded. "We will have to meet again to finalize our plan. The departure of the *Lady Elgin* with a boatload of young Irish soldiers will draw a huge crowd. It will be a gala event. We might even get the mayor to attend, maybe even speak. Why don't you approach him, Dan? If anyone can get him to do it, you can."

Dan's nose began to glow. "I'll give it a try, councilman. Maybe the mayor will start trading at O'Mara's Grocery Store."

"Given your gift of gab, I'm sure you'll talk him into it."

Everyone started talking, congratulating Barry, who was beaming. Garrity stood, making a great exertion to haul his three hundred pounds into an upright position. He raised his voice, but that didn't get anyone's attention, so he banged on the table.

"That's it, then. So much for business. Would anyone care to go over to Feeney's and hoist a few?"

"Sure," said Jack, ignoring his father's disapproving glare.

"I'll join you," said the elder O'Mara, "if only to keep an eye on my son. No hoisting for me, though."

"Ah, well, I thought you might break your rule this once. How about you, Captain Barry? Will you join us at Feeney's?"

Barry was dying for a whiskey. It took all the willpower he could muster to reply, "Feeney's? Count me out."

Chapter Eight

WHEN BLEVINS ARRIVED HOME, THE light was still burning in the print shop. He found his father in a raging drunk.

"One thing those lazy peckerheads do know is when to quit."

"Dad, it's midnight. Your printers quit because they were finished. They went home to their families. So should you."

"Lackadaisical louts. They're behind, you know. Don't you think I want to get home and be with your ma? I have to stay to finish their work."

"No, you don't. Come on, Dad, let's go."

Bill tilted a pint bottle to his lips, but it was empty. He flung it to the floor, where it smashed into smithereens. He tried to say smithereens, but it came out "smitheens."

"Dad, don't worry about it. Call it a night. If you really are behind, I'll help you in the morning."

"What do you mean 'if I am behind'? Don't condescend to me, boy."

Blevins sighed. This was the second time that someone had accused him of condescending. He didn't have the patience for this. "Good. Stay all night, for all I care."

"Sorry, son. I'm a mean bastard, aren't I?"

"Dad—"

"No, no. I am. You don't know what a low-down louse your old man is."

"I suppose you're going to tell me."

"My own mother used to say to me, 'Bill, you're a bum. You'll never amount to anything.' My own mother, for God's sake."

"Dad—"

"Don't try to stop me. It's time you heard the truth. After I married your mother, there was this woman—" Wild Bill looked at Blevins with a blank expression, having lost his train of thought. "Ah, yes. This woman … what was her name?"

"This is your story, Dad. How should I know? I don't want to hear any more. Let's lock up."

"She called me 'Billy Boy.'"

"Who?"

"My ma. Pay attention. Never wanted me to grow up. Broke her heart when I married your ma. Called me 'Billy Boy' until the day she died."

"You're not making sense. Let's go."

"Ah, you go ahead, son. Tell Dorothy I'll be in shortly." Bill sat on a stool and yawned. "Go ahead. Don't wait for me. You need your beauty rest. Go."

"Dad, I wish you'd—" Blevins stopped in midsentence. Bill was snoring. Blevins gave up and slipped out the door.

In the house, his mother was sitting in a rocker, reading a book of poetry. The house was always cluttered with her books, the desk drawers crammed with her writings. She had been educated at one of the better eastern schools, but she did not allude to that often. When Bill— handsome, boyish, and witty—had come along, she had thrown it all up and eloped. In time, her parents had forgiven her, but they had not forgiven Bill.

The early years of the marriage had been heady and romantic. Bill started drinking. His good looks dissipated, and his cheerful wit turned to biting sarcasm. In spite of it all, he maintained the boyish charm.

"Hello, Blevins, is your father still in the shop?"

"Yes, and he'll be there the night."

"Then there's no point in my staying up any longer. A letter arrived for you today," she said, handing Blevins a scented envelope sealed with wax, "and it smells lovely. It must be from that fair colleen."

Blevins hadn't been expecting a letter. The handwriting was Flynn's, but he'd not seen Flynn since Lookout Hill, and she'd mentioned nothing about a letter. "Thank you, Ma." He started up to his room.

"Aren't you going to open it?"

"Yes, Ma, in my room."

"I don't mean to pry. After all, you are an adult."

"I've been old enough to open my own mail for a long time."

"Flynn is a nice girl, but—"

"But what?"

"Nothing."

"No, not nothing. What were you going to say? Flynn is a nice girl, but—"

"She's a Catholic."

"So?"

"If you plan to marry her, you'll have to become a Catholic. Is that what you have in mind?"

"I hadn't given it much thought."

"Do so. The pressure on Flynn will be intense. If you don't convert, you won't be allowed a church wedding. You won't be accepted in the Irish community, and Flynn will be an outcast in her own family. Your children will have to be raised in the church or Flynn will be excommunicated."

"Excommunicated? I doubt it. Outcast? Dan O'Mara would never cast out his favorite child. Oh, there would be some gnashing and grinding of teeth, but not what you say. I understand your concern, but you've been misled."

"Maybe so. Just be sure you're not misled. We Protestants can be narrow-minded, even among ourselves. You know that I am not narrow-minded. Once, before I met your father, I almost converted. I was impressed by the pageantry and stirred by the drama of the high mass. Ah, there is more to it than that. Blevins, if I have unintentionally spoken any untruth, seek the truth yourself. Give the matter a lot of thought."

"It's obvious that you've given it a lot of thought."

"I'm just trying to help."

"Flynn and I are in love. We have each other. We can deal with this. There's nothing we can't face together."

"The two of you against the world, eh? For your sakes, I hope so. The world is full of hate, not the least of which is right here in Milwaukee. You want an example? Just recently, there was the case of

Leahy, the Trappist monk. You remember that. You wrote an article about it."

Ma was a stickler for examples. She, more than any of his teachers, had taught him to write, and she had taught him to back up his statements with examples. The Leahy incident was an extreme example of local religious bigotry. Leahy, a fallen Trappist monk, had been invited to speak at a nearby Methodist church. The topic was the evils and shortcomings of Roman Catholicism. The lecture was attended by a group of Methodists, eager to believe the ex-priest's scurrilous lies.

The lecture was also attended by a group of uninvited Catholics with clubs concealed under their garments. At a given signal, they started to swing their clubs. The Methodists tore planks from the pews to bash the Catholics. This "holy war" ended after an alderman fired a shot into the air, scaring the participants, who fled the meeting.

"Mother, we are not going to base our life decisions upon the behavior of others."

"Do what you must do. Just do it with your eyes open."

"Thank you, Mother. Now I would like to go upstairs and read my mail."

"Go on with you. Get the letter and the aroma out of here. Good night, son."

"Good night, Ma."

In his room, Blevins sat at his writing desk facing the window. Using a silver letter opener, he carefully broke the seal to preserve the envelope. He removed the letter and unfolded it.

Dear Blevins,

> Thank you for a lovely moonlit evening. Thank you, dearest, for sharing your secret place. I was touched and deeply honored. I, too, once had a secret place. I wish I could take you there, but I can't. Instead, here is my poem, which I have shared with no one else. The poem is yours, and so am I. Oh, by the way, I can't wait to see *The Merchant of Venice* with you on Saturday.
>
> All my love,
> Flynn

The poem was on a separate sheet of paper. Blevins put the letter in the desk drawer. He supposed anyone with a nose for perfume could find it. He needed to get a strong box with a lock to secure his personal correspondence. He read the poem, written in Flynn's meticulous calligraphy.

"Pond in the Wood"

A place to retreat to
a place to explore.
Cool and quiet with sun-streaks
filtering through the leaves of trees overhead.
'Twas but a quick child's pace to the
tadpole-filled pond nestled at the
far edge of the wood.
Little tadpoles squiggly and
undeveloped like the child
observing them.

The day starts to pass and the child
must leave a bit reluctantly.

A short way down the path she
stoops to lift the green-and-brown-
striped hood of the Jack-in-the-
Pulpit to say hello and to wonder
what his Sunday sermon to the
creatures of the wood will be.
"Good-bye until we meet again
Mr. Jack-in-the-Pulpit."
She pauses, gently strokes his head,
and continues on.

The next friend she spies is the
soft, pink delicate one
known as "Lady Slipper."
How pretty and gentle she seems!

Her voice, too, is soft and bell-like.
It almost seems to break into
tiny crystal-like pieces.
She tells the girl-child to be ladylike.
The child seems for the moment
to be transformed into
an elfin princess.

The spell ends.
The child breaks free and scampers
from the darkened wood into the
sun-drenched field of tall
yellow grass and perky white daisy.
She sees her wood-framed home
snuggled just ahead and runs
toward it and the safety of reality.

Marion O'Mara heard the stifled sobs of her daughter and softly opened the bedroom door. "Flynn," she whispered, but there was no response. "What is it? What's wrong?" The shapeless mound beneath the quilt stopped shaking and the sobs subsided. "Flynn, we have always been able to talk. Please don't hold this in. I want to help."

It was silent beneath the quilt. "Are you there, Flynn?" She resisted the urge to tickle her daughter, a ritual that had taken place at bedtime when Flynn was a little girl. "It's Blevins, isn't it? Blevins and you." The sobs began again, and the form under the quilt heaved. "You don't want to talk about it. Good. I'll leave."

"Oh, Mother," Flynn cried, head emerging turtle-like from under the quilt, "I don't know what to do. I love him so much."

"Does he love you?"

"Yes. He says he does. He wants to marry me."

"Then why are you so unhappy?"

"It's impossible. Da will never accept it. He'll go through the ceiling and never speak to me again. Then there's Jack and Maggie and my friends in the parish and Father Delaney and ... and you, Mother ... and ..."

"At least Blevins isn't German." They both laughed at that. If there was anything worse than a Protestant, it was a German.

"Or a German Protestant," Flynn chortled and started sputtering with laughter, but the laughter went on too long and soon she was wracked with sobs again.

"For goodness' sake, Flynn, get yourself under control."

"I'm sorry, Mother. What do you think? What should I do?"

"If I were choosing your mate, I would choose a Catholic. I would choose a church wedding in the presence of friends and relatives, and, of course, a priest. Will Blevins convert?"

"I wouldn't ask him to do that."

"Then you have a difficult decision, which could involve your living in sin and being denied the sacraments. You will have to tell your father."

"I can't confront him."

"Then don't, at least not now."

"You've always said, 'Yes him to death and then do what you want,' but this is different."

"It is. Sooner or later, you'll have to tell him. Things may work out. Postpone the inevitable. Wait. I will try to soften the blow. Flynn, I am a traditional woman. It would never be in me to do what you contemplate, but I am not you. You are a grown woman. You must not consider disappointing others. Be strong and be true to yourself. You will live a long time with whatever choice you make. I can't help you with this."

"You have helped. Now I want to go to sleep. Thank you, Mother. I love you."

Marion kissed her daughter and left the bedroom, shutting the door behind her.

The Gaiety Theater was a cultural oasis in a city of commercial enterprise that not long ago had been a frontier town. Drawing together the multiethnic elements of Milwaukee, it was one of the few places where Germans and Irish could gather together under the same roof without assaulting each other. It should be noted, though, that they didn't mingle during intermissions.

Flynn loved the Gaiety. Her earliest memories were of her father sending her, Jack, and Maggie to the minstrel shows on Saturday afternoons. The shows had been funny and entertaining, with black-faced men dancing, singing, and banging on tambourines, and she had delighted in the jokes told by the man they called "Mister Interlocutor." Then she learned that the black men were really white men wearing black makeup. It seemed to be a put-down, a caricature of black people. When she thought about the jokes, she realized many of them were racial slurs. She didn't agree with slavery, either. She stopped attending the shows. Then a Shakespearean troupe arrived in town. Flynn was fourteen. The play was *A Midsummer Night's Dream.* She was captivated by the magic of the language. After that, she attended every Shakespearean production at the Gaiety.

How pleased she had been to discover that Blevins also enjoyed Shakespeare. It was another of the many things they had in common. (How sad if the one thing, religion, which they didn't have in common, were to spoil everything else.) With what anticipation they had awaited this evening's performance of *The Merchant of Venice,* starring the great John Jefferson as Shylock.

"Wasn't that exhilarating?" said Blevins afterward, as he took Flynn's white-gloved hand while they strolled to the waterfront. She didn't respond. They paused on the bridge over the Milwaukee River, gazing eastward toward the mouth where the river emptied into Lake Michigan.

"Poor Shylock. How sad for him."

"Shylock? He was a loan shark. He got what he deserved."

"He had to give up his faith. He was a Jew and he was forced to become a Christian. No one should be coerced. I would never expect you to do that, Blevins. I would never want you to give up your faith for me."

"I'd do anything for you. I don't want to lose you. I'll become a Catholic, if that's what it takes."

"I don't even like to hear you say that. That's not what it takes, and you aren't going to lose me. I just wish it were easier."

A hansom cab started across the bridge. Blevins hailed it. "Take us along the waterfront." The cab proceeded down Huron, once the city's main street. They passed the Lake Brewery, the first brewery in Milwaukee. It was owned by three Welshmen: Owens, Paulette, and Davis. The Welshmen, who owned land along the waterfront, had built a pier that extended way out onto the lake, allowing the big ships to dock and unload. Eventually, a river entrance had been cut and dredged to allow the ships to sail into the heart of the city. After that, the pier had fallen into disuse.

Now there were twenty-five breweries in Milwaukee, most of them German, including the Empire Brewery, brewer of the popular Melms Beer, and Braum's Brewery, owned by a Bavarian named Valentine Blatz.

They clip-clopped along the waterfront, cuddled like two peas in a pod. The tears began to flow. "Oh Blevins, what are we going to do?" He kissed her hair, drawing her close to comfort her. The driver asked for directions because they had reached the end of the main section of the waterfront. "Fourth Ward Park," Blevins responded.

"I have a plan. On September 7, the *Lady Elgin* sets sail for Chicago. Well, you know about that. Your father helped plan the excursion. I'll be going to cover the parade and rally. I want you to come with me. That shouldn't arouse suspicion. It's a big event and nearly everyone's going. We'll get married on the *Lady Elgin*.

"How can—"

"Captain Wilson has the civil authority to marry couples aboard his ship, and he owes me a favor. It will be legal and binding. We won't let anyone know. When we return to Milwaukee, we'll be man and wife. The families will not approve. Sure, there'll be a terrible uproar, but it'll be too late. What's done cannot be undone. Marry me, Flynn. Marry me on the *Lady Elgin*."

There was a silence for several miles. The hansom slowed as they reached the park. "Let's get out and walk," she said. They stopped and disembarked. Blevins signaled the driver, who followed at a discreet distance. Opposite the park loomed the four-story brick house that was the residence of John Plankinton, who, with his partner, Philip D. Armour, owned the largest meatpacking plant in Wisconsin. Dim lights flickered in the darkness of the city. Flynn stopped and looked at Blevins. Her eyes were shining.

"Oh, yes. Yes, Blevins. Let's do it."

They kissed for an eternity. Blevins motioned for the hansom. They climbed in, and he directed the driver. Flynn sighed happily. "What an evening—from Shakespeare to King Arthur."

"King Arthur?"

"Do you remember who gave the sword *Excalibur* to Arthur?"

"No."

"It was the Lady of the Lake."

The hansom went on through the night. As they approached the Third Ward, it began to rain.

Chapter Nine

OLD NED WAS STARTLED BY a thunderclap followed by a scream. He nearly fell off the limb of the apple tree where he was picking apples. In the stable yard, the captain's white stallion was loose and bucking wildly. Astride the horse was young Willie, yelling and hanging on for dear life. At the window of the house Mary Barry shouted, "Willie! Willie!" A moment later, the captain ran out. There was another clap of thunder and a sudden downpour.

The horse stopped bucking and galloped directly toward the apple tree, the captain chasing in hot pursuit. Old Ned crouched on the limb. As Willie and the horse approached, Ned leaped, soaring through the drenched air like a wet, black crow. Time stopped for a split second. What was a cotton-picker doing picking apples? Wasn't he too old to be doing this? Was this flight his final moment? Why was he risking life and limb for an impetuous white boy?

He grunted as he spread-eagled on the back of the glistening horse, keeping his balance long enough to grab the slippery Willie and fall into a lake of mud, his body a cushion for the boy. The captain, racing straight at them, was caught short and lost his balance, toppling on Willie and Ned. The last thing Ned heard before passing out was Mary's voice sobbing, "Willie, Willie …"

"Is he dead?" asked Willie. Ned heard the voice in a cloudy distance but didn't open his eyes. When he had climbed into the tree, he had felt young and spirited. Now he felt his age. Every bone in his body ached.

"He's breathing. His chest is going up and down."

Ned smiled inwardly. He was alive at that. The aching diminished as he remembered why he had risked his life for young Willie. It had nothing to do with black or white, slave or master. Ned had had a son of his own. The last time Ned had seen him, his son had been Willie's age. The slave owner had taken him and sold him. How Ned missed his son! He had searched but never found him. If he was still alive, he'd be a grown man now.

"No, dear, he isn't dead. He's resting. He saved your life. Your father will get him into the house, and I'll make some hot broth."

Ned basked in the deep comfort of the guest room bed. Somehow, the captain had gotten him undressed and into a nightshirt that was clean and fresh. He had never known such luxury. The Barrys treated him well, mostly at Mrs. Barry's insistence, providing him with a cot and a chair in a corner of the stable, but he had never slept in a big bed in a big house. He didn't want to open his eyes, never mind get up. He groaned with pleasure.

"He groaned, Mother. Are you going to send for a doctor?"

"No, dear, we mustn't do that. No one must know that Ned is here. There are bad men who might come to the house and take him away. The same men would try to get your father and me into trouble."

"I know, but if he needs a doctor—"

"He'll be fine. You'll see."

Captain Barry arrived with a steaming bowl of chicken broth. The aroma reached Ned's nostrils, and he opened his eyes. Everyone made a fuss. Mary spoon-fed him the broth, and Willie brought him an extra pillow. Ned tried to get up, but the captain said, "Stay in bed. We do not have a guest. Be our guest. There's time enough for work tomorrow or the next day."

"Come, Willie, we'll go downstairs and let Ned rest."

"I was hoping Ned would tell me one of his stories."

"No, Willie, he's not up to that."

"It's all right, Mrs. Barry. I can handle one story."

"Good. Tell me the one about Moses in the bulrushes."

"One story, young man, and then come downstairs. We need to discuss what you were doing on your father's horse."

"Yes, Mother."

As Mary and Garrett went downstairs, Garrett remembered the words of Marshal Doughty. "They call him Moses. No last name. Just Moses."

"He's got to go. Ned has got to go."

"What!"

"The man is a runaway slave and a leader of runaway slaves."

"We've been over this before. I thought we were in agreement."

"No, I never really agreed. Ned must leave."

"How can you say that?"

"Mary, his name's not even Ned. He calls himself Moses."

"I don't care if he calls himself Jesus Christ."

"Listen to me—"

"No, you listen to me. How could you? How could you betray Ned, or Moses, or whatever you choose to call him? He saved our son's life. Our Willie—Ned saved his life! For God's sake, Garrett."

"Federal marshals are on his trail."

"They won't find him. Anyway, talk about timing. Here he is, recovering from bruises suffered while snatching your only son from the jaws of death, and you say we have to get rid of him. Good timing, Garrett."

"It's not that I don't appreciate—"

"Fine. Do it. Do it now, my brave captain. Go up there this minute, while Ned is telling our child a lovely Bible story. Let's see, how will you phrase it? 'Thanks, I appreciate what you did. Get dressed and leave and don't come back.' Is that what you'll say? Or will you offer him a few coins and fresh clothes to make him feel better?"

"Mary—"

"Will you also tell him to forget that he was ever here? 'If you are captured, Ned, don't tell anyone we let you stay here.' What will you tell Willie? You'll have to explain it, because I won't."

"Please lower your voice. They'll hear us. The children will hear us."

"You mean they'll hear you. I will not support you in this. You'll have to take all the initiative."

"Very well. I will do that."

"No, you will not. I won't let you."

"Won't let me?"

"Ned's welcome in my house."

"This is our house."

"Purchased with my money. I have never thrown it up to you, but now I do. Ned stays."

Barry tried to control a surge of anger. The pitch of his voice shot up as he attempted to keep the volume down. "The house may be yours, but the career is mine. I have made a public stand against the governor on the issue. Now I am harboring a fugitive. A federal marshal is breathing down my neck. If Ned is found here, I'll be a laughingstock."

"Is that what you're worried about? Being a laughingstock? Garrett, I know the pressure you must feel, but Ned is like a member of the family. He belongs here. We owe him for Willie's life."

"It's convenient, this whole episode. It really puts us in his debt, doesn't it?"

"Are you suggesting that the apple tree incident was staged? That's stupid, really stupid, and unworthy of you."

"Ned doesn't belong here. He is not a member of the family. He belongs to a plantation owner in South Carolina."

"No one belongs to anyone."

"You belong to me, Mary." Garrett helped himself to a generous swig of whiskey, which he poured from the decanter on the counter.

"You belong to that! Talk about slavery. You are a slave to whiskey. I do not belong to you, Garrett. I love you. I have never loved anyone else. However, I am not your property. I am your wife."

"Why don't you act like a wife and accompany me to Chicago on the *Lady Elgin*? I need you by my side."

"Take Willie with you. It would be a wonderful experience for him. You and he need time together. I will stay with the girls. Besides, I don't support Stephen Douglas. I'm happy for you and for what he's doing for the brigade, but I'll not go to a rally and cheer for a candidate with whom I so strongly disagree."

"Since when did your opinion matter?"

"Well, my opinion matters to me. Abraham Lincoln is going to win, Garrett."

"What do you know about it? The new Republican Party doesn't have the numbers to defeat a solid Democratic opposition. Lincoln's going to win? That's a joke."

"Ah, but my dear, the Democrats aren't solid. The South is pulling away from Douglas. Lincoln doesn't need a majority to defeat a split party."

"Oh, Mary, leave politics to the men. Women can't vote. A woman's place—"

"Don't you dare finish that sentence, Garrett Barry."

"All of that aside, my mind is made up. Ned is a liability. He must go."

Willie came bounding down the stairs. "Who must go, Father?" Mary glared at Garrett. There was a long pause. Garrett sighed.

"No one, Willie, at least not now. But the matter is not closed."

"The matter is closed. There's nothing further to discuss. Did Ned finish the story?"

"No. He fell asleep in the middle of it."

"I told you he was tired. Now, young man, you have a lot of explaining to do. What were you doing on your father's horse?"

———————

The alley stank of garbage. Maggie sat on a crate that had been discarded by Plankinton Meat Packers. She was alone. Everyone else in the ward was down at the dock to see off the *Lady Elgin*. That's where she was supposed to be, but she didn't care about that crap.

Da had closed the store so that everyone could go. Da never closed the store. *It wasn't fair*, she thought, *that Flynn was getting all the attention*. Flynn—the favorite. She hated Flynn. Flynn got to go on the trip with that sissy Blevins. She guessed she knew what the two of them would do on the trip. She hoped Flynn got pregnant. Maggie thought about that for a while, relishing the idea of a disgraced Flynn.

Jack was going to Chicago, too. She didn't hate Jack. It was just that Maggie was the only one to stay home. What really got her nanny was that those two brats Brian and Liam were able to go because Jack invited Maeve. She hoped Jack wouldn't marry Maeve. She couldn't bear the thought of having Brian and Liam around all the time.

Maggie pretended to go to the parade down to the ship. If she'd refused, she'd have been stuck minding the store. Before they'd all left, she'd sneaked into Jack's room. Jack hid a bottle of whiskey in his closet. She'd found the bottle and slipped it into her bag. So what if Jack got mad? What could he say? Besides she knew about his secret meetings and his little war games out in the woods. She was the only one in the family who knew. The others were so dumb. They all thought

Jack was an angel. Even Da thought so, in spite of the hot arguments they often had.

She'd wandered away from the crowd and walked into this dead-end alley, and now she tipped the bottle to her lips. The rush of the liquor entering her bloodstream made her feel warm and toasty, so she took another swig. She figured that after she finished, she'd go home. The store would be locked, but the house would be open. If she got home before the others, she'd go to bed and sleep it off. No one would be the wiser. She laughed and guzzled the remainder of the bottle, after which she smashed it against the wall of a building.

Then she saw the thing coming down the alley toward her. It was big and pink with huge nostrils and made vulgar grunting sounds. This wasn't the first time Maggie had gotten drunk, so she knew this wasn't a hallucination. Whiskey didn't give you hallucinations, did it? She stared at the animal. The animal stared back. For a moment, her vision blurred and there were two of them.

Her vision refocused, and Maggie saw what it was. It was a pig. "Get out of here, pig!" She'd seen pigs on the streets before. A couple of years ago, a law had been passed prohibiting animals from running loose on the streets. Cows, pigs, sheep, and geese had been allowed to run freely, but with the growth of the city, they had become a nuisance. The law hadn't done much good, Maggie thought.

This pig was being uncooperative and would not go away. Instead, it searched for garbage. Maggie shrugged and slid off the packing box. She felt light on her feet and dizzy. The pig was nosing through garbage and slurping on dead tomatoes. "Ugh," thought Maggie, unsure if her nausea came from the whiskey or the pig.

Maggie had an idea. If she could get the pig home, she could shut it in Flynn's room. What a delightful surprise would await Flynn. Even if Ma found the pig before Flynn returned, it would be a hoot. The pig would do major damage to the room, maybe even destroy that pesky cat. Maggie, of course, would deny everything. The question was, could she get the pig home?

"Here, piggy," she coaxed. Her voice slurred, but no one was there to notice except the pig, who munched vapidly on a mouthful of rotten cabbage. The animal was not very big, really. If she could get a good hold on it, she could carry it home. She got down on her knees beside the pig and put her arms around it, crooning in a soothing voice, one arm around its back and one arm around its belly. Mustering all of her strength, she lifted it and staggered down the alley with the beast squealing and squirming in her arms.

Reaching the end of the alley, she stepped in a mud hole. Down she went like a sack of potatoes. The pig bolted around the corner. Maggie managed to get up, mud-covered, and lurch around the corner in pursuit of her quarry, but the pig was nowhere to be seen. Several pedestrians stared at her.

"Jesus, Mary, and Joseph," she said. If she were lucky, she'd have time for a quick bath before she crawled into bed.

The world loves a parade. Why is that? What is it about marching down a street in formation that so stirs the emotions? Whatever it is that thrills people, whatever mysterious chemistry creates the catalyst that releases such passion, the parade to the *Lady Elgin* had all the ingredients. Perhaps it was the pride of the families who turned out to watch their sons in dress blues and shiny brass buttons, or perhaps it was the youthful exuberance of the lads themselves, off to a grand adventure.

It had started with an address by the mayor himself at St. Patrick's Hall. The mayor had been introduced by Dan O'Mara. People who knew Dan observed that his nose was luminous. Although the mayor wasn't Irish, any Irishman would agree that his speech was a fine example of blarney. The affair was concluded by Father Delaney, who gave a benediction and blessed the excursion.

The glow from a hundred torches gave the late evening an illusion of daylight, as the parade proceeded down Wisconsin. At the head of the brigade marched the proud Captain Barry, looking more a general than a captain. The color guard bore two flags: Old Glory and the flag of Ireland. The flag of Wisconsin was conspicuously missing. The band led the parade with tin whistles, bagpipes, and bodhrans. The music was Celtic. Spectators exchanged knowing glances, recognizing music they'd heard when the *Lynne* had been set ablaze.

Some of the marchers carried banners with emblems. One emblem, carried by Jack O'Mara, was the fierce wolfhound representing the hound of Ulster. At the rear of the parade two men and a boy marched abreast with a wide banner reading: Union Guard For Douglas. The boy was Garrett Barry's young son, Willie.

Following the brigade was a long, flat, horse-drawn wagon upon which girls from the parish danced high-steps. "Johnny!" a proud parent called, and other parents called the names of their sons as they passed by. "Sean! Seamus! Paddy!" were some of the names called. The so-named marchers did not turn, for to do so would have been a disgrace, but there were smiles on their faces and pride in their eyes.

Usually after a parade passes by, the spectators go home. Tonight, they followed the parade down Wisconsin. By the time the parade turned on Huron, its following had ballooned, filling the streets and wooden sidewalks. As it headed down Huron to the dock, the crowd continued to grow. When it reached the dock it was met by another crowd, most of whom had booked passage.

The magnificent *Lady Elgin* lay in waiting, three hundred feet of elegance graced with swooping arches and a giant paddlewheel, looking like a regal luxury hotel. The ship was scheduled to leave at 7:00 pm, but there were delays. The porters, dining staff, and crew hustled in preparation, and the band, struggling with instruments, headed up the gangplank. Dock workers loaded freight. There wasn't much personal freight, since most of the passengers were returning the following night. Commercial freight included cases of meat on ice from Plankinton and Armour, cases of Melms beer, food for the galley, and lumber to be used on plank roads.

The plan was that the brigade would march up the gangplank as a grand finale of the parade. The idea had been abandoned when they reached the dock and found the gangplank closed to passengers. By the time the ship was ready to board, it was an hour later than scheduled. The soldiers had become part of the crowd, which had become restless and angry. People started boarding, while soldiers had to push and shove, searching for wives and sweethearts, some of whom had already boarded and were yelling down from the guardrail of the ship.

Maeve struggled with her harp up the gangplank, wondering why she had brought the thing with her. Brian and Liam, of little help, were already on board. Maeve saw no sign of Jack. She noticed that Blevins and Flynn were right behind her.

Deputy Marshal Joshua Doughty was at the dock, keeping an eye on who boarded. It seemed unlikely that an attempt would be made to smuggle Moses aboard, but there was a large crowd. It didn't hurt to be watchful. Captain Barry and his son had been among the first to board. Doughty noticed that Mary Barry wasn't with them. Hmm. So Mary was staying home. Trouble in the Barry household? It was common knowledge that the captain's wife was an influential abolitionist. He'd have to pay Mrs. Barry a visit, perhaps first thing in the morning.

Soldiers were still searching for their partners when the whistle blew, warning of imminent departure. Just as the crew was about to raise the gangplank, three latecomers arrived.

"Hold it!" yelled Flaherty, dressed in fancy plainclothes and dragging two River Street girls in tow. "We have tickets. Let us aboard." The crew held the gangplank as the three revelers, none of whom were sober, crossed. The gangplank was pulled up, the mooring ropes removed, and the *Lady Elgin* moved away from the dock. It was now after 10:00 pm, more than three hours later than scheduled.

There was excitement and laughter as passengers waved from the railing. "Good-bye! Good-bye!" There were shouts from the families on shore. "Bon voyage" and "Take care" and "God bless Stephen Douglas" were some of the well wishes, not to mention "Erin go bragh." The crowd stayed a while. When the *Lady Elgin* reached the horizon, people started to leave.

Dan O'Mara was watching the ship, wondering what had happened to Maggie, when he noticed that Marion was crying. "Why would you be crying, darlin'? They're just goin' to Chicago, not the end of the world. Jack will be in seventh heaven, marchin' in the big parade, and Flynn can take care of herself. They'll be home in a couple of days. So why the tears?"

"I ... I don't know. I have a bad feeling."

"You and your bad feelings. The saints preserve us. 'Don't be putting your shoes on the table, Dan. Throw the spilled salt over your shoulder, Dan. Watch out for the black cat, Dan.' You're full of superstition, my girl. 'Tis a sin, you know. Do you confess it to the priest?"

"It's none of your business, what I confess. Admit it. My premonitions are often right."

"True, and your premonitions are often wrong. I hope to God that this is one of them."

"Oh, so do I, Dan. So do I."

The parade was over and the *Lady* had sailed. The ward had returned to normal, causing Lieutenant Hogan to breathe a sigh of relief. With so much focused on the waterfront and half the population down on the docks, felons were likely to crawl out of the woodwork. It didn't help that Flaherty was gone. No major crime had occurred so far, thank God. The night wasn't over, but he'd put in a day and a half and was headed home. The boys at the precinct would have to deal with it.

Home was within walking distance of the precinct station. Most nights he preferred the brisk walk. Often he would jog. Hogan spent more time than he liked behind a desk. He loved physical exercise, taking advantage of every moment he could to work out. Although in his midforties, he was in better shape than most of the younger men who frequented the gym where he spent his spare time training to maintain his status as champion of the Third Ward Amateur Boxing Society. In all of Milwaukee, there was no one more feared than Padraic T. Hogan

Tonight, though, he wished he had his horse. If he took a cab, he'd hear about it the next day. He took a lot of ribbing about his walking, but the routine was established and breaking it would be perceived as a sign of weakness. So he would walk, no matter how exhausted he felt.

He decided to pay Feeney a visit. Feeney wouldn't be open for business this late, but he'd be home and probably awake. The pub didn't open for business until midmorning. Feeney stayed up late and slept in. Maybe Hogan could talk him into an after-hours pint. A quick pick-me-up would motivate him to finish his walk.

The pub was dark, but a light glowed in the room above, where the proprietor resided. From the street, Hogan saw Feeney looking out the window. Feeney spent a lot of time looking out the window. "Hey, Feeney! Is that you?" There was no answer. "Feeney? It's me, Hogan. How about a short, after-hours libation?" Maybe he was asleep. "Feeney? I'm comin' up." Strange bird, that Feeney. Hogan suspected that he was behind a series of fires that had plagued the waterfront, but there was no proof. He entered the building.

The door at the top of the staircase was ajar, which was peculiar, the light spilling out and dimly illuminating the hallway. On the way up, he slipped on a dark puddle and fell on the steps. His hands, extended to break the fall, came away wet and sticky. Wiping his hands on his trousers, he stained his uniform with blood. After regaining his balance, he drew his pistol and rushed through the door.

"Feeney!"

The room was neat as a pin. The safe in the corner was wide open and empty. A trail of dark stains led from the door to the chair facing the window. The corpse of Feeney reposed in the chair. Dead eyes stared unseeing at the waterfront. One hand, in rigor mortis, clutched a long, black telescope. Protruding from his back, and deeply embedded therein, was a gory shaft. The carved face of a wolfhound grinned from the tip. Hogan recognized the symbol. Feeney had been murdered with the spear of Cuchulain.

Part Two

Chicago

Chapter Ten

IN THE PILOT HOUSE, CAPTAIN Jack Wilson relaxed, now that the *Lady Elgin* was underway, albeit hours behind schedule.

"Right full rudder and full steam ahead!" barked First Mate Davis to the wheelsman. The ship made a ninety-degree turn, heading due south, next port of call Chicago. As the *Lady* glided through Lake Michigan, propelled by two giant paddlewheels, the light from scores of kerosene lamps beamed from the ship's many staterooms, parlors, and passageways. The light encircled the steamer, reflecting from the glossy lake surface like a halo.

Three hundred fifty passengers enjoyed the varied amenities offered by the luxury liner, including a band, a dance hall, social parlors, a dining room, a gift shop, gaming facilities, a barber shop, and a bar. The bar was an independent enterprise, contracted by a man named Lacy. If Lacy had a Christian name, he divulged it to no one. With the money he would make from a boatload of thirsty Irishmen, he could retire.

Wilson was proud of the "Queen of the Lakes." Three hundred feet in length, thirty-five feet of beam, weighing 1,037 tons, she had cost $96,000 when she was built in Buffalo in 1851. The *Lady Elgin,* named after the wife of the governor-general of Canada, had served Canadian ports on Lake Superior before being purchased four years ago by Gordon S. Hubbard and Company of Chicago.

Hubbard couldn't have selected a more qualified man than Jack Wilson to be captain of the floating resort. Wilson was a seasoned sailor with twenty-four years experience on the Great Lakes, which included other paddlewheel steamers. He had guided the side-wheeler *Illinois* through the Soo Locks, the first voyage of such a vessel through the locks.

"Looks like a clear night and smooth sailin'," said Davis, a wiry, energetic man in his thirties, who had been with Lewis since the beginning days on the *Lady Elgin,* and who had worked with Wilson on other ships. When Wilson had been offered this job, he had accepted on condition that Davis be hired as first mate. They made a good team.

Davis had taken to the ship when he had first seen her, impressed by her shape and her huge longitudinal arches. The *Lady* was built entirely of wood, but she had uncommon strength, part of which was provided by the arches. It would take a mighty storm to damage her.

"With any luck at all, Cap'n, we'll make up for the lost time."

"On the mark, Davis, but don't forget that we now carry a heavy load of passengers and freight."

"We'll arrive with time to spare for the Stephen Douglas shindig. The passengers won't notice what time we get there. They'll be havin' too much fun." Wilson ran a tight ship, demanding much from the staff. The passengers were encouraged to do as they pleased, within reason.

Davis gave one or two orders to the wheelsman to keep him alert, but the run from Milwaukee to Chicago on a night like this was a cinch, which was why an inexperienced seaman was on the wheel. Give him a chance to learn. Davis or Lewis would be there with him most of the time, taking the wheel if conditions worsened. Otherwise, the seaman could handle this segment of the voyage.

Wilson surveyed the vast flat expanse of water, knowing how treacherous it could be, how fast it could transform from a docile, predictable friend to a fierce, erratic monster capable of swallowing a whole ship. Seagoing crews were frequently saved by precautions taken out of respect for the power of nature. Many who made the mistake of trusting Lake Michigan rested eternally on the bottom.

At the moment, the flat, calm surface reminded Wilson of his farm in Coldwater, Michigan. He had grown up in Michigan. Had it not been for the lure of the Great Lakes, he would have become a farmer. He'd purchased a farm in anticipation of an early retirement. Ironically, the mortgage payments kept him from retiring, that and the family he supported.

He thought of them now, his wife Meg and his daughters May

and Maureen. Maureen was an invalid requiring constant medical care and attention, another drain on his income. He loved them all but felt profoundly guilty that he spent so much time away from home. The fact that he had trouble remembering their faces haunted him.

"Begging your pardon, Cap'n, I can keep an eye on the wheelsman here and keep up the log, if you want to go below. Just a suggestion, sir."

"Davis, you read my mind. We've come a long way together, mate."

"Just what I was thinking, Cap'n. Just what I was thinking."

———————————

"You'd better be saving some of that for the return trip," said Maeve, as Jack tilted back another jar. "You may be my young Celtic god, but too much nectar will be your undoing."

"Nectar, is it? Nectar's a Greek libation. A Celt's drink is mead. Is that what you mean? Too much mead will be my undoing?"

"Melms. Too much Melms. You've been swilling that brew since we left. Are you trying to keep up with your hard-drinking idol, Captain Barry? You'll be staggering in the big parade, falling down drunk, the lot of you."

"Ma," said Brian, "play a sailor's hornpipe."

"Yeah, said Liam, "play a sailor's ... ah ..."

"Hornpipe."

They were seated in chairs on the quarterdeck, Maeve with her harp. She struck up a hornpipe. Jack performed a burlesque of a hornpipe, grimacing and winking and missing a step here and there. The boys clapped, and a group gathered to watch. Suddenly there was a loud blast on the whistle, causing Jack to lose his balance and fall on the deck. Embarrassed, he sheepishly rose to his feet for a bow, but the audience had disappeared. They were all at the rail watching a three-mast schooner heading north. It was too dark to make out the schooner's name. She moved slowly, the mild breeze barely filling her sails.

"Ship ahoy!" Liam shouted, but there was no reply.

Soon everyone was settled again. Maeve decided Brian and Liam needed haircuts, a service provided by the ship's barber on a continuous basis.

"A haircut after midnight?" asked Brian.

"Why not?" replied the intrepid Liam. "There's nothing else to do."

Jack wondered if it was wise to send them unchaperoned to the other end of the ship. "They have to learn responsibility," said Maeve. Jack gave them money, and they ran off without thanking him. This relationship was getting serious. If marriage was imminent, he was going to have to explain his philosophy of child-rearing. Dan O'Mara had always been the boss in his family, and, by God, Jack would be the boss in his. Brian and Liam would toe the mark. Well, he'd deal with the issue later. He took another swig of Melms.

Maeve patted the seat next to her. "Come, Jack. Sit beside me. Regale me with wild tales of Feeney, and tell me again how you lost your spear."

In a parlor, a poker game was in progress. It was the quietist parlor on the ship, the men intent upon playing. A cloud of cigar smoke hung over the gamblers, but no one coughed. A pile of chips on the table meant high stakes. The players were upper-class passengers to whom the game meant little more than a way to pass time. Money was not important. Winning was. None of these players were good losers.

Thomas Cummings, the ship's law enforcement officer, noticed one man who seemed like a fish out of water. Mike Flaherty, a policeman like himself, did not earn enough money to be in a league with the others. Sometimes a poor man would get lucky, but Flaherty had been losing steadily, yet continued to ante up. How could he do that? At the end of each hand, except when it was his deal, he would leave briefly and return. Cummings had the impression that when Flaherty returned, he had more money.

Cummings suspected something nefarious, but he couldn't make a move until he knew. Captain Wilson had a laissez-faire attitude when it came to the behavior of the passengers but wouldn't tolerate anything illegal. Cummings smelled a rat, a criminal rat, in Flaherty.

For one thing, the man had rented a stateroom. The staterooms were occupied by people like School Commissioner James Rice, Registrar of Deeds Samuel Waegli, Chief Engineer of the Fire Department Thomas H. Evanston, and other members of the Milwaukee social register. Flaherty did not fit into this group. Most of the passengers on this cruise couldn't even afford passage without the group rate Captain Wilson had given them. Of course, on such a short trip, a stateroom was a luxury.

An exception would be made for Blevins Morgan and his soon-to-be bride, Flynn O'Mara. The captain had arranged for them to have the most luxurious stateroom, for which they would not be charged. Blevins was a friend of Wilson's and promoted the *Lady Elgin* in his newspaper. Blevins and Flynn were to be married by Captain Wilson. Davis and the wheelsman would be witnesses. A quiet wedding would take place in the pilot house. Because Cummings was security, he had been informed. He assumed that no one else knew.

Flaherty was another story. How could he afford a stateroom on the "Queen of the Lakes"? How could he afford to keep losing at poker? Cummings vowed he would get to the bottom of it.

Barry sat morosely at the bar, nursing another drink, having lost track of the number. He'd been at the bar a while, but Lacy was busy, so Barry'd been sipping slowly. Mary was right; he was a slave to alcohol. Mary was right about Old Ned, too. It irritated him how right Mary could be about everything. He didn't like the position in which she'd put him. He didn't like her involvement with the abolitionists and worried about her activities in the Underground Railroad. He was sorry, though, that he'd behaved loutishly in their fight about Ned. Woman or not, she had a right to her opinion. Damn it, why couldn't she leave it at that?

Barry was against slavery and philosophically agreed with his wife, but she was an activist. In time, he was sure the institution of slavery would die a natural death. There was no need to break laws or go to war over it. The law was the law. If the law was wrong, let them change it. Mary didn't see the possible consequences of her activities, or if she did, she chose to ignore them.

The sight of couples entwined on the dance floor depressed him. He wished Mary were here with him. He missed her. It wasn't that he couldn't bear to be away from her for a short interval, but there had been a strain on their relationship lately that an outing like this might have repaired. In its best moments, their marriage contained a closeness that many marriages would never know. The expression "straight as an arrow" could have been coined with Barry in mind. Honor, though, wasn't what kept him faithful. There was room for no one else but Mary. She occupied his mind and heart. It pained him that she'd refused to come on the trip, but she was right about one other thing. This was a chance to get to know his son better. Lacy came with another drink. Barry pushed it away and went in search of Willie.

———

"C'mon, Brian, let's find Ma and Jack. If we report back to them now, Ma will know we can be trusted and she'll let us explore. Besides, I want to show Ma our new sea haircuts."

"You go. I'll be there in a while."

"Ma'll have a fit if I show up without you. She'll be mad. She'll blame me. Say, what's wrong?" Brian's face was white as a sail. "What's the matter, Brian?"

"I ... I feel sick." In fact, Brian felt very dizzy. His head was spinning like a top, and his whole body felt weak. He couldn't remember feeling this badly before. He wanted to die.

"Brian?"

Brian motioned his brother to be quiet. Then he threw up all over the deck.

———

Blevins and Flynn were the sole patrons of the dining salon, an exclusive room away from the main dining area. The salon was designed for intimate dining, available only to the occupants of staterooms. Reservations were required, and the menu was expensive.

"What's gammon?"

Blevins didn't know. "It rhymes with salmon. Maybe it's fish."

"Would you mind changing places with me?"

"Why?"

"When I am dining, I like to face the front of the boat. It settles my stomach."

"There," said Blevins, changing places. "Is that better?"

"Much better, thank you."

"By the way, you don't say 'front,' you say 'bow.' You don't say 'rear,' you say 'stern.' We aren't on a boat, we're on a ship."

"Are you going to be like this after we're married?"

"Like what?"

"Always correcting me."

"I worship you."

"Please don't say that."

"Are you having second thoughts?"

"Not at all. If I'm sure of anything, it is that I want to spend the rest of my life with you. There are things we are going to have to resolve when we get home, not the least of which is that we don't have a home. I don't want to think about that now. Tonight is the happiest night of my life. I want to block out the past and the future. I want to wrap us in a warm cocoon of now."

Immersed in flickering candlelight, gleaming silver, lacy linen, and plush carpeting, they made love with their eyes and toasted each other. A waiter appeared and they ordered gammon, not asking what it was. It was baked ham and very good. They nibbled at it slowly, having nowhere to go. Their bags were in the stateroom, which they chose not to occupy until after the wedding. When they entered that room, they would be starting a new life.

The waiter brought rice pudding, the dessert of the day. Flynn was delighted. "This will be our rice, the rice that people would throw if there were people. Not that I care that there won't be people," she added hastily, seeing the look in his eyes. They ate tiny mouthfuls of rice pudding from elegant dishes.

Captain Wilson arrived and sat at their table. "Are you resolved to go through with it?" They nodded happily. "In that case, how about right now?"

"Here?" Blevins blurted. "In the dining room?"

Wilson laughed. "It's a fine place, isn't it? Truth is, couples have been married in this room. In this case, discretion dictates otherwise. You'll exchange vows in the pilot house. The first mate and the man on the wheel will be witnesses. Are you ready? Last chance to change your mind," he said without smiling.

"Lead the way," said Flynn.

Chapter Eleven

NOTHING WAS WORSE IN TOM Cummings's book than a corrupt policeman. Tom's father was a dock worker, and Tom had been raised in a poor, lower-class family with middle-class values. As a child, he had believed the bromides taught by his teachers and parents. Truth will prevail. Crime doesn't pay. Money is the root of all evil.

Tom's father had once said, "If you can't trust a policeman, who can you trust?" That had become Tom's credo when he joined the Chicago police force. The idealism of youth seldom survives the gritty reality of everyday life. The bromides did not hold up. Honesty was not necessarily rewarded. Crime was often lucrative. Some policemen were untrustworthy. For Tom, the latter was the unkindest cut of all. He had the common sense not to wage a one-man crusade against his peers, but he remained a tower of personal integrity.

Integrity earned him the respect of his colleagues but taught him a bitter lesson. He'd been passed over for promotion. The corrupt cops he detested cheated on tests, took credit for the legwork of others, accepted bribes, and worked their way dishonestly up the ladder, while he remained on the bottom-most rung.

To his credit, he kept the faith. Then along came the offer to be in charge of security on the *Lady Elgin*. He'd jumped at the chance, and it had changed his life. The pay was more than he'd ever earn as a public servant and he was his own man, responsible only to Captain Wilson, who'd been impressed by his spotless reputation. Cummings was the man in charge. There was no need for compromise, no on-the-take colleagues.

Cummings had observed a steady stream of men going in and out of Flaherty's stateroom. He spotted one or two standing in the passageway, as if waiting for an appointment. It hadn't taken much intelligence to deduct what was going on. He waited until he was the only one in line. He knocked softly on the door. The door opened a crack. A woman stood there. She was young, rather plain, with a hard edge to her voice.

"May I help you?"

"Oh yes, I think you may."

"Well, then, what's the password?"

"Password?"

"The word that will open the gates of paradise." There was a pause. She eyed him suspiciously.

"I don't know. I saw you when you boarded and I—"

"I guess you're all right, dearie, so come on in." She wore a lacy, cotton shift with long, red-ribboned drawers of the same material. The corset, petticoats, and bell-shaped crinoline were piled in a heap on the chair. He stepped toward her, but she crossed her arms and wouldn't move. "Wait. The money first. One hundred dollars, if you please, sir."

"One hundred dollars! For what?"

"Anything you like."

"That's all I need to know. You're under arrest."

"So that's your pleasure. You're the policeman and I'm your prisoner. I can do that." Opening a bureau drawer, she produced a pair of handcuffs. "We could use these, or maybe you'd like to tie me up. I must have the money first."

"You don't understand. I really am a policeman." This girl lacked brains as well as virtue. He showed her his identification. "Tom Cummings, ship's security, and you are under arrest. The charge is prostitution."

"A cop! You're a cop!"

Something in the way she said this made him turn. Sneaking out of the toilet and heading for the stateroom door was the largest man he'd ever seen. Bald as an ostrich egg, naked body shaped like a partly deflated hot air balloon, he tiptoed across the room. In his arms he hugged a shirt, trousers, and underwear, which failed to conceal an enormous belly and rather small appendage.

Although Cummings didn't wear a uniform, he carried two props which made him feel like a policeman. One was a pistol, which he wore in a shoulder holster under his jacket, and the other was a silver whistle that would jolt a felon straight in his tracks. Mustering all of his lung power, he blew the whistle so hard that his lips went numb.

The fat man dropped his clothes and threw his arms into the air, body quivering like raw salt pork. His pink face reddened and his mouth gaped. Simultaneously, there was a loud yelp from the open bathroom, where a woman struggled to get into a pair of bloomers.

"Don't anyone move!" Cummings barked, brandishing the pistol. "You are all under arrest." He stared at the unadorned mountain of flesh. "Aren't you Herman Goetz, owner of Goetz Brewery, and husband of Mabel Goetz, prominent Milwaukee socialite? Isn't she with you on this cruise?"

"Please give me another chance. Keep quiet about this, I beg of you. The scandal would ruin me. Mabel would be devastated."

Cummings considered. In his neophyte days, it wouldn't even have entered his mind to let the man go. On the other hand, he didn't want to open a can of worms. A full-blown scandal involving a rich and powerful Milwaukee businessman wouldn't be good for the *Lady Elgin*, not to mention Cummings himself. The culprit he was after was Flaherty.

"Go."

"What?"

"Get dressed and get out."

"I can give you money."

"I don't want your money. Get out, before I change my mind and charge you with bribery."

Goetz heaved a sigh, causing waves to ripple across the ocean of his torso. After struggling into his clothes, he managed to squeeze out the narrow door with surprising haste. Cummings wondered how far down the passageway the beer baron would get before he realized he was barefoot. What kind of story would he tell his dear Mabel?

The prostitute in the bathroom, an older woman with ample endowments, had donned a robe. The idea of this woman and the portly Goetz doing what they were doing in the confines of the cramped water closet boggled Cummings's mind.

It made him calculate. Flaherty's little enterprise must be flourishing with two customers in the room at the same time. How many customers, he wondered, had passed through these portals, and how many more would there have been?

"Get dressed, ladies, and pack your unmentionables."

"We goin' someplace?"

"You betcha."

"You gonna make us walk the plank?"

"No. You're going to jail."

"There's a hoosegow aboard this scow? What if we don't wanna go?"

Cummings waved the pistol. "Here's something to convince you. If you don't cooperate, I'll step into the passageway and blow my whistle, which will bring help as fast as you can wink."

"You're a real blowhard, ain't you, dearie?"

"Follow me, and don't try to get away." They followed him down the passageway to the last stateroom on the port side. He opened the door and ushered them inside.

"This ain't no hoosegow."

"Yes, madam, it is. The door locks and unlocks only from the outside. There is only one way to escape and that's through the porthole. Feel free to consider that option. *Au revoir.* I'll return shortly with your pimp, Mr. Michael Flaherty, Esquire."

When Flaherty stepped into the passageway, Cummings was waiting. "Michael Flaherty, you're under arrest. Come with me. The gentlemen at the table will be notified that you'll not be returning to the game. In case you hadn't noticed, there's a gun in my hand. I would love an excuse to use it."

"In the name of Jaysus, what's the charge?"

"Soliciting."

"What's that?"

"You may be a disgrace to your badge, but you're a cop, and you know what soliciting is. You're under arrest for operating a brothel on the *Lady Elgin.*"

"You don't know what you're talkin' about, boyo."

"Two females locked in the brig say I do. One of them's a minor, which means that when they lock you in prison, they'll throw away the key. Don't 'boyo' me, you contemptible swine. You're a poor excuse for an Irishman. Although not a bona fide brig, this is our detention room, which you will occupy with your lady friends until we reach Chicago. You will be pleased to know that you are our first inmates. We are unaccustomed to clientele of your ilk."

"Wait, wait. Listen. I know you're not interested in my girls, a man of such character, but if you forget about this, I can make it worth your while."

"I'll bet you can, maggot. I don't want your dirty money."

"I have friends in high places."

"You'll need them for the trial."

"Isn't there anything—"

"You don't get it, do you? I'm proud of what I do. You are offering me a bribe. That offends me."

"What are you going to do with me, with us?"

"The girls will be left in Chicago to fend for themselves. How or if they get back to Milwaukee is no concern of mine. I don't care about them. They are being exploited. How much of the money do they get to keep? What's your take? If I followed my instinct, I'd throw you overboard and let you swim back to Milwaukee. Cold fish that you are, you'd probably make it.

"You will remain locked in this room for the duration. When we get back to Milwaukee, you will be handed over to your own boss, Lieutenant Hogan. He'll be so very proud. I hear he has fists of steel and a fierce temper. Why, you'll be lucky to make it to trial in one piece. Have a pleasant cruise, and enjoy your lovely companions. You deserve one another. Erin go bragh, boyo."

He slammed the door and locked it, heading down to the gaming room. The poker players had left, but the heavy cigar smoke hung over the table like a thunder cloud. Cummings was not sorry he had spoiled the sport.

In all of the years he'd been a captain, Jack Wilson had never performed a wedding. He was more nervous than the bride or groom. He wouldn't have agreed to this, but he liked Blevins and owed him one. He sympathized with the dilemma of the Catholic-Protestant issue, believing that the church was too arbitrary, especially in its demands on the non-Catholic party. This marriage would not be acknowledged by the church, a fact with which Flynn would have to deal. Father Delaney was a liberal, but a rule was a rule. Life would not be easy for the newlyweds, a fact that Wilson had pointed out to them. They would not listen, but what could you expect? They were so young. The wedding would be legal, anyway. No parental permission was required, since they were both of age. In spite of Wilson's efforts to keep everything hush-hush, he wondered how in the world they would keep the secret from Flynn's brother Jack, who was on board.

They were dressed simply, to avoid calling attention to what they were doing, but they could not conceal their bliss. Wilson, correctly assuming that Blevins wouldn't think of flowers, presented Flynn with a bouquet, which he had bought in Milwaukee. Blevins had thought of the ring, thank God, which the first mate would produce at the right moment.

Captain Wilson read the vows and they repeated them. It was done by the book, with no homilies and no music. Even so, when the captain said, "I now pronounce you husband and wife," Flynn was as radiant as any bride he had seen and Blevins was transported. They kissed for a very long time and were much congratulated by Wilson and Davis. Even the wheelsman timorously proffered his best wishes, letting go of the wheel long enough to kiss the bride and shake hands with the groom. For that brief moment, the *Lady Elgin* was on her own.

Wilson cracked open a bottle of champagne to toast the bride and groom. Then it was over and the newlyweds departed for their honeymoon a few short corridors away. They stood in front of the stateroom door and embraced. Unlike the tender nuptial kiss, the embrace was deep and arousing. "Oh God," gasped Flynn, "can't you wait until we're inside?" Blevins fumbled for the key and opened the door. They lost their balance. He had planned to carry her over the threshold, but a great need overwhelmed him.

The door closed, shutting out the passageway and shutting out the rest of the world. Mr. and Mrs. Morgan were attending to the business of being Mr. and Mrs. Morgan.

Maeve played the harp and passengers carried deck chairs to the forward section to listen. The partying had concluded, and the band no longer played. People rested, asleep on benches or in chairs, snuggled in blankets or listening to the hissing of the prow and the sloshing of the paddles as the *Lady Elgin* plowed through the night. The only intrusive noise was the distant argument of several drunken firemen at the bar.

And Maeve—it was as if an angel had alighted on deck. People listened quietly, soothed by the serene music of the harp. The boys slept. Brian's equilibrium had returned after his attack of *mal de mer*. ("How can anyone be seasick on a lake?" Liam wanted to know.) Maeve kept on singing and playing. It was as if each song was the fuel that fired the next, and Maeve's untiring eyes shined.

Jack supposed she could go on forever. He was sick of it. It was as if he didn't exist, only the music, the damned music. He wasn't in love with a woman; he was bewitched by a musical enigma, the eighth blamed wonder of the world. She was too much for him.

Flynn—he'd search for Flynn. He needed to unburden his soul and his sister would lend a sympathetic ear. There had been an unspoken agreement that they wouldn't get in each other's way on this voyage, but that didn't mean they couldn't talk. Where in the hell was she? She was with that good-for-nothing Blevins.

Jack was soused, saturated with Melms and barely conscious of where he was, except that it was in a hallway, or, he supposed, since he was on a ship, a passageway. The doors along each side were to the staterooms in which the well-to-do clientele took their ease. He didn't belong here and he certainly wouldn't find his sister here. When he turned the corner, he froze.

There, a few doors ahead, were two lovers entwined in a deep embrace, oblivious to his presence. He cleared his throat as they started groping one another, but they didn't hear him. He leaned against the bulkhead, nearly falling asleep. Finally they parted. They didn't look his way, but he got a good look at them. He was drunk, but not so drunk that he didn't recognize his own sister and that scalawag newspaperman. Before Jack had time to react, they had entered the stateroom and closed the door.

"Hey! Hey!"

Several people came by, entering different rooms. Doors opened and closed. Jack's head spun and he became confused. He tried to remember the room number, but it eluded him. Unable to focus, he looked down the passageway, but it was a blur. He was angry and his helplessness increased the anger.

"Flynn! Come out at once!"

He must save his sister's virtue. He couldn't believe it. She had gone into a bedroom with a man, for God's sake. His own sister. She was so moral and upright. How could she? Maybe it was a mistake. No, there was no doubt in his mind about whom he had seen.

Where did they go? He headed down the wrong passageway, in the opposite direction. He would rescue her. He was Cuchulain, the Hound of Cullen, so named because he had killed the vicious dog of his host. Now he would kill another dog. To affirm that, he let out a fearful howl. Then he started pounding on doors.

"Flynn! Flynn! Come out, Flynn! Blevins … I … I know you're in there, you … you Welsh rapist."

He'd kill the seducer, kill him with his bare hands. Better still, he'd run Blevins through with the spear of Cuchulain. Where was the spear? Then he remembered that he'd left the spear with Feeney for safekeeping. No matter, he didn't need it. He could take care of Blevins with one hand tied behind his back. He pounded on another door. If he had to, he'd pound on every door until he found the right one. A door opened a crack. Someone peeked out to see what the commotion was about.

He heard a loud police whistle. A second later, he was on the deck, strong arms pinning him. Then he passed out. Somewhere under the darkness he was aware of someone snoring. It might have been Cuchulain.

Barry sat in the bow, a steaming cup of black coffee in his hand. Willie picked at a bowl of oatmeal. It was beginning to get light. He smelled breakfast cooking in the galley and heard the slam-bang of pots and pans and other busy sounds that announced the arrival of morning. The cook had told him that by the time breakfast was ready, the ship would be docking. The dining area would be open all morning for the convenience of passengers in no hurry to disembark. It isn't customary for ships to offer breakfast on a short sail, but the *Lady Elgin*, renowned for her culinary amenities, never allowed passengers to leave hungry, unless they chose to do so.

He was queasy after all that drinking, but no stranger to mornings after. He'd be all right, although food wouldn't hurt. He and Willie roamed the deck, taking deep breaths of fresh air. Barry kept himself awake by checking the lifesaving equipment. He counted four yawls and three lifeboats, and wondered if that was enough. It hardly seemed adequate on a ship carrying this number of passengers. A lot of the life preservers were made of two-inch planks, twelve-to-eighteen inches wide and five feet long with rope at each end.

He wondered about the lads. Many had been up all night drinking. Well, the lads were young and robust, and Barry wasn't their caretaker—far from it. There would be a few hours' wait before the parade, giving them time to spruce up. Once the parade was over, all they had to do was attend the rally, where they could blow off steam. In all, it shouldn't be a tasking day.

Traffic on Lake Michigan was increasing. Barry noticed a variety of types of craft coming and going. Gallant four-masted frigates, schooners, steamers, lumber barges, and freight ships abounded. The hustle and bustle of a busy port might be a routine sight to a world traveler, but it filled him with excitement. In the distance, Barry saw a sight that stirred him even more. It was the skyline of Chicago.

Chapter Twelve

SWEAT GLISTENED ON PADDY HOGAN'S body as he went for the kill. Up to now, it had been an even match, a slug fest with no rules. Paddy had been on the receiving end of a few wicked blows, but now there would be an end to that. He had one advantage over his opponent: a driving motivation. He wanted to remain chief of police. In the brutal neighborhood of Milwaukee's Bloody Third, he had to prove himself again and again. The ward wanted its cops to be fighters.

"Kill 'im, Hogan!" roared the crowd. A surge of adrenalin pumped through his system. The blood on Paddy's face and the bruises on his ribs were forgotten as the mob urged him on. He smiled coldly as he charged. His opponent displayed a glimmer of fear. Paddy seized the moment. With a mighty swing, he cracked the opponent's jaw, and it was over.

To the victor, the spoils. He was king of the mountain. Fearless Paddy, protector of the ward, a good man to have on your side; that's how he was perceived. He'd fought to keep his reputation. It was worth it for the respect generated among the criminals with whom he dealt. He took on all comers, but he knew a downfall was inevitable. He wasn't getting any younger and years of smoking "long nines" had given him shortness of breath, even though he claimed that he didn't inhale.

His wife, Bridget, took in laundry, and all seven of their children went to work as soon as they were physically able. He appeared to be a good, churchgoing Catholic, a decent God-fearing man with few apparent flaws. That he frequently beat his wife was known only to

Bridget, who bore the affliction silently, lying about the bruises when anyone cared to notice. His children knew, but they were afraid of him. If they questioned him, they received a harsh blow for their trouble.

Hogan didn't care for liquor. He had a drink with the boys now and then to prove that he was a man. The macho image was calculated. He wanted control. John Barleycorn took it away. He was a physical man, prone to settle arguments with his fists, expecting people to buckle under his authority. Bridget was not a buckler. She stood up to her husband, in spite of his brutishness, but he beat her into submission.

He tried to make up for it afterward. In public, the Hogans were a perfect pair. People remarked how kind Chief Paddy was to his darlin' Bridget. He was deeply ashamed of the truth. He'd confessed to Father Delaney and done penance for his sin, but, like most sin, it would not go away that easily. Hogan had a quick temper and didn't deal well with frustration. He was sensitive to issues involving his manhood, with clear ideas about what a man should and should not be. A real man was tough and a real man was always in charge.

A man who allowed a woman to boss him was a sniveling coward, a weak nancy. Bridget, God love her, had a sharp tongue, and when it stung he slapped her as he might slap a mosquito. Sometimes he slapped her too hard. When she really asked for it, he used a closed fist. Sure he felt bad about it, but that made him do it even more.

Now, in the room above the pub, Hogan stared at the dead man in the chair. He blinked, but the corpse didn't go away. Feeney wasn't well liked, but who could have hated him enough to drive a spear through his heart? Feeney's empty eyes stared back at Hogan. Hogan shut the eyes for the last time. "Damn you, and damn your eyes for allowing yourself to get killed like this. You've put me in a tight spot, old fella. What am I to do now?"

He didn't know what to make of the situation. He was good at what he did, which was enforcing the law. Solving crimes was another matter. Hogan was no sleuth. His powers of deduction were limited. Investigations gave him headaches. Oh, there had been no lack of murders in his precinct, but most of them were cut-and-dried, a barroom brawl, a domestic quarrel, a thief caught in the act. The perpetrators were of low intelligence, breaking easily under interrogation.

This case didn't add up. To complicate matters, it couldn't be swept under the rug. Feeney was not well liked, but he was well known. The pub was a popular watering hole. A Fenian connection was rumored. If that were true, the crime could have international implications, creating even more pressure. Hogan groaned. It would be big news. Blevins Morgan would be nosing around, making life difficult. Things would be blown out of proportion, especially the bizarre weapon that had dispatched the victim.

The spear had been driven into the body with such force that it had penetrated all the way through. The stone tip was painted with an ornate Celtic design. Carved into the shaft was the face of a wolfhound. Hogan had a passing familiarity with ancient lore. The wolfhound represented Cuchulain, legendary warrior of Ulster, and brought to mind the recent torching of the *Lynne* by the mysterious rider they called Cuchulain. If Cuchulain's namesake did this, who was he?

Some said the rider was Jack O'Mara. There was no proof. Hogan trod lightly when it came to the O'Mara family, who had prestige in the community. He didn't like Jack, but he was reluctant to stir up a hornet's nest, especially lacking hard evidence. Not only that, there was no motive. Why would Jack kill Feeney? Certainly not for money. There was no need for that.

Yet there was the empty safe. Hogan had no idea what the safe contained, although he'd heard rumors about a satchel full of money. Hmm. Rumors. Rumors were in the air, if only he could bring them down to earth. The motive would seem to be robbery. If that were the case, why the spear? A thief would more likely use a knife or gun or even a club. Common sense would have dictated it.

Were the robbery and murder separate events? That idea had possibilities. Maybe Cuchulain (or Jack, as Hogan was beginning to think of him) did kill Feeney. Someone came in later, discovered the body and robbed the safe. One thing bothered him about that. Would Cuchulain use his own spear and incriminate himself by leaving it behind?

Hogan knew that Feeney and some of the lads were involved in a secret Fenian organization. It wasn't a well-kept secret. Respectable Irish in the community pretended to be shocked, but many inwardly approved. Anyway, no one wanted to do anything about it. Was this connected to the killing? Whoever offed Feeney must have been an acquaintance, since there was no sign of a struggle. Hogan's head was spinning. He was nowhere, with lots of questions and no answers.

One thing was certain. He couldn't leave Feeney's skewered corpse sitting there in rigor mortis. He'd go over to the precinct house and find help to get the body to the morgue, and then he'd have the pub boarded shut. The act of closing the pub would grieve more men than the death of its proprietor. He had no idea what the final disposition would be. As far as he knew, Feeney had no relatives in Milwaukee. Feeney didn't trust lawyers and didn't attend church, so he wouldn't be buried in holy ground.

The headache was getting worse. He'd do what had to be done and go home to a good night's sleep. The *Lady Elgin* would return in a couple of days. He'd start the investigation then. Flaherty would be back. He could question Flaherty, who knew Feeney well. He needed time to think. Right now, he and the killer were the only ones who knew Feeney was dead. Tomorrow the whole ward would know. Hogan's head was killing him. He hoped Bridget would be asleep when he got home.

Those damned abolitionists, Deputy Marshal Doughty thought as he rode past the Milwaukee jail made famous by the Glover incident in 1854. Glover had been a runaway slave. His owner, accompanied by a federal deputy, tracked him down, caught him, beat him, and locked him in this jail. Abolitionist Sherman Booth, with an illegal posse, stormed the jail and freed Glover, who fled to Canada with the help of the Underground Railroad.

Glover's owner was arrested by a local sheriff, but a federal judge upheld the owner's right to do what he wanted with his own property. Sherman Booth was arrested by the federal authorities, but the Wisconsin Supreme Court freed him, declaring the Fugitive Slave Act unconstitutional. This was the beginning of the Booth Wars between Wisconsin and the federal government. The federals arrested Booth again, finding him guilty. Booth paid a fine and continued to break the law. The federals continued to charge him and Wisconsin continued to free him.

Doughty didn't give a rat's ass about the issue. He did what he did for the money. He didn't like blacks in general and slaves in particular. He disliked slave owners even more. This Clayton, who owned the runaway Moses, was a despicable son-of-a-bitch. Moses was a dead man if Doughty caught and returned him. Clayton wanted revenge more than he wanted the slave. Doughty imagined the pain Moses would suffer before he died. Not that Doughty cared. He might even stick around and watch, for the entertainment of it.

It amused him that he was on the right side of the law. It hadn't always been that way. He'd grown up in a dirt-poor district of Atlanta. His people were considered trash, probably a fair depiction. Violence was a constant in his existence. He'd given it and taken it. In his adult life, he'd given more than he'd taken. He had no regard for the law. The reason he'd never been in jail was that he'd never been caught.

He wasn't without wit or resources. Sometimes he thought he was invincible now that he was a deputy. In normal times, a man like Doughty wouldn't qualify for the job. The Fugitive Slave Act changed that. The government needed manpower to enforce the law, especially in states like Wisconsin. It was supply and demand. The requirements to be a deputy had been lowered. Now anyone could be a deputy. "Good thing, too," Doughty chuckled. He liked the job. It made him feel important, superior to the people he tracked and for whom he tracked.

Another thing, he liked the pay. It wasn't much, but he didn't have to steal, which is not the same as saying that he didn't steal. He was never above accepting bribes, although his captives didn't have much to offer. When he did apprehend slaves, he felt proud, imagining himself a soldier, his captives prisoners of war, even though they were docile and afraid. Sometimes they were women. He took advantage of the women, pretending that they wanted him and forcing them to go along with his fantasy. Never mind that they were black. Hell, tip them upside down in a barrel and all women looked alike.

He enjoyed a good game of cat-and-mouse, as long as he was the cat. In this case, the mouse was Captain Garrett Barry. Oh yes, yes, indeed. He knew the captain didn't like him. Most people didn't like him, and liked him even less when they got to know him. That wasn't what tipped him off. No, it was the expression on Barry's face when he saw the drawing of Moses. There was a flicker of recognition. Barry knew the runaway.

A few days after meeting the captain, Doughty had been in the park watching an abolitionist rally. It always helped to know your enemy. Police had to arrest several rowdies who were throwing rocks at the speaker's stand. There was a time when he would have thrown rocks, too. Mary Barry took the stand. She spoke so eloquently that even he was moved by her words. Suddenly he knew. It was all so clear. The runaway Moses was being hidden in the Barry home.

These thoughts occupied Doughty's mind as he rode through town. The usual midmorning clamor was absent, perhaps because so many people had gone to Chicago. Stephen Douglas was a major attraction. The *Lady Elgin* had carried a boatload, but many others had gone down via rail or coach. Even Republicans went down, just to hear what Douglas had to say. As for Doughty, he didn't much care. Whichever way the wind blew, he figured he wouldn't have this job much longer.

After a while, he was in the outskirts heading toward the Barry homestead. He came to the rise of a hill. The house would be at the bottom of the other side of the hill. He daydreamed of Mary Barry, a stunning Irish lass. He visualized her undressing slowly before him, making love to him in a large four-poster, the same bed in which she and the captain dallied. As he reached the top of the incline, he scratched his crotch and noticed that he had become aroused.

He looked down the hill and saw the house. There was a woman in the yard near an apple tree. She wore a robe and was hanging clothes on a line. Even from a distance, there was no mistaking her. The woman was Mary Barry.

Mary had lounged around the house all morning in her robe, feeling guilty about not going to Chicago with Garrett. Johanna and Mary Anne were off on a picnic. Elizabeth was writing in her diary and little Maria was sleeping in. She could have gone with her husband. The girls could have stayed with neighbors. She'd been rough on him, taunting him about his drinking and bringing up her father's money.

Stephen Douglas notwithstanding, she should have gone with her husband. Some people, enemies of Garrett, would misconstrue her not going. It was the wife's place to be at her husband's side. How she hated to be told what her place was. She should have bitten her lip and gone. It had meant a lot to him. She had let him down.

Perhaps, though, Garrett and Willie would connect. Willie had a great admiration for his father, almost to the point of hero worship, mesmerized by stories Garrett told about his military exploits in the

Mexican War and of his friendship with Ulysses Grant at West Point. Lately Garrett had been drinking more than usual, dismissing his son and becoming self-absorbed. Maybe this trip would bring them closer together.

She had a sudden impulse to have a drink. If Garrett could do it, why shouldn't she? It was silly, at this hour in the morning, but she couldn't get the idea out of her head. She poured herself a double and gulped it. She gagged, the liquor invading her head, making her dizzy. She thought she might pass out. Mary's friends would be shocked at her behavior. She was no drinker, not even a closet drinker. This was quite unlike her.

She glanced at the grandfather's clock, which Garrett had bought for their anniversary. It was 10:00 am. He would be in Chicago now, leading the parade. He'd look so fine in his sharp uniform, and she not there to cheer him on. She'd make it up to him when he got home. She had another drink. What if Garrett came home and found her passed out drunk? She giggled. This would never do.

She had to clear her head. Why not go out and hang up the laundry? She could have Old Ned do it, but he was busy cleaning Garrett's gun. Besides, Garrett had a thing about another man touching her underwear. Garret could be such a prude, but she guessed she shouldn't complain. She was lucky to have him.

The fresh air helped. She staggered ever so slightly to the clothesline. Whew! If three drinks made her react this way, she should avoid the stuff entirely. She knew some people were allergic to alcohol. Maybe she was one of them. She concentrated on pinning the clothes to the line and didn't hear the horse and rider approach. A man's voice startled her. She dropped a pin and spun around.

"Sorry to startle you, ma'am. Deputy Marshal Joshua Doughty, at your service. Investigatin' a runaway slave. Like to talk to you about it." He winked. "P'raps we could go in the house and discuss the matter."

"That's out of the question." He started to dismount. "No. Don't get off your horse. Say what you have to say and leave. State your business and be brief." She could smell his body odor and the yellow stain on his teeth disgusted her. He dismounted. "Please leave at once. You are on my property."

"Ayeh. There's someone else on your property, too. Black man named Moses. Care to tell me where he is?"

"Get out of here."

"In the house, p'raps? In the stable?" He scratched his crotch. "In the bedroom?"

"In case you don't know it, my husband is—"

"In Chicago," he smirked. For the first time, she began to feel panic. She could run for it, but the house was too far. She'd never make it.

"I would ask you to leave," she said, but her voice slurred.

"You would 'ashk' me to leave? What a naughty girl. You've been drinking. When the cat's away. Don't worry, I'll keep your little secret. Why, I'll even forget about the runaway, if you're nice to me."

He approached her with a look that could not be misinterpreted. She backed against the clothesline pole. He grabbed a handful of her robe and ripped. The fabric came off in his hand. She screamed and lost her balance, falling onto her hands and knees. In her struggle to get up, she lost the rest of her robe. Doughty, transfixed, watched with glazed eyes, a fleck of saliva appearing at the corner of his mouth.

She threw the basket of laundry at him, which knocked him off balance and scattered the clothes all over the lawn. He fell near her, laughing and cursing. She grabbed a towel to cover herself, but he caught her ankle and she went down again. He had her. This is it, she thought. But I will fight him. I will fight him with every last ounce of strength that I have. He will have to kill me.

He crawled toward her like some obscene beast and he was over her. She looked up into his face and the strangest thing happened. There was a thunderclap. Doughty's head exploded. Blood was everywhere, all over her, dripping from the clothesline, soaked into the clothes on the grass. His headless body lay twitching beside her on the ground.

Over by the stable stood Old Ned. He held Garrett's favorite rifle. Smoke poured out of the barrel.

Chapter Thirteen

From his perch atop the Tremont House, One-Eyed Bird could see everything. The vast panorama of the city of Chicago was accessible to his telescopic stare. He hawked a huge wad of chewing tobacco and spit it off the roof, watching the globule float gracefully past windows and splatter on Randolph Street narrowly missing a pedestrian. The pedestrian looked up and shook his fist. "Hey, Bird! Do that again and it's open season against you and your avian colleagues!" Bird laughed and flicked him a distinctly bird-like gesture.

Bird's given name was Wolfgang Meyerhoff. His grandfather had been a Hessian mercenary in America's War of Independence. Instead of returning to the fatherland after the war, he had enlisted in the Continental Army, where he had served with distinction. Wolfgang's father had been born on a farm in Pennsylvania, which he'd left at an early age to seek his fortune. The quest had led him to Chicago, where, instead of a fortune, he had found a wife. Wolfgang was born in 1800, followed by a sister and two brothers.

Wolfgang had watched Chicago develop from a swampy settlement to a boom town, grain hub of the continent, lake port, stockyard, shipper of lumber, hardware, molasses, rum, and whiskey. The growth had been rapid, accelerated by the McCormick reaper, and boosted by "Long John" Wentworth, flamboyant promoter, land developer, and mayor.

With the growth of the city had come the growth of crime, and Chicago had every type of crime known to mankind. Chicago was no place for the timid. Wolfgang was a scrapper and a hustler. As a youth, he had worked a variety of jobs: stockyard worker, rail hand, stevedore, and grocery boy. Then he went to work for Tremont House as a porter, meeting ships and loading baggage onto hotel omnibuses, transporting the baggage and the passengers to the hotel.

Competition among the porters and omnibuses at the dock was fierce. As passengers disembarked, porters would vie for the bags, jostling each other and hawking the merits of their respective establishments. Fights erupted, during which passengers lost their valuables to pickpockets. The Matteson House, the Sherman House, and the Tremont House were rivals, each hostelry having its own fleet of omnibuses. Independent cabs added to the turmoil, trying to steal customers. Some of the independents stole not only the customers but the luggage as well.

Wolfgang was the Tremont's best porter. Although a hustler, he was honest and intolerant of cheating, and he reported others who did. A porter's income depended entirely upon gratuities. His reputation permitted him to earn a modest living. Then, as an omnibus driver, he earned larger gratuities and a small salary.

The years passed. He married and sired a child. His blond hair turned grey. Wolfgang became cantankerous, finding more in common with whiskey and chewing tobacco than with his wife. He was a favorite driver among the hotel's regular patrons because of his salty, irreverent humor. However, age was taking its toll and the hassle of driving was for a younger man.

So Wolfgang had become a roof man. On the roof of the Tremont was a cupola, a white-domed structure with windows all around it. The roof man stood guard in the cupola. With a telescope, he watched the docks and railroads for incoming ships and trains. When an arrival was spotted, the roof man would give the word. An omnibus would be dispatched and the hotel staff would prepare for business.

Ships and trains arrived frequently, often unscheduled. Roof man was a soft job and the pay wasn't bad. Wolfgang liked to joke that now he was high in the hotel business. It was an ideal job for an "old" man of sixty, and it afforded him hours of watching his beloved city. He earned the reputation of being a great spotter, reporting ships long before they docked and trains long before they stopped.

He spotted other things, too. Once he spotted bank robbers leaving the Mechanics Bank with bags of money, watching their escape through the telescope and reporting their location to the police. As another result of his one-eyed vigil, guests had recovered luggage delivered to rival hotels. Also, fires had been identified and extinguished, and changes in the weather correctly predicted. Wolfgang's eye had become so famous that he had become known as "One-Eyed Bird." For brevity folks called him "Bird." If he resembled a bird at all, it was a turkey or buzzard, but he was so used to the appellation that he even started to think of himself as "Bird."

———————————

It was a clear day, but Bird had a feeling it might rain later this afternoon. He peered in one direction and another with his trusty telescope. He scanned the retail stores along Lake Street, which would soon teem with shoppers. Beyond was the familiar spire of the Plymouth Congregational Church on Madison and Wabash. By moving the telescope slightly to the left, he could see the grain elevators along the Chicago River and Illinois Central Station. Situated on the lakefront near the mouth of the river, the station was 504 feet in length, 84 feet high, and 162 feet wide with eight tracks.

In another direction, he eyed the US Post Office and Customs Building. Marvelous invention, the telescope. If he squinted, he could see parts of the forty-five-acre tract that had been the site of the United States Fair attracting 69,000 tourists to Chicago last September. What a week that had been! Hotels filled to capacity, culminating in a fire that had leveled ten buildings at Canal and Lake.

"Let me look through the telescope, Gramps," piped the voice of his twelve-year-old grandson, Hansi, who came up to the cupola as often as possible to help his grandfather. Hansi was known affectionately by the staff as "Young Bird."

"Yah, sure, give me a break. Be careful not to drop the telescope."

There wasn't a chance that Hansi would drop it. The telescope was more important to the boy than a favorite toy. He was as good a watcher as his grandfather, who had taught him well. He had a good eye and was a reliable messenger, saving the old man from running up and down the stairs when a ship or train was spotted.

"Be back in the wink of an eye. Don't lay a hand on my chewing tobacco while I'm gone."

Bird stepped out of the cupola onto the roof. Darting a furtive glance, he unzipped his fly and watered the roof, shaking his bird before tucking it back into his pants. Then he noticed a colleague on the roof of the Sherman House shaking a finger at him. Bird waved and laughed so hard he had to go again. Walking to the edge, he stared straight down, which gave him a sense of danger, an insecurity which he didn't feel inside the cupola. He thought crazy, irrational thoughts on the brink. The idea of flying entered his mind. He fantasized leaping off the roof, flying across Randolph and landing on the roof of the Sherman House, scaring the hell out of his wiseacre colleague.

He noted a balcony directly below. From the same balcony, Stephen A. Douglas would address a crowd of supporters this afternoon. Douglas had spoken from the balcony in 1858, and Lincoln had spoken from it the next day. The event had been followed by the Lincoln-Douglas debates throughout Illinois, resulting in the reelection of Douglas to the US Senate. Now they contended for the presidency. Bird hadn't decided which candidate he favored, but Douglas would be no shoo-in this time.

His reverie was shattered by the shrill sound of Young Bird's voice from the cupola. "Ship ahoy! Ship ahoy!" Bird ran back to the coop as fast as his old legs allowed. His grandson handed him the telescope, and he peered toward the lake. On the horizon, he saw the long paddlewheel steamship. He didn't need to squint to read the name. He would have recognized the ship from any distance. It was the *Lady Elgin*.

———

"Whew!" exclaimed Brian. "What a smell!" The *Lady Elgin* was entering the Chicago River, into which a dozen packing plants poured stinking offal. The river was a forest of masts. Brian had never seen that many ships in his life—at least that he remembered, for he had been an infant during his Atlantic crossing. Chicago was a big city and noisy. The clang of the grain elevators and the slam of lumber being unloaded from barges made him block his ears.

Liam pointed to a huge structure with a name painted on it that he couldn't read. "Ma, what does the sign say, the sign on the building?"

"The sign says 'McCormick Reaper Works.' They make machines that harvest wheat. The harvested wheat is sent to Chicago and from Chicago all over the country."

Maeve was about to explain about the stockyards and the railroad, but the boys' attention had wandered, so much to take in. Their eyes were like saucers. They had been born in the tiny village of Killibegs and had never even been to Dublin. A sadness filled Maeve to think the boys might never see that ancient city with its cobbled streets and Viking wall.

"Ah, Dublin," Maeve sighed, a tear forming in a corner of her eye. She dearly loved the mountainous west coast of Ireland, especially her native Bundoran and County Donegal. She'd left that behind, and it left a void in her soul. Yes. But Dublin—how she did miss Dublin. She had pursued literature and music, specializing in the harp. She'd learned Gaelic in secret from an old professor who taught the forbidden language evenings in his home. If the professor had been caught, he would have been fired and the handful of students expelled.

Maeve delved deeply into the roots of her native land, spending hours researching Celtic mythology in the vast, musty, arched library at Trinity. Among the artifacts displayed at Trinity was a harp that may have belonged to Brian Boru, the bardic king who defeated the Vikings at Clontarf in 1014.

Maeve's favorite pastime had been strolling the city streets, a dangerous diversion for a woman. Dublin, or in Gaelic *Dubhlinn*, had grace and charm, with its Georgian houses, fancy brass door knockers, round towers, open markets, and quaint bridges. She liked to stand on the Ha'penny Bridge spanning the Liffey and admire the ships moored along the quays. On weekdays she would go to the seashore and run barefoot along the glistening strand, letting wind blow through her hair and pretending she was Brian Boru battling Vikings or the pirate Grace O' Malley, the one they called Grania.

One day when she was daydreaming on the Ha'penny Bridge, she was approached by a man who introduced himself as James Stephens. They talked awhile, discovering they had much in common. Stephens courted her in the traditional way, ever the gentleman. They drove over the green in a fancy brougham, cuddled, held hands, attended concerts, and took long walks. Stephens, an eloquent speaker and raconteur, spinner of spellbinding tales, was shy and tongue-tied with Maeve. He confessed that he had followed her to the bridge the day of their "chance" meeting, the closest he'd come to a declaration of love.

When she and Stephens got into Celtic history, there was magic in their relationship. Stephens would lose his reticence, and they would explode together in bursts of language, poetry, and folklore.

It followed that when Stephens led the Fenian movement, Maeve would be involved. He introduced her to O'Mahony, Doheny, and O'Donovan Rossa. She traveled to Killarney and Kerry to attend meetings of the Phoenix National and Literary Society. She made friends with O'Mahony. Once, she and O'Mahony hiked to Kerry and climbed McGillicuddy's Reek, which commanded a dazzling view of the sea and the deep valley below. They shouted Gaelic words into the valley and the echoes bounced back. When they had returned to Killarney, Stephens had been jealous and angry. There had been an argument, but the issue had passed. They were the most exciting men she had known, the men of the Phoenix National and Literary Society, revolutionaries with bright-eyed intelligence and a penchant for marathon talk-fests.

One summer when Maeve was home in Bundoran and Stephens was in Paris drafting the charter of the Irish Republican Brotherhood, she'd met the virile young fisherman who'd swept her off her feet. After an intensely physical relationship, they married. She'd been happy, but he was at sea most of the time, while she played the role of fisherman's wife in the quiet village of Killibegs. Whether the marriage would have withstood the test of time will never be known. If opposites attract, the union would have survived. The man had a small intellect and no ear for music. Early on, the sea had made a widow of her.

Maeve hadn't known Feeney then, although they had moved in the same circles. When she had come to Milwaukee, she'd avoided him and didn't think he knew who she was. When O'Mahony was in the ward recently, he had visited her. They'd spoken of old times, of Stephens and the Phoenix Society, of Kerry and McGillicuddy's Reek. O'Mahony had implied that Feeney was in trouble with the Brotherhood, but he wouldn't be specific. Maeve didn't press him. She didn't want to know.

Toot! The whistle blew, and the *Lady Elgin* glided toward her berth. Jack had wandered off last night and she hadn't seen him since. Jack would disembark with the brigade and they would meet after the parade. The boys were hanging dangerously over the rail. She roughly pulled them back.

"Look lively now. We're here."

The Union Guard gathered with multitudes at the fairgrounds where the parade would begin. Captain Barry stood on a platform with Willie, who waved a sign indicating that this was the muster area for the brigade. They were surrounded by a sea of faces belonging to militia from the far reaches of Illinois and Wisconsin. Many of the faces were Irish. Stephen Douglas had multiethnic support, but he was a favorite of the Irish.

People were milling about. Barry wondered how the parade organizers could create order from this chaos. In addition to the uniformed soldiers were several bands warming up, creating a dissonance loud and unpleasant to the ear. One of the floats was in a state of disrepair, and carpenters pounded on it, adding to the din. Barry wondered what Mary was doing now. At least she'd be enjoying the peace and quiet of the manor.

Mary and he had attended the 1859 United States Fair last September. They'd had a marvelous time at the races, where Barry'd won ten eagles on a horse named Mary. They had been impressed by the array of railroad and farm equipment on exhibit, including the latest inventions in household appliances. They considered buying one of the newfangled stoves on display. Mary admired a lockstitch sewing machine. On the last day, Barry bought Mary a coffee grinder, which he'd lugged on the train all the way back to Milwaukee, feeling guilty because it was he, not Mary, who drank coffee.

The most exciting event of the fair had been a plowing contest between two behemoth steam plows. The winning machine plowed a whole acre in seventeen minutes. The new technology was incredible.

The parade, which was to begin at the fairgrounds and proceed down Lake to Randolph and the Tremont House, was scheduled to start shortly. Excitement filled the air. Damn! Barry wished he'd prevailed upon Mary to come. This was a rowdy crowd, though. Perhaps she was safer at home. Meanwhile, he didn't see how this maelstrom would ever be ready on time.

Boom! A huge explosion shook the ground, and then another. All eyes turned in the direction of the sound and saw two smoking cannons. Barry knew the story about Douglas's love of cannons. During the Lincoln-Douglas debates, a cannon was fired each time Douglas scored a point on his opponent. Today the cannons riveted attention upon the parade marshal, who summoned the leaders of each segment of the parade and gave them brief instructions.

In no time, to Barry's surprise, the parade was organized and ready to begin. This was nothing less than a miracle. He stood at the head of the Union Guard. This was the largest parade in which he'd ever marched. Looking backward or forward there was no beginning and no end.

Boom, ta-ta-boom, ta-ta-boom! Drums beat and bugles blared. Huge crowds mobbing the wooden sidewalks cheered and applauded. Signs announced: Douglas for President and Illinois Loves the Little Giant. Other signs proclaimed: Let the Territories Decide and Popular Sovereignty.

Maeve, Brian, and Liam searched for the Union Guard. In a while they spotted the signs, which read: Captain Barry's Union Guard for Douglas. They recognized the Ward Three for the Little Giant banner, which had been hanging outside Feeney's Pub. The banner had been vandalized, but someone had repaired it. Maeve noticed Jack and waved.

Jack heard them and grinned, surprised that he could grin after last night's debauch. He was buoyant, caught in the spirit of the grand event. Two hours ago, his head felt like a watermelon, his mouth full of peach fuzz. The ship's security man had dumped his wasted body on a bench to sleep it off. When the lads awakened him, Maeve and the boys had left the ship. Breakfast was being served onboard, but he couldn't face breakfast. Now he was hungry.

Jack loved the glory of the military, relishing the camaraderie, the *esprit de corps*, the thrill of combat. He longed to be in a real conflict to test his courage. If war broke out, he would be in it, fighting for the North. If the North wouldn't have him, he'd fight for the South. Ideology had nothing to do with it. He wanted to be a warrior.

Maeve and the boys would be at his side. He loved those boys. They were like brothers to him because there was something of the boy in Jack. The boys would not be a challenge. Maeve herself was the challenge. She was a free spirit, independent, and unconventional. She avoided the subject of marriage. Jack tried to pin her down, but she was evasive. There was a lot about her that he didn't know, a fact that made her even more attractive.

Flynn was a different matter. The incident on the ship preyed on his mind. Oh, he was drunk, and he was glad he'd passed out before committing an act of violence. He acknowledged the hypocrisy of his moral dilemma. Flynn was sleeping with Blevins. Jack was sleeping with Maeve. Was it any different, what they were doing?

In his mind, there was a difference. Jack was a man, and it was all right for a man to sow wild oats. Maeve was a widow. The standard wasn't the same. A widow, after all, was not a virgin. There was another distinction. Maeve hadn't been brought up in Irish Milwaukee. She didn't have a reputation, one way or another, to uphold. Flynn, on the other hand, had everything to lose. Jack had thought Blevins to be trustworthy. He thought Flynn to be a rock of virtue. How could he be so wrong about her? She wasn't the type to go off on a wild fling.

What if Flynn got pregnant? The shame of it would disgrace the family. It was too late to talk to her about it. She had a stubborn streak. In time, he could make her listen to reason, but there was no time. What if she were already in the family way? He had to find a way to save her. Religion was not the way, not now.

He thought about Catholicism, and how far he had drifted from it. How could he talk to her about that, preoccupied as he was with Celtic nature worship? Sometimes he thought the spirit of Cuchulain was within him, and he fantasized about crows, druids, and spirits in trees. Catholicism lurked beneath the surface, making him feel guilty about his drinking and fornication. He avoided confession because he couldn't bring himself to stop the behavior. He agonized.

What if he went to heaven and God said, "Jack, you could have had it all. You could have had the sex, the booze, the Celtic dreams, and all would have been forgiven. It's too bad you lost all that sleep over it."

A wagon load of politicians brought up the rear of the parade. Leaders of the Midwestern Democratic Party carried signs indicating support for Douglas. The politician most conspicuous by his absence was "Long John" Wentworth, once a force among Chicago's Democrats, a controversial figure who, during his tenure as mayor, had developed the city by building canals and bridges and clearing slums. Wentworth had changed horses in midstream, become a Republican, and supported Lincoln.

Damn traitor, thought Garrity, waving and smiling at a cluster of children. "Garrulous" Garrity, whose own ethics had never been a strong point, could forgive most human failings, but he could not forgive disloyalty. That Democrats had jumped on the Republican bandwagon alarmed him. It didn't occur to him that Lincoln projected a moral force that Douglas did not. Garrity never thought about moral forces.

Lincoln's direct style had a fresh, folksy, backwoods appeal, in contrast with Douglas's familiar bombastic eloquence, the style of oratory people had come to expect of politicians. Douglas was immensely popular in Illinois, having been a judge and a senator. Douglas was from Vermont and Lincoln was from Kentucky, which didn't seem to matter. Neither candidate appealed to the South, which did matter.

It mattered because of slavery. The Kansas-Nebraska Act, brought to the Senate by Douglas, had been the catalyst that stoked Lincoln's fire. Lincoln might not have entered the arena had it not been for his opposition to Douglas's concept of popular sovereignty giving each new territory the right to decide on slavery. The act was an attempt to compromise in an effort to please the largest amount of voters. Lincoln had polarized the issue by demanding that all states be free. No wonder they didn't like him in the South.

Douglas defeated Lincoln in the senatorial race of '58. Meanwhile, John C. Breckinridge split the Democrats in the South. The Southern Democrats angered Garrity, who followed the party line. He believed in cronyism, rewarding loyalty, tit for tat, quid pro quo, mutual back-scratching. Being malleable allowed him to survive at the gut level of politics, but when it came to party loyalty, Garrity was inflexible.

He didn't have the charisma of his old pal Dan O'Mara, who could have risen to dazzling heights in the political arena had he not been tied to business and raising a family. Garrity had to be content with backroom politics. No speaker, he was at his worst in front of crowds. Behind the scenes, he had influence, wielding power as a ward boss. A manipulator extraordinaire, he had markers everywhere, which he could call in at any time. That's how he'd negotiated with Douglas on behalf of the Union Guard. Douglas owed Garrity and Garrity called in the marker. It was as simple as that.

He didn't always cover his rear and recently had been living under the black cloud of another master manipulator, the publican Seamus

Feeney. One night, in his cups, Garrity had been indiscreet and blurted out a secret deal he had made with a contractor involving the building of a city bridge. He'd bragged, and Feeney had drawn him out, extracting how much profit Garrity had gained from the kickback. Feeney had demanded a share of the kickback in return for his silence. Since then, Garrity had paid ... and paid ... and paid.

Lugh Finnegan was certain that his presence wouldn't be missed on the return voyage. The lads would be tired and inebriated and no one would be checking on anyone. It would be a few days before they realized he hadn't returned. "Where's Lugh?" they would ask. "Did anyone see him board in Chicago?" They would speculate as to why he missed the ship. Someone would swear to having seen Lugh passed out in a pub and someone else would attest to having seen Lugh in a knock-down, drag-out fight with a German bully. Rumors would abound. A mysterious woman would certainly come into it. Several lads would claim to have seen Lugh fall off the ship after they were underway. Then they'd forget about him and swap anecdotes about their own exploits in Chicago. The bloody fools.

It would be a while before it occurred to them that he wouldn't be returning at all. Feeney's Boys would be well rid of him. He'd never been a convincing Fenian. He couldn't swallow that tribal Celtic nonsense. What a crock. He'd played along, even to the point of assuming the role of Lugh, the Sun God.

It made him laugh, especially the Cuchulain charade. Jack O'Mara had never fought in a real war and had never killed anyone. Fierce in staged battles, Jack demonstrated a degree of military leadership, but the grocer's son had never been put to the test. Lugh was sick of pretending. It was good that he was pulling out now, before they learned that he couldn't speak a word of Gaelic.

The Stagecoach Inn, south of Chicago, was noted for its superb meals of wild game. Residents made the jaunt for the meals alone, returning home stuffed. Lugh was bloated with pheasant, wild rice, and wine. His uniform was in his valise. He'd changed into civilian clothes suitable for traveling.

Lugh had felt obliged to march in the parade but departed directly afterward, not staying to hear Douglas's address. He'd taken an omnibus from the Tremont House, which he'd shared with an elderly couple who'd quarreled during the entire two-hour drive. They would no doubt quarrel on the return trip. Lugh didn't care. He wasn't going back.

Exhausted, he was tempted to spend a night at the inn, but he had an agenda. The inn was a terminal for stagecoaches traveling east and west. Near the Illinois-Indiana border, the inn yard was always congested with incoming and outgoing traffic.

Valise in hand, he found the coach he needed, which would transport him east, with several changes, to New York City, where he would catch a ship that would take him to Dublin. His father would be waiting.

Chapter Fourteen

YOUNG BIRD ALMOST HAD IT. The billfold was hanging out of the man's back pocket. It was an easy mark. Hansi only went for easy marks. He was a novice in the art. In his circle of friends, there were a few thieves whose fingers were incredibly nimble. Others less skillful landed in jail. He wasn't taking any chances. Old Bird, who didn't have a dishonest bone in his body, would be furious to learn of his grandson's larceny.

The portly mark bent to pick up a suitcase. *Plop!* The bulging billfold dropped to the ground. Young Bird snatched the billfold and was about to run when a voice came seemingly from nowhere. "Psst! Boy. Hey, psst!" The mark heard the voice and turned, spotting the boy with the billfold. The boy thought fast. Smiling earnestly, he looked straight at the mark, handing him the billfold.

"Your billfold, sir? I believe you dropped it."

"Why, thank you, lad. Good boy, good boy."

The old duffer returned the billfold to his pocket and walked away. Fat tub of lard! The least he might have done was to proffer a small reward. Whew! The boy felt weak all over. What if he'd been caught? The thought of jail filled his heart with fear, but the thought of Old Bird's wrath terrified him. He'd been given a sign, a second chance. He would never try it again.

"Psst! Boy!" It was the disembodied voice again. "Over here, boy. Behind you. On the *Lady Elgin*."

Young Bird looked behind himself where the ship was moored. A beckoning arm was extended from a porthole. He knew he should just leave, but curiosity consumed him. He walked to the ship. The arm disappeared and a smiling face appeared at the round window.

"Listen, boy," said the voice of Flaherty, "you'll never get rich pickin' pockets, and you'll get caught for sure, goin' about it the way you do. New at the game, is it?" Young Bird said nothing. "Ah, I see by your look that you are a novice. Stick with me, boyo, and you'll have untold riches." The arm came out of the porthole again with a handful of greenbacks. "For starters, take the money in my hand. Take it, lad. It's yours."

"What's the catch, mister … mister …?"

"Rafferty," Flaherty lied. "Rory Rafferty. What's the catch? Why, there ain't no catch. I can see you're an enterprisin' young buck who'd not object to earnin' an eagle or two. Is there a catch? Not really. I want you to sell somethin' for me, that's all."

"Mr. Rafferty, why can't you come out of the ship?"

"Just call me Rory, son. Why can't I come out? You might say that I'm … ah … indisposed. But here, now, you haven't taken the money. Take it."

"What do you want me to sell?"

"Listen, you're a hotel boy, are you not?"

"I've been known to run errands for the Tremont."

"Ah, the Tremont, yes. So you know the lay of the land."

"I've lived here all my life. What do you—"

"Good boy, good boy. So. What do I want you to sell? See those pretty ladies standin' over there by the pilings?"

Two women stood by the pilings, giving Young Bird a funny look. To say that they were pretty was stretching the truth. One was overweight and the other had a hard, tawdry look that belied her youth. The fat one grinned and winked at Hansi. Hansi had spent most of his young life on the streets. It dawned on him what Rory wanted him to sell.

"You want me to be a pimp."

Flaherty winced. The boy was smart. He caught on fast. "No, boy, not you." He grinned sheepishly. "If anyone's a pimp, it's old Rory. Listen, they know you at the hotel. You can hang around without anyone being suspicious. Why, it's a perfect scam. All you have to do is spot a gentleman and ask him if he'd like to meet a fine lady. I can tell you how to judge if the gentleman is a good prospect. You'll get a percentage, of course, and you won't have to pick a single pocket."

"Well, I don't know."

"It'll be all right. Trust me. Take the money. It's an advance." The two women walked seductively toward the boy. "Here come the ladies now." The shrill of a police whistle pierced the air. "Damn!" shouted the voice behind the porthole. A man brandishing a pistol ran down the ramp of the *Lady Elgin*. The two women ran and disappeared into the crowd. The boy snatched the money from the outstretched hand before Flaherty had a chance to pull it back. "Hey, boy! Wait a minute!"

Young Bird took flight. He didn't run toward the hotel. Fear propelled him. Running until the pain in his side was too much to bear, he stopped to look back. He'd left the waterfront and was alone in an alley in an unfamiliar neighborhood. A barrel leaned against one of the buildings. Chest heaving, he collapsed onto the barrel, lost—but not hopelessly lost.

Having scanned the city from the top of the Tremont, he had a general idea of where he was now. He knew he was in a bad part of town. He was shaken and disoriented. It started to rain, but his perch on the barrel beneath the overhang of a roof protected him. He'd never go down to the docks again. Not only had he almost been caught picking pockets, he'd nearly been drawn into a serious crime. The more he thought about it, the more scared he became.

So much for a life of crime. From now on, it would be straight and narrow, but he wouldn't return the money to Mr. Rafferty, if that was his name. After all, didn't Mr. Rafferty tell him to keep it?

Gasping for breath, her sweat-soaked body cold and shaking, Adele raced down the railroad tracks as fast as her bleeding, splintered feet would carry her. Her heart was pumping and her bladder was ready to burst. The train was right behind her. The light of the train grew brighter and brighter, bathing her in a blinding illumination. Her mouth was a gaping maw of terror. A scream filled her soul, but no sound escaped from her mouth.

"Rise and shine, my dear. Rise and shine."

Adele opened her eyes. It was morning and her husband stood at the hotel window, the curtain open to let in the sunlight. She'd dreamed about trains before, awakening in other rooms. What room was this? What train brought her here?

"Where are we? What day is it?"

Stephen Douglas looked at his wife, a faint smile curling the corners of his mouth. "Why, we're in Chicago, Adele. Wake up, dearest. Surely you remember the Tremont. We've stayed here many times. Are you all right?"

"Oh yes, of course. I had a bad dream. The same bad dream. I see you're dressed already."

Douglas was a smart dresser. Compared to Abe Lincoln, he was a dandy. This morning, he wore a bright blue brocade coat, a fancy vest, and gold cufflinks. In his hand he held a stovepipe hat, but he was too much of a gentleman to wear it inside. The stovepipe had become identified with Lincoln. It was curious that Douglas favored stovepipes, too.

"It will be a busy day. I'll be breaking fast downstairs with party leaders. Later, I will speak on the balcony. Sorry you can't join me."

"Stephen, I can join you. You won't have me."

"We've discussed that. This is Chicago, and it's not safe, the way it used to be. Chicago is a powder keg. It's far too dangerous."

"Pshaw! If it's dangerous for me, it's even more dangerous for you."

"The matter is closed. I'll expect you to join me later at the press reception."

"Don't go, Stephen. I had a bad dream."

"How can I not go? You and your dreams ..."

Adele sat on the edge of the bed in her shift. Stephen gave her an appraising look. She was a stunning woman. With great effort, he forced his thoughts away from her. "I ordered breakfast for you, which will arrive shortly. I promise to be careful. See you at the press reception."

"Good-bye, Stephen."

"Good-bye, my love."

In the silence following her husband's departure, the image of the train and the foreboding mood of the dream lingered. She was no stranger to trains. If tracks extended the width of the continent, she could have crossed the country and back and still not equaled the miles she'd traveled on the campaign trail with Stephen.

In 1858, there'd been the Lincoln-Douglas debates, seven debates throughout Illinois in the towns of Ottawa, Freeport, Quincy, Charleston, Jonesboro, and Galesburg. Her Stephen was the most popular man in the state, hailed the "Little Giant," although Adele failed to see anything little about the love of her life. She guessed that the towering, gangling height of Lincoln made Stephen appear shorter than he was.

Adele loved the debates and basked in a glow of warm approbation attending the arrival of Stephen's private train, announced by the firing of a cannon he took with him everywhere he went. She hated loud noises, blocking her ears when the cannon was fired. Stephen was developing a hearing problem caused by the deafening explosions. She'd tried to talk him out of it, but he had a boyish enthusiasm for the weapon and couldn't be dissuaded.

The friendly faces, hospitality, and deference shown them in those rural communities made her feel important and proud, enjoying the personal fuss people made over her. Not a political person, she never talked about issues, many of which she did not understand. She was happy to live in the shadow of a great man and provide for his needs.

She was a domestic creature, a hostess comfortable playing a wifely role in the social whirl. It didn't trouble her that she was a second wife. Stephen's first wife had died when Stephen was still a young man. Adele had been with him during the best years.

For Adele, the debates had been social events, which included picnics, parades, teas, and dances. Gracious and beautiful, she was an asset to the ambitious senator, which was acknowledged by the press. Even the staunch Republican paper the *Chicago Daily Press Tribune* extolled her virtues. Reporter Horace White wrote, "Her presence gained votes for her husband without any effort of her own." She still had the clipping.

"Breakfast for Mrs. Douglas."

The boy came in with the steaming meal. It was way too much. Stephen had a large appetite, ordering for her what he would have ordered for himself.

"Thank you, Johnny."

She handed the boy a generous tip. The Tremont was their favorite hotel and she knew most of the staff on a first-name basis. The Tremont went out of its way to accommodate the senator and his wife. In honor of today's balcony speech, the hotel lobby displayed a bust of Douglas created by the renowned sculptor, Leonard W. Volk.

In spite of her husband's concerns, Adele felt safe in Chicago. The whole nation was heating up over the issue of slavery. There had been outbreaks of violence. She worried about Stephen, who was so deeply involved, but because of the city's familiarity, she did not feel threatened here.

Washington was another story. That cosmopolitan city had intimidated her when they had moved there. She'd never learned to like Washington but had adapted well enough. At first, she'd fretted about her ignorance of politics, until she discovered that even in the capitol women were expected to be ignorant. Washington was an old boys' club, which suited Adele just fine. Small talk was the province of wives and she was good at that. She didn't spread gossip, but she listened to it and passed it on to Stephen for whatever advantage it might have.

She wondered what it would be like to be married to Abraham Lincoln, to share life's intimate details with such a man. She thought of the dour Mary Todd Lincoln and Adele thanked God she was married to Stephen. But she worried—oh, how she worried. The slavery issue was so inflammatory it was banned from discussion on the Senate floor. The pressure had intensified. It was taking its toll.

She'd had unspeakable dreams. There was the train. Sometimes, like this morning, the train was a bright light that pursued her and consumed her. Other times the train was filled with slaves and moving slowly, dragging her from a rope in the rear.

The worst nightmare did not involve a train. Her husband was president. At the inauguration ball, women with hour-glass figures wearing crinolines danced with long-trousered men wearing dark waistcoats. The sentiment-drenched music of Stephen Foster saturated the air, which was moist and warm. Suddenly the music stopped. There was an expectant hush. A slave walked into the room. He had white hair and walked with a limp. In one of his chained hands was a pistol. He walked up to Stephen. No one moved to stop him.

"This is for you, Mr. President," the black man said. Aiming the pistol at Stephen A. Douglas, he fired it into the president's head.

Old Bird peered over the edge of the roof to better view the crowd.

He scanned the square to see if he could spot Young Bird, who had been gone quite a while. The boy was probably caught up in the excitement. No matter. The hotel had all it could do to handle the Douglas crowd today. It would be a learning experience for his grandson to see a presidential candidate, if that's what Hansi was doing. He may have returned to the flat where he lived with his ma. Usually, no one was home. Hansi's ma scrubbed floors during the day, while the boy attended school. Today school was closed. Hansi didn't care much for school.

The boy's father had worked in the stockyard where a tragedy occurred. Bird's son had fallen into a pen. He'd been kicked in the head, and the blow had been fatal. Since then, Bird had been a substitute father to his grandson, which would have been difficult under any circumstance, but his daughter-in-law made it even more difficult. He was never sure where he stood with her, disapproving of her lifestyle since his son's death.

He worried about the company the boy was keeping. The waterfront and railroad teemed with pickpockets, pimps, and thugs, a few not much older than Hansi. The neighborhood was no improvement. The daughter-in-law entertained a scurrilous lot of lowlife gentlemen during the evening, leaving the boy to fend for himself. More than once he appeared on the roof with bruises. Bird had complained once to his daughter-in-law and had not seen Hansi for a month after he complained. So he shut up and helped the boy any way he could.

A sea of people inundated the square. Even with the telescope, it was impossible to find Hansi. Bird decided to relax and enjoy the spectacle. The variety of hats struck his fancy. Such a cluster of toppings he'd rarely observed: straw hats, bell-shaped bonnets, feathered-nest hats, pillbox hats, stovepipes, visored caps, and bowlers.

What if a huge gust of wind blew off all the hats? He imagined hats filling the air, sailing over the horizon as far as the eye could see and landing in neighborhoods all over Chicago. He and Young Bird would run all over town collecting hats. They would collect enough hats to start a haberdashery. They'd be rich and buy a home in the country.

He wondered if he'd become senile. He daydreamed a lot lately. Now that he thought about it, he'd always been a dreamer. How far had it gotten him? He thought about flying again and looked over at the roof of the Sherman. Something was going on over there. A group of men were busy doing something out of the ordinary. What were they doing?

He focused the telescope. It took a moment to realize what was happening. They were moving a large object that appeared to be—that was—a cannon. How in the hell did they get a cannon onto the roof of the Sherman? He froze in horror when he realized that the men were preparing to fire and were aiming at the Tremont, the barrel of the cannon pointed directly at him.

"Holy Christ!" The explosion shook the roof, throwing Bird to the floor. The cannonball whizzed over his head, landing harmlessly on the far end of the roof. Bird crawled on his hands and knees to the cupola. When he was safely inside, he let out a stream of invective, using words he'd forgotten he knew. It took a while for him to calm down. He hadn't been the target. The cannon was part of the celebration. The men now were laughing and slapping each other on the back. No harm intended. Even so, Bird would remain inside the cupola.

A band was playing a loud rendition of the ever-popular "Camptown Races." The music was followed by wild cheering, thunderous applause, whistling, and stamping. The cannon was fired again, the ball dropping dangerously close to the cupola. Bird imagined the collapse of the hotel. He imagined bricks raining on the square burying the spectators, and himself landing birdlike on the rubble.

The cheering went on. Stephen A. Douglas stepped out on the balcony.

The whole of Stephen A. Douglas was greater than the sum of his parts. An aura surrounded the silver-tongued orator like a magnetic field drawing objects toward its center. He exuded power and heat. Folks took to him immediately. He treated the humblest voter as an equal, appeared to listen, and rarely forgot a name. During his tenure in the Senate, he considered the smallest request of any constituent and answered all correspondences personally. Nothing was too trivial. A compromiser, Douglas looked at the whole picture and tried to strike a middle ground. If not the idealist Lincoln was, he was a good man, not lacking in principle.

The balcony oration was at the heart of the issue, a message he had spoken before, underscoring the philosophical disagreement between him and his Republican opponent. "There is but one path of peace in this republic, and that is to administer the government as our fathers made it, divided into free and slave states."

It was a shame, Blevins thought, *that Douglas had become embroiled in the slavery issue.* To some degree it had been unavoidable. Douglas had exacerbated his own involvement by spearheading the inclusion of popular sovereignty into the Kansas-Nebraska Act, which had brought Lincoln out of the woodwork. If Douglas lost, it would be on this single issue. If he became president, he'd have to deal with a Southern Democratic bloc, which threatened to secede. If Lincoln won, war would follow.

The crowd's enthusiasm belied the broad reality that the Douglas campaign was in trouble. Not only had the "solid" South split, but the Buchanan Democrats, labeled the "Danites" by Douglas, had withdrawn support. Buchanan wanted Kansas to be admitted as a slave state. Douglas held that since not all of the residents of the territory had voted on the question, the requirements of popular sovereignty hadn't been met.

Blevins couldn't concentrate on the oration. He couldn't keep his mind off Flynn. She'd almost dragged him out of the stateroom, admonishing him that he had an obligation to cover the parade and rally. Phrases of the speech floated by his ears, "Black Republicans ... noninterference ... local control ..." The crowd shouted "hip-hip-hurrah" and other affirmations, causing Douglas to beam expansively. The Little Giant basked in the applause, letting it soak in like warm rain before continuing.

Blevins supported Douglas. Blevins was a Democrat, and his newspaper reflected that, although he didn't necessarily support the party line. He had a mind of his own, now and then expressing a dissenting point of view. Some opinions he kept to himself, aware that most of his readers were Democrats.

In 1860 America, a journalist had to choose. Newspapers, by and large, were partisan. Going against community standards could be disastrous to a newspaper's survival. Elias Lovejoy came to mind. Because Lovejoy stood up for abolition in a proslavery community, his press had been burned to the ground and the man had been murdered.

Stephen Douglas had decried the brutal murder, speaking on the floor of the Senate. His colleagues didn't have the guts to publically condemn the act. If there were no other reason to admire Douglas, this would be reason enough. Now he was concluding the oration, most of which the love-struck Blevins had missed.

"Let's go back to the ship," Blevins whispered, as if whispering were necessary. Flynn frowned and shook her head. Before she could put the response into words, Douglas's voice rose in a shimmering crescendo.

"My friends, there never was a time when it was as important for the Democratic Party, for all national men, to rally and stand together as it is today."

The crowd roared and a demonstration continued for five minutes. Douglas raised his arms and luxuriated in the welcome response. Then he left the balcony. The crowd cheered a while, and when Douglas did not return, started to disperse.

"Let's go back to the ship."

"Wicked man. I know what you want."

"Well?"

"You are invited to Douglas's press reception. I think you should go."

"Wives are invited, too."

"No one knows you have a wife. Next time I will go."

"But—"

"It's your job. You go now. I'll do a little shopping and return to the stateroom. I'll be waiting for you."

"All I can think of is you."

She kissed him and had to gently push him away. "Don't worry about me. I've never shopped in a big Chicago store. I need to buy a gift for my sister. Maybe it will patch things up between us. She was sullen when Jack and I got to go on the cruise and she didn't. Not that she deserved to go, mind you."

"Speaking of Jack, we haven't seen much of him."

"We haven't seen much of anyone, Blevins. Jack and I made a mutual promise not to spoil each other's fun."

"Thank God for that."

"I'm not sure that Jack will keep his side of the promise. The trip isn't over. Look, the newsmen are crowding into the hotel. You'd better go."

"Will you miss me?"

"Miss you?" she laughed. "I'm wearing you over my heart, my love." She fingered the gold locket that he had given her. Inside the locket was a tintype of him. "When you return to the ship, I'm going to cut a piece of your hair and put it inside the locket."

"I can't wait."

"Go now. When I have finished shopping, I'll take a hack to the ship. I'll be waiting in the stateroom. I promise I won't fall asleep before you return."

"You'd better not."

Chapter Fifteen

CLUTCHING A TOWEL TO COVER herself, Mary ran into the shed off the kitchen, which was the washroom, and vomited into the sink. She needed a bath, but there was no time for that. The Barry homestead wasn't within the city limits, so the family didn't benefit from Milwaukee's new municipal water system, which now piped water into city homes.

Garrett had built a windmill, which pumped water to the attic. The water was dispersed by gravity to the sinks, tubs, and water closets throughout the house. The system was an improvement over hauling water from a cistern or well, but to take a bath—a real bath that would cleanse the dirtiness that Mary felt required hot water—was time consuming. Mary rinsed her vomit down the drain and wiped globs of Doughty's blood from her arms and face. The act made her vomit again.

She walked into the main part of the house, still clutching the bloody towel, and climbed the stairs to the bedroom, grateful that the children were preoccupied in the other room. She rocked in the slat-backed rocker in the bedroom and cried, body shaking with uncontrollable sobs. A horse whinnied outside. "Oh my God, Ned!" She threw the towel into the closet, slipped into a robe, and raced down the stairs two or three steps at a time. She rushed to the yard, uncertain of what she would find, dreading the faceless corpse and having no idea what to do.

The corpse was gone and so was Ned. The rifle was gone and Doughty's horse was gone. All gone. The blood-soaked laundry was still on the grass. Mary gathered it into the washroom and rinsed off the blood, fighting the urge to vomit again. She left the wet clothes soaking. Later she would rewash them and burn items with permanent stains.

Returning to the house, she entered the parlor, reclining on the rosewood Hitchcock chair, careful to avoid staining it. She stared vacantly at the Currier and Ives hanging above the medallion-back sofa. The painting had been a wedding gift from her parents. Inside her was a labyrinth. She'd done no wrong, but she felt shame. That evil man had seen her nakedness. The way he'd looked at her. Ned had seen her, too. She felt so violated. Icy hot rage mixed with fear and disgust made her tremble. She'd never seen a man die, never mind getting his face blown off.

She felt responsible. If she hadn't guzzled the drinks—if she'd been fully dressed when she went out to hang the clothes—if she'd run into the house before that monster got off his horse—maybe it wouldn't have happened. Ned had saved her from being ravished. Then he'd left, taking the horrible burden with him. Ned would be a fugitive again, in much more danger than before.

He had done what he had to do. If he were free and white, no court would convict him. The killing had been justified. No matter. A runaway slave who had killed a federal deputy had no rights and would be executed without trial if caught. Furthermore, Mary's activities in the Underground Railroad would be exposed. She and Garrett would be discredited for harboring. Mary could only pray that Ned would conceal the evidence and get far, far away.

The noise of the children upstairs brought her back to reality. Collecting herself, she went into the kitchen and called them down to breakfast.

Deep in the Wisconsin woods, in the shade of dark pines, was a cemetery known to few. A lonely spot, far away from the nearest farmhouse, its tranquility was disturbed only by infrequent hunters who stumbled across it accidentally. The graves were marked by plain wooden crosses having no inscriptions.

Old Ned dug, the shovel digging easily into the soft, mossy, coniferous soil. In a while, there was a deep hole, not as deep as the others, but deep enough. He struggled with Doughty's blood-soaked corpse, covered with blankets and stretched across the horse, and managed to roll it into the hole, where it dropped to the bottom with a dull thud, landing on its back, the remains of its pulpy, featureless head facing upward.

As he shoveled dirt into the hole, he softly hummed a song he'd heard the white folk sing, a gentle, ironic grin on his face, as he recalled the words.

> There was an old darkie and his name was Uncle Ned,
> And he died long ago, long ago.
> He had no wool on the top of his head,
> The place where the wool ought to grow.

Ned stomped on the dirt. No wooden cross would mark this grave. He rested against a tall pine. The cawing of crows made the woods seem even more isolated by emphasizing the utter lack of human sound. Black crows were not human. Black slaves were not human. Ned was tired, really tired. It wasn't so much physical. For his age, he was in good condition, but he had never killed anyone. The act diminished him. In killing a man, he killed something in himself. It didn't matter that Doughty got what was coming to him. A steep price had been exacted.

Ned patted his breast pocket and felt the book that had been a gift from young Willie. It was the *Narrative of the Life of Frederick Douglass*. Willie had read parts of it aloud to Ned, who couldn't read. Willie was a good reader. He wasn't old enough to understand the power of the words, but Ned understood. He would carry this book with him. Someday he'd find someone who would read more of it to him. He'd like to meet the famous ex-slave who wrote it.

Wearily, he stood and flung the shovel far into the woods. He had taken Barry's rifle, in case he was stopped on his way out here, but he'd not followed a road and had met no one. Now the gun was a liability, so he flung it in the same direction as the shovel.

He couldn't return to the Barry home after what had happened. The Barrys had been good to him and protected him. Now he was at large. He would ride the horse until he reached the outskirts of Winnetka, avoiding the main thoroughfares. A black man on horseback, especially as fine a horse as this one, would arouse suspicion. Eventually, he'd have to ditch the horse. Mary Barry had once given him a letter of introduction to a man in the Winnetka Underground Railroad who would help him. With this man's help, he would escape to Canada.

Mounting the horse, he took one final look and chuckled. A slave cemetery, what an ideal resting place for a federal deputy marshal. If Doughty's spirit rose here, the spirits of the slaves would have a score to settle. It was midafternoon as Old Ned rode out of the woods.

"Death," he mused, "is the great equalizer."

"The speech is boring. Let's get out of here, Ma. Let's walk down by the boats." Brian tugged at Maeve's sleeve, but Maeve, mesmerized by Douglas's eloquence, failed to notice. "Ma," he persisted, but she ignored him. "Come on, Liam, let's go down to the boats."

"We'll lose Ma."

"We'll be back in a while. This guy's going to talk for an hour. Ma's in another world. She'll be standing right here when we get back. Won't even know we were gone. C'mon, Liam."

"We've seen the boats."

"Then let's see the trains. The station's just a few blocks down the street."

"Trains! Man alive, that'd beat all."

"Let's do it."

The crowd burst into applause, and there was stomping and cheering. Brian and Liam slipped through the crowd and headed down Randolph. Brian looked back. Ma stood near the Tremont House entrance, near the omnibus station. It would be easy to find her when they returned, if they didn't take too long. They'd see a few trains and hurry back. They could have asked, but Ma would have said no.

"What if Ma's gone?"

"She won't be."

"But what if she is? What if she's looking for us?"

"We'd just go to the ship. I mean, it's not going to happen, but she knows we have common sense. It'd be the first place she'd look."

They crossed a bridge and stopped to look at the Chicago River. An old derelict was sitting on the ground, his back against the bridge. He opened a toothless mouth to take a pull of whiskey from a brown bottle. The liquid dribbled down the dark stubble on his chin.

"Hey, mister, which way to the train station?"

The man stared at the boys and muttered something like, "Get the hell out of here."

"C'mon, Liam. Let's go. You don't ask someone like him directions."

"Why not? He lives here, doesn't he?"

"C'mon, c'mon. Let's turn left at the next street. The station's not on Randolph. You can see that. We'll go down Lake. If we don't find the place, we'll return."

They continued their exploration, making several turns. They passed a church under construction, but no workers were there today. The boys each had the same thought at once: they were lost. Ahead was a street of shacks, a bad neighborhood, worse than the Third Ward. The shacks were elevated on stilts with jackscrews. Much of Chicago had once been a swamp. This area was two feet above the water level.

The sky darkened, casting a pall on the city and dampening their spirits. "We've got to get back," Brian said. "We've been too long." It started to rain, slowly at first, then a deluge.

"Run!" yelled Liam, who started to run without thinking of where he was going. Brian chased after him. The wooden sidewalk was rotted and cracked as the boys tramped over it. Mud oozed beneath them and scurrying rats scared them into running faster.

"Over here, Brian. Over here!" Liam ran into an alley between two buildings to seek shelter beneath the overhanging structures. The two of them pressed their backs against the wall, dry for a moment. It only took that moment to become aware of another presence. A few feet away, sitting on a barrel, was a boy. He glared at them and held a knife in his hand.

Douglas had the gift of gab, Maeve had no doubt. He must have kissed the Blarney Stone. She'd heard the best of them, and he ranked high. The audience was eating out of his hand. A tap on the shoulder gave her a start. It was Jack, who had just found her.

"Maeve, where are the boys?"

"Why, they're right here …" she faltered. "Brian? Liam?" She looked around frantically. "Brian! Liam!" She raised her voice. The spectators shushed her. "Oh my God, where are they? They were right here. Jack, they were right here."

"Calm down. You'll never find them in the crowd. The speech will be over shortly. They'll find us."

"I ... I lost track. I was caught up in the speech, and I guess they wandered off. I didn't notice. How could I not have noticed?"

Douglas concluded, and, after a prolonged ovation, the crowd started to disperse. People were milling, cursing, and pushing as they headed for the many diversions that Chicago had to offer. Newsmen crowded into the hotel for the press reception. Women were eager to shop at Palmers, T. B. Carter and Co., M. and T. Doherty, Titsworth, M. P. Ross and Co., and other popular merchants on Lake Street. The uniformed men headed to the southwest corner of Clark and Lake to the Saloon Building, Chicago's famous watering hole.

Visitors spending the night could enjoy elegant hotel dining and a play at McVickers Theater, a concert at Metropolitan Hall, or a lecture at Mechanic Institute. Fundamentalist Christians could attend revival meetings held in huge tents at various locations. Other options for visitors were available, including a circus.

Omnibuses and taxis lined in front of the Tremont. Vendors, eager to make last-minute sales, hawked their wares.

"Yeddy go, sweet potatoes, oh!"

"Raaaspberries!"

"Hot corn! Lily-white corn!"

"Peaches here!"

An organ grinder played "My Old Kentucky Home" and passers-by dropped coins into the little red hat of his monkey. Newsboys, selling the latest edition of the *Tribune*, cajoled, "Get your paper here!" A paperboy boldly walked up to Jack and held out a paper, which Jack declined.

"Jack, what are we going to do?"

"Let's ask around."

They asked the doorman at the Tremont. They entered the hotel and asked the desk clerk, who dispatched a messenger to the roof. Old Bird sent a return message that he hadn't noticed two boys who fit the description but would keep his telescopic eye open. They went out to the cabs and alerted the coachmen to keep a watch at the hotel and to keep a lookout as they drove their fares around the area.

"Ride? Take you somewhere?"

"No."

"Yes," said Maeve. "Take us to the nearest police station. Come along, Jack."

Jack climbed into the cab beside Maeve. "You heard the lady." As the hack pulled away, rain began to come down, and by the time they turned a corner it was pouring.

"My God, dear God, what kind of a mother am I, who cannot keep her boys out of the rain?"

Young Bird carried a knife for protection, although he'd never had to use it. He knew how to defend himself, having taken lessons from his pickpocket friends. Chicago was safe for hotel patrons if they did not venture far from the hotel, and the city was safe for residents of Terrace Row, who lived in big houses among orchards and flower gardens. Young Bird lived in Conley's Patch, where you had to stand on your own two feet or you didn't stand at all. Having a weapon went with the territory.

The district into which he had blindly run was Gamblers' Row, south of City Hall, a dangerous area of hovels inhabited by whores, pimps, gamblers, and hoodlums. He'd lost his pursuers, but this was no place for him. This was worse than Conley's Patch. If he were in rags or filthy looking, no one would bother him, but he was clean-cut as befitted a boy who worked for a hotel. The occupants of Gamblers' Row would creep out of their lairs and murder him just for his clothes. He had to get out of here. As he was about to do so, it began to rain, and then these two kids showed up.

"Hey, kid," said Brian, "we're lost. Can you help us find a way out of here? And by the way, I hope you won't try anything with that knife. There are two of us, and we don't scare easily."

"Maybe you should scare easily." Young Bird put the knife in his pocket. "You picked a fine place to get lost. You're in Gamblers' Row, the meanest section of town. People around here eat kids for lunch."

"What are you doing here? Do you live here?"

"Nah. I work for the Tremont House. I took the wrong turn, but I'm on my way back there now."

"That's where we're going. There was a parade and a speech by Stephen Douglas. We got bored and decided to look around. It rained, so we ran in here to get dry."

"The rain is over. Come with me."

The going was slow, because they were ankle-deep in mud. Liam's shoe came off, so they had to help him extricate it from the mud. It came out with a sucking sound. Liam made a face when he slid it back onto his foot, the mud oozing between his toes. A pack of rats scurried under a stilted house, causing the boys to shudder. Loud talking and cursing came through the shattered window of a peeling saloon. The rain had diminished to a drizzle. They turned several corners, Young Bird in the lead. At an intersection, they stopped to stare at a man lying on the wooden sidewalk. The man didn't appear to be breathing.

"Is he dead?"

"Nah. Passed out."

"Shouldn't we do something?"

"Nothin' we can do."

An old woman appeared in an open window. In her hands was a chamber pot. She opened her toothless mouth and cackled a mirthless laugh.

"Run!" shouted Young Bird.

They ran, getting out of the hag's range. She dumped the contents of the chamber pot out the window. The disgusting liquid landed near the derelict's prone form, splattering him with offal. The harridan whooped and shut the window. The boys paused near a corner to catch their breath.

"Hey, pal, what's your name?"

"Hansi. People call me Young Bird. What's yours?"

"Brian."

"And I'm Liam. We're brothers. Why do they call you Young Bird?"

"Tell you later. Where are you from? I can tell by the way you talk that you're not from around here."

"We live in Milwaukee, but we were born in Ireland."

"My great-grandfather was born in Germany."

They heard the sound just before they turned on Randolph. *Moo! Moo!* A cattle pen on a wagon was stuck in the mud. There must have been twenty head, and they were all bawling. "Haw!" shouted the red-faced drover, whipping the straining horses. Six men grunted as they pushed the wagon. Suddenly it broke loose. A man fell, disappearing into the mud. The drover cracked the whip. The wagon proceeded down Randolph.

"I wonder where they're going," said Liam.

"Down to the waterfront. The cattle are being shipped, probably on your *Lady Elgin.*"

"It seems strange to see cows in the middle of the city."

"How many times you fellows been to Chicago?"

"Only this once."

"Chicago is a cow town. Say, you boys want to do some real sightseeing? Take you to the stockyards. Why, you'll see cows you never thought existed. There are so many steers the horns go as far as the eye can see." Young Bird warmed to the subject. It had never occurred to him how proud he was of his hometown. "And smells. You should smell the stockyards. Once you've been there, you can smell those cows forever."

"I don't think I'd like that," said Liam.

"You'd love it. You shouldn't leave Chicago without seein' the yards. We could go now. What do you say? It'd only take a while."

"Thanks, but we haven't got a while," said Brian, noticing that the sky was darkening. It was later than he thought. "We have to get back to the Tremont. We're going to be in big trouble."

"You're almost there. There it is, two blocks away. You can see it from here."

Indeed they did see it, and Brian realized, with a lump in his throat, that they were back where they had started and the square was empty, the people gone.

"Ma!" shouted Liam. "Ma's gone!"

Chapter Sixteen

SHE OPENED THE BUNDLE, SPREADING the gifts on the unmade bed. It was hard to believe that she'd found gifts she could afford at Palmers. There had been so many items in this celebrated store that were beyond her means. Ma had hinted that she wanted a bottle of lilac water, her favorite scent. Flynn had no trouble finding it. With the lilac water, she purchased a sachet, which would be an added surprise. On a whim, she bought lilac water for herself.

Choosing a gift for Da was more difficult. Da would give away his gifts or say not to spend hard-earned money on gifts, but he'd be hurt if she bought him nothing. She selected a handkerchief of Irish linen. A handkerchief was practical (she thought of his red nose), and he'd like it because it was Irish.

Her sister was another story. There was no pleasing Maggie, who would find fault with whatever she was given. She chose a leather-bound diary, something which she knew Maggie didn't have. Maybe if she started recording her thoughts, she'd become more introspective. She bought Jack a warm scarf, which he could wear on deck. That is, if she could find him. She bought Blevins a picture frame because she didn't want to slight her new husband, and because he wanted a picture of her. All she needed was a picture.

Flynn prepared for Blevins's return—undressing, washing, slipping into her delicate white nightgown and peignoir, powdering and perfuming her body, and sitting at the mirror brushing her luxurious blonde hair. She thought about last night, the first time, the feverish lovemaking that had swept them, and later a slower, more tender, intimacy. It had required willpower to leave the stateroom in the morning and self-restraint to convince him to stay for the press reception. She hoped he'd return soon.

Flynn insulated herself from thinking of the repercussions that the elopement would have at home. So far, she'd been able to prevent such thoughts from invading the cocoon that she'd spun around her and Blevins, putting her finger to his lips whenever he mentioned the future. But now that she was alone, uninvited thoughts intruded. In spite of her concerns, she did not feel guilty. Everything seemed so right, although her family wouldn't see it that way. "Mrs. Morgan." She spoke the name aloud, liking the sound of it. It was more Welsh than Irish, but it had a nice ring to it.

Da would be hurt and angry, but he never stayed angry. It was he who had taught her to be true to herself. In Ma she had an ally, albeit a secret ally. Marion wouldn't openly confront Dan, but would quietly work on him to gain support. Maggie would be true to form, making snide comments every chance she got, but that was Maggie's way. The person whose reaction most worried Flynn was Jack. In the O'Mara family, the one who struggled with guilt was her brother, in spite of his efforts to hide the feelings. During childhood, Flynn had been Jack's sole confidante.

"What if I leave something out when I go to confession?" he would ask. Or he would ask, "Do I have to confess my bad thoughts?" One day Flynn had snapped, "Why don't you ask a priest?"

Jack was a secret reader. He hid books in his room. Da thought reading was a waste of time. Jack loved the old tales of the Celtic heroes. He and Flynn would play games in the yard. Jack would be Finn McCool, Brian Boru, Rory O'Rourke, or Cuchulain, and Flynn would be a maiden in distress. One day Jack stayed in a tree until dark, claiming to be the legendary Sweeney, who was cursed by a monk and turned into a bird.

Once they went bathing in Lake Michigan with a group of childhood friends. Jack spent the entire afternoon building a sand replica of the Rings of Tara, ancient seat of the High Kings of Ireland. A schoolmate had destroyed the replica. Jack had nearly killed the boy.

The nuns had taught them Gaelic, which they spoke often, at Jack's insistence. Jack was continually making toy weapons: axes, bows and arrows, spears, and clubs. Once she had helped him capture a crow. The hero Cuchulain carried a magical crow on his shoulder. Jack had kept the crow in a cage. Finally, he let it go because, he said, "It wouldn't talk to me."

Once she and Jack had stolen three boulders from a stone wall. Jack had built a dolmen in the yard. Da found the dolmen and was furious. He'd knocked down the Celtic burial symbol and returned the boulders to the stone wall. "Pagan nonsense!" he had fumed.

Flynn worried that her brother had never put aside his childhood fantasies. She knew that he had been responsible for torching the *Lynne.* That night when she and Blevins had raced to the waterfront, something had been disturbingly familiar about the painted Celt on horseback. Later, she'd realized who it was. It frightened her that Jack was involved with Feeney, a terrible man. She'd heard the rumors about Fenians in the Third Ward. She really didn't know much about Fenians, but she knew they were in dead earnest, not just grown-up children playing romantic games.

Since the *Lynne* incident, Jack had become secretive. He knew that Flynn disapproved of Maeve, so he had not confided. In recent months, Flynn and her brother had hardly spoken. This worried her the most. Jack needed a confidante. He was a bundle of inner conflicts. He needed someone to share the burden. Flynn suspected that Maeve was not that person.

Of course, Flynn also had been secretive. Here they were, she and Jack, on the same ship, and she covertly married, under his nose, so to speak. She knew that she could make Jack understand, but she had to tell him soon—before the end of the voyage. If Jack discovered she was staying in a room with a man, there was no telling what conclusion he would reach or what he might do. Thinking again of the childhood games, she was sure Jack would try to "rescue" her.

Worrying about Jack was giving her a headache. This was her honeymoon. She dismissed the bad thoughts, concentrating on Blevins. She stretched on the bed. When he entered, she would be the first sight he would see. Smiling seductively, she'd say, "See, I told you I'd be awake." He would be so struck by her appeal, he'd be at a loss for words. He'd come to her and … and …

She felt herself slipping. The bed was so soft and thoughts of Blevins made her feel so warm. Blevins—her protector—her husband.

Her lids drooped. She couldn't keep her eyes open. Melting into a glowing oblivion, Flynn fell fast asleep.

"Hey, cabbie," said Brian, "How fast can this claptrap go?" The hack clip-clopped down the cobbled street, its passengers having a lark.

"It ain't no claptrap, and it'll go as fast as I want it to go."

"Aw, you're all talk. The only wind you make is with your mouth. Why, the old nags aren't fit to do more'n hobble."

"Says you."

"How do you make them go fast?" asked Liam.

"You use this," said the cabbie, waving a whip. "Haw!" he said, lightly cracking the whip. The horses picked up the pace.

"Could I try it?" asked Brian.

"Not a chance."

Brian pulled money out of his pocket. "Not even for an eagle?"

"You ever drive?"

"Sure. Don't worry. You can stop me if I don't do it right."

The cabbie took the eagle and pocketed it. He pulled on the rein and the horses stopped. "We'll change places." The cabbie got out and headed to the other side to take a passenger seat. Before he could accomplish that, Liam grabbed the whip and gave the horses a good hard crack. "Haw!" he yelled exultantly. "Haw! Haw!"

The horses took off like a shot, bolting down the street so abruptly that Liam fell back into the seat. The cabbie was crawling on the ground screaming "Stop! Police!" The hack raced by another hack with a single woman passenger. The woman was Maeve.

"Ma! Ma! Beat you to the ship!" shouted Brian. Liam was choking with laughter.

When Maeve and Jack had left the police station, they had parted company. Jack returned to the hotel area to continue the search. Maeve hired a hack to return to the ship. Jack reassured her that the boys would show up one place or the other. Maeve was not reassured. Chicago was a big, unfriendly city. She was frightened.

Now, seeing the laughing boys pass, she was angry. "Follow them!" she shouted furiously, and her driver cracked the whip.

"Ma's racing us!"

"Give the horses a couple of cracks again."

"Haw!" Brian gave them each two hard cracks. The horses were straining at the bit, the waterfront a blur. The hack, which was not the latest model, creaked and groaned, heading directly toward the edge of the wharf and not slowing.

"I don't know how to stop."

"Pull, Brian! Pull on the reins!"

"Whoa!" yelled Brian, pulling on the reins with all his might. The hack screeched to a halt and collapsed, throwing Liam to the ground. A wheel came off. It rolled to the edge of the wharf and flew into the lake with a loud splash.

"Are you hurt, Liam?" shouted Brian, body shaking with fear.

"Nah. Here comes Ma." Maeve's hack careened to a halt. Maeve leaped out.

"I guess we beat you, Ma." Liam grinned sheepishly.

"Beat me! Land sakes, I guess you did, and unless there's a good explanation, it's my turn to beat you. Where have you been? What happened?"

"We got lost and—"

Just then the cabbie arrived, gasping for breath, followed by a policeman on horseback. "My cab! What have you done?" The cabbie ran over to the collapsed hack. "The wheel, where is the wheel?" Liam pointed to Lake Michigan.

"Are you the mother?" asked the policeman. Maeve nodded, holding in her anger. "This man says the boys stole his cab. By the looks of it, they did."

Maeve glared at Brian, who still sat in the driver's seat. "Well, what do you have to say?"

"We didn't steal it. The cabbie stepped out and said I could drive."

The half truth calmed everyone. "Well, mister," the policeman said, "is that how it was?"

"Aw, I ain't got nothin' against the boys. They wanted a little fun, but they'll have to pay for the fun. It'll cost somethin' to repair the hack, including a new wheel."

"How are they going to pay? They're children, and I don't have the money."

"Beggin' your pardon, ma'am, but your boys do have money." The cabbie looked at Brian. "Two more eagles should do." All eyes were on Brian as he handed the cabbie two eagles. Maeve's mouth dropped in astonishment.

The policeman looked at Maeve. "I see that the money is a surprise to you, lady. I won't make an accusation, but I'd keep a close eye on them."

"That's just what I intend to do."

The policeman nodded, and trotted away on his horse. The cabbie went in search of a wheelwright. Maeve yanked Brian off the decimated hack, pulling him over beside Liam. "All right," she said fiercely, "I want to hear it all. Before you start, first things first. Where did you get the money?"

"Young Bird."

"Don't be smart. What do you mean, young bird?"

"That's the name of our friend. Well, his real name is Hansi. He showed us the way when we were lost."

"His grandpa works on top of a hotel. We met him."

"This boy gave you money?"

"He gave us money for the cab and a little more."

"It was a loan. He said we could repay him the next time we were in Chicago."

"It will be a long time before you're in Chicago again, young man. Where did this Hansi get the money?"

"I don't know," Brian shrugged, "but he said not to hurry paying him back. He said he didn't want it."

"Where's Jack, Ma?"

"Jack is looking for you. He'll be here soon. Now that you've spoiled our time in Chicago, you will follow me onto the ship, where we will remain until it's time to leave. March!"

Jack and Old Bird burst through the swinging doors of the Randolph Saloon. Old Bird paused to expectorate into a spittoon, but his aim was off, causing the wad to splatter on the sawdust floor. No one noticed. The Randolph was not one of the cleaner establishments in town, but Jack wanted to buy his new friend a drink, and the saloon was near the Tremont. In a while, he would have to head back to the ship, but there was time for a brief diversion. They pushed their way across the smoke-filled room and found two stools at the end of the bar.

Jack ordered a tankard of blackstrap for himself and Bird, and then he lit up a long nine, nearly gagging after inhaling the cheap cigar smoke, which he blew into the face of his companion, who coughed and turned away. A table of rowdies sang "Buffalo Gals," accompanied by a drunken musician who banged on a dusty old piano in the corner. Laughter erupted after a member of the group vomited on the table and a waiter hurried over with a towel.

"Them're two fine boys, them sons of yours," shouted Bird over the din. "You must be proud of 'em."

"Not my sons. May be one day. Mother's a widow."

"You plannin' to get hitched?"

"That remains to be seen." Jack quaffed a gulp of blackstrap and wiped his mouth. Gas formed at the base of his throat. The pressure made him feel uncomfortable, so he let go an enormous burp that resonated throughout the saloon, causing unfriendly stares. "Excuse me." Bird guffawed, taking a generous swig of his own blackstrap.

"Bird … ah … Wolfgang. Do you mind if I call you Wolfgang?"

"That's my name."

"Wolfgang, I do fancy the widow Maeve. Indeed it would be no exaggeration to say that I am smitten with her." He drained the tankard and signaled for another, indicating that the barkeep should refill Wolfgang's tankard. "Should we tie the knot, I'd take a firm hand with the two boys."

"Ah, boys will be boys. Give 'em some slack. Hansi needs a firm hand. Today a stranger on the waterfront gave him money to pimp for him. Hansi would never do that, but he did keep the money. He told me about it. I can tell when he's done something wrong. My grandson tells me everything. Well, maybe not everything."

"Why was your grandson down at the waterfront?"

"Young Bird is self-reliant. He lives with his mother in a bad section of town. He hustles the waterfront, portering and running messages, and he helps me on the roof. I worry 'bout him getting mixed up with a gang of thieves or pickpockets, but I don't think he's doin' that. He ain't much for school, but Hansi's a good boy."

Jack ordered another blackstrap and munched on Saratoga chips.

He hadn't eaten for hours, and the beer was making him woozy. "What did you do about the money?"

"Well, it didn't seem right, his keeping it. It should be used for a good cause is what I thought. The money was given to your boys for cab fare. But then, you know that. There must have been money to spare, but don't give it a thought."

"Wolfgang, I am in debt to you."

"Not at all. It was a pleasure to meet such fine young men. Hansi brought them to the roof, and they got to see Chicago through a telescope."

"A unique perception, I am certain. By now they are getting a warm reception from their mother," Jack said dryly.

"Say, do you gamble?"

"I do, in moderation. Chuck-a-luck, craps, and draw poker, if there's a game."

"Let me show you something, a sight few out-of-owners have seen. It won't take long. Follow me."

Jack guzzled the last of his blackstrap and rose unsteadily to his feet. He expected to be led upstairs to the blackjack tables, but Bird led him to a shadowy corner and knocked on a door. They were greeted by a giant of a man wearing galluses, which held up loose-fitting knickerbockers. Jack considered himself large, but he was diminutive compared to this Cyclops, a hairless Neanderthal with a moon face and a black patch over one eye. One kick from this man's huge brown brogans would send a man flying. The giant grunted and let them pass. Clearly, Bird's was a familiar face.

They descended damp cellar stairs. At the bottom was another entrance. The dim glow of gaslight flickered though the portal, and the sound of yelling and cursing greeted their ears. Jack heard growling— inhuman growling—and he wondered if he were entering hell.

Men were seated around an octagonal pit in the center of the subterranean room. Chained to a wall, below the men and at a safe distance, was a bear. The bear wore a metal collar. An attached chain had a few feet of slack, allowing the animal a limited range. The bear growled and strained at his tether.

"Savage as a meat ax," said Bird. "Did you ever see such an ornery, pug-ugly critter?" Jack allowed that he had not. The crowd was getting rowdy. Groups of men were huddled to make bets. "Do you dip?" He offered Jack a wad of snuff, which Jack declined.

Two dogs slunk into the arena. At first they kept a distance from the bear, circling and growling outside the range of the tethered beast.

"Care to make a bet?"

"What could I bet?"

"You could bet on the bear to win, or you could bet on the dogs. You could bet on one dog, or you could bet on the time it takes, or which animal dies first. There are endless possibilities."

"I'll pass for now." The crowd was hollering, urging the dogs on. Men were feverishly exchanging money.

"Get 'im!"

"Sic 'im!"

"Ratters! Worthless mongrels!"

The din was deafening. Spectators threw objects into the arena, hitting the dogs and arousing them. The cellar reeked of stale liquor and acrid cigar smoke. One of the dogs leaped at the bear and gouged it. The bear roared and shook the dog off. The men cheered. There was more huddling and wagering.

The second dog crouched for an attack and leaped. With a mighty swing, the bear cuffed the dog in midair. The dog yelped and flew through the air, landing outside the arena, body bloodied, neck broken. The first dog licked its wounds, just outside the bear's reach.

"One on one," said Bird. "Still time to wager." Jack shook his head. "Maybe this ain't your pleasure. You like rats? Know a place where you can bet on the number of rats a dog can destroy. If that don't suit your fancy, there's cockfights a plenty. You can find them anywhere."

"Is any of this legal?"

"Illegal as hell, but the law don't pay no attention. Gaming goes on regular-like. No one does anything. But look, if you could stay until tomorrow, we could go down to the stockyards and watch bull-baiting."

The limping dog circled the bear, and the bear made several unsuccessful swipes. The cur made a desperate leap, tearing a flap of flesh from the bear's hide. Leaping again, he bit the bear and wouldn't let go. The bear roared and danced around in the confined area, trying to shake off the dog.

Mesmerized, Jack stared at the spectacle, revolted and horrified.

The animals performed a dance of death, a blur of blood and hair. The men were lustful and bloodthirsty, their greed palpable. "Thanks for showing me around, Wolfgang, and thanks for helping the boys. I can't watch this any longer."

"You're leaving? You ain't seen it all."

"I've seen enough."

"Hey, Jack. Look me up the next time you're in town."

"Count on it. Good-bye, Old Bird. Keep a sharp lookout."

Old Bird did not answer. He had turned back to the pit, where the dog and the bear were staring at each other. Neither dog nor bear had much enthusiasm left. Jack headed for the stairs, tripping over the carcass of the other dog, which had not been removed. Jack's one thought was to get out. Near the top of the stairs, he stopped to catch his breath. The Cyclops eyed him suspiciously. Entering the saloon, he crossed to the swinging doors and stepped outside, breathing the cold, fresh air and shaking his head to rid himself of the horrific image of the barbaric subterranean spectacle. Jack was claustrophobic. The cellar had closed in on him, giving him a feeling of panic.

There were other lurking feelings that Jack had trouble identifying. Underneath it all was the guilt, which was always there and which he could never shake. Guilt faded after confession but returned later. Jack felt guilty about everything. He even felt guilty about feeling guilty. The bear-baiting had repelled him, but he had stayed to watch most of it. Why had he done that? Why hadn't he left as soon as he saw what was going on? The worst of it was that he had actually enjoyed it, in a perverse way. The game stirred him in a way he didn't like.

He'd had a similar feeling when he had torched the *Lynne* and again when he grasped the spear of Cuchulain. He wished he had the spear now. Jack was restless. He felt like doing something, but he didn't know what.

"Lincoln said, 'A house divided against itself cannot stand.' That's a well-turned phrase, much quoted. I ask you, why can't it stand? What's wrong with diversity? This house has been standing since our forefathers built it. Many of our forefathers were slave owners. Thomas Jefferson owned 140 of them. The founders believed that 'all men are created equal' didn't apply to slaves. Let the people decide. In our house there is room for free states and slave states. That's for you to decide. It is Lincoln who is polarizing our great nation, Lincoln and his agitating cohort, Lyman Trumbull."

Stephen Douglas's dislike of Trumbull, a pro-Lincoln Illinois senator, was well known. Members of the press were gathered in the crowded ballroom of the Tremont. Douglas's voluminous voice rose above the hubbub of the informal congregation. Although the guests were mainly newsmen, a few prominent Democrats were present, as were a few nonpolitical guests, including Cyrus Bentley, founder of the YMCA, and George P. A. Healey, the portrait artist who had painted likenesses of European kings and queens.

Leonard Volt, whose bust of Douglas was on display in the hotel lobby, was having an animated conversation with photographer Alexander Hessler. Hessler had done a daguerreotype of Lincoln that portrayed him with rumpled hair. Lincoln had insisted upon the rumpled hair, claiming dryly that he wouldn't be recognized without it. Douglas wanted Hessler to do a portrait of him.

Reporters crowded around Douglas. It was so congested that Blevins couldn't get close to the great man. Questions were being volleyed faster than Douglas could respond, and the responses were aimed at representatives of the major dailies.

"Do you think you can win without the support of Breckinridge and the Southern Democrats?"

"May I remind you that Lincoln was nearly scalped at the Republican Wigwam? He was running neck and neck with Seward and nominated by a narrow margin on the second roll call." The Wigwam was what Chicago called the National Republican Convention Hall at Lake and Market. The structure, built specifically for the convention, resembled a huge wigwam.

Joseph Medill, publisher of the *Chicago Tribune*, picked up the gauntlet. "Lincoln may have beaten Seward by a narrow margin, but now Seward stands solidly behind Lincoln."

Medill was the most powerful publisher west of New York and a staunch supporter of Lincoln. The *Tribune* was the only Republican paper that had seen fit to attend this reception. Blevins deemed it ironic that it was in the lobby of this very hotel that Joe Medill and Bill Raymond had signed the papers that had made them co-owners of the *Tribune*. The two men were friends of Horace Greeley, who had encouraged the enterprise.

"Isn't it true, Mr. Douglas," he continued, "that the Dixie delegation walked out of the Democratic Convention in Baltimore?"

"Yes," snapped Douglas, "and Dixie will walk out of the Union if Lincoln is elected." There was laughter among the Democratic newsmen. Medill had rubbed a sore spot and they all knew it.

The orchestra played Stephen Foster, causing Adele Douglas to drop her teacup. The black waiter who had poured the tea mumbled an apology, wiping the liquid with a cloth and removing the broken china. The waiter was old and white-haired. Adele stared at him. Another waiter came by and offered tea, which she declined.

Blevins had seen Adele Douglas on several occasions. In 1858, Blevins had made a trip to Galesburg to attend a Lincoln-Douglas debate. The debates had stirred interest beyond the borders of Illinois, and he had written an article about the event for his local Milwaukee paper that had pleased the Democratic subscribers.

Adele was a beautiful woman, as stylish as her dapper husband. Blevins had a sense that something had startled her into dropping the cup and that the white-haired black waiter was somehow involved. In Galesburg, Adele had seemed relaxed, spirited, and sociable. Now she seemed tense. Blevins wondered what bedeviled the woman.

Maybe the Douglas campaign had something to do with it. Douglas stumped the nation and dragged his wife with him. It must be a strain. In a presidential campaign, trail stumping was not the norm. Lincoln, for the most part, limited his travels and let the record speak for itself. Douglas's goal seemed to be to shake the hand of every living American of voting age.

Blevins circulated among the newsmen. In this rarefied atmosphere, he was a little fish in a big pond. Milwaukee, a scant seventy miles north, was a frontier town in the boondocks of journalism, there being no newspaper receiving national attention. Joe Medill and Vic Lawson were standing by the punchbowl. Blevins poured himself a cup and eavesdropped, which wasn't difficult, since Medill spoke in a conspicuously loud voice.

"A newspaper ought to be the organ of no one man, however high, no clique or ring, no matter how influential, no faction, however fanatical or demonstrative, and in all things to follow the line of common sense."

Lofty rhetoric, thought Blevins. If any newspaper was the organ of one man, it was Medill's *Chicago Tribune*, and if anyone diverged from the line of common sense, it was Medill, who went to any extreme to get a story and who was no stranger to being out on a limb.

"Have you been talking to 'Uncle Horace' again?" laughed Vic Lawson of the *Chicago Daily News*.

"Horace Greeley is redefining the penny newspaper. The *New York Herald-Tribune* competes with you and me in Chicago, our own backyard. It's read nationwide by Republicans and Democrats alike for its nonpartisan reporting of the news."

"Nonpartisan? Greeley, more than anyone else, helped get Lincoln nominated. Some say that Greeley founded the Republican Party. Horace Greeley: Mr. Republican."

"Even so, Greeley doesn't follow a party line. His critics call him inconsistent. He speaks to what he believes. 'Uncle Horace' is his own man, not beholden to any pressure group."

The music of Stephen Foster continued to sway. Blevins recognized "Jeanie with the Light Brown Hair." It was a small irony that Douglas had selected music so identified with the South, which had deserted him. In a corner of the room, he found a Buchanan Democrat, and tried to draw him into an argument. The man was drunk and went on about Buchanan's white neckties.

"How many white neckties do you think Buchanan owns?" Blevins asked politely, knowing somehow that the man would have an answer.

"One fer every day of the year."

"Three hundred and sixty-five?"

"Wrong. B'god, you forgot to count the holidays."

Blevins scratched his head. The smoke in the room was oppressive. He hated smoke. Stepping out into the night air, he took a deep breath. He was alone, and the darkness made him realize how late it was. He had to get back to the ship. Poor Flynn. What a way to begin a marriage. A loud activity outside the Randolph Saloon across the street distracted him. Then he heard a familiar voice behind him.

"Blevins!"

Blevins turned. It was Jack. Before Blevins could speak, Jack's fist plummeted into his face. The world began to spin. Blevins blacked out.

When he had stepped out of the saloon, Jack had noticed Blevins standing by the entrance of the Tremont. The bottled-up rage he felt about Blevins and Flynn, the violence of the bear-baiting, and the effects of far too many drinks built an inner combustion that required only the appearance of Blevins to ignite. Even when Jack spoke Blevins's name, he wasn't sure what he would say or do. When Blevins turned, Jack exploded.

It had happened in a second. The moment Jack's fist had come in contact with Blevins's face, Jack felt a release, a euphoria that passed an instant later when Blevins slumped to the ground. Jack looked around. A few drunks were causing a disturbance in front of the saloon, but no one had witnessed the assault. Kneeling by his unconscious victim, he took a pint of applejack from the pocket of his uniform and poured the golden liquid over Blevins until Blevins reeked of it. Then he signaled a cab, knowing that most independent cabs were unscrupulous.

"My good man! My friend, here, is under the weather. Help me get him into your cab. It's worth an eagle if you do."

At the mention of money, the driver brought his horse to a stop and helped Jack lift the liquor-soaked form of Blevins into the cab.

"Now, cabbie, take my sotted chum to the railroad station. Buy him a ticket and get him onto a train to Milwaukee."

"Aw, listen, soldier boy, ain' t that askin' a lot?"

Jack gave him an eagle. "That should cover the fare. Oh, and here are two eagles for yourself. By the way, my good friend here may become violent when he comes out of it." Jack winked. "John Barleycorn makes him fighting mad. For your own welfare, if he awakens, give him another good crack."

"Well, sir, I don't know. It's beyond the pale."

"I've paid you handsomely, damn it. You are doing the man a favor. God knows, he may give you an eagle himself, in gratitude for getting him on the train."

The cabbie considered. The sum total of what Jack had given him was more than he would earn in a week. The cabbie saluted and departed. Jack watched the hack clip-clop down the road. Then he walked around the corner to the front of the hotel.

The last omnibus to the *Lady Elgin* had just departed but was still in sight. Jack raced after it and hailed it. The vehicle slowed to allow him to board. As the omnibus journeyed toward the waterfront, the winded Jack caught his breath. Would the cabbie put Blevins on the train, or would he keep all the money, including the fare? It didn't matter. Either way, Blevins would not be returning on the *Lady Elgin*.

Part Three

The Lady Elgin

Chapter Seventeen

BARRY WATCHED HIS SON SKIPPING rocks into the lake as they stood dockside waiting for the arrival of the rifles. It had been a grand day, although not the kind of day he'd anticipated. Since the trip had begun, Willie had been swollen with pride to be a part of it all. When the parade had ended, he had asked if he could keep the banner and had lugged it around with him for the rest of the day. He'd been greatly impressed by the oratory of Douglas, although Barry doubted that he understood much of it. "After all, Da," he exclaimed, eyes brimming, "he may be the next president!" Barry smiled. It had been a good idea to bring his son along.

After the oration, Barry had met briefly with Councilman "Garrulous" Garrity, who would be personally delivering the promised rifles late in the afternoon. He was disappointed not to meet Stephen Douglas himself to thank him. Douglas, he understood, was footing the entire bill. Well, the boys of the brigade had done their part. Now, he was sure, they were all off celebrating. Normally, he'd be off with them, drinking them under the table. No more of that. From now on, his priority would be Willie. He painfully realized that in recent years he had been self-absorbed. He had missed much of his son's childhood. He'd try to make it up to him.

They'd spent the next few hours cruising around Chicago and talking about things. He regaled Willie with tales of his exploits in the military, and Willie shared his adventures with school and friends. They both laughed about the runaway horse. "Old Ned saved your life, son," said Barry in a sober voice, which brought them to the issue of slavery.

By then they were back at the dock. Neither father nor son had paid much attention to the sights of the city.

People were milling about, some of them boarding the ship. As members of the brigade arrived, Barry detained them. "We'll need you when the guns get here, lads. Stay." Barry was worried. It was near departure time. Where were the guns? An omnibus unloaded passengers, including Jack O'Mara, looking worn and dissipated. Jack had seemed quite distracted lately. Barry would have to have a talk with him after they returned.

"Da," said Willie, "if there are any extra rifles, could I have one?"

Barry laughed and clapped him on the back. "Those rifles are not mine to give. They are gifts for the brigade. Well, not gifts, exactly."

"But couldn't you just buy one of them?"

"No, son, I could not. When you are ready, I will buy you a rifle. Maybe when we get home, I'll take you to the range and teach you how to use a gun safely. Then you and I can go hunting. There's more to a gun than loading and shooting."

A rickety wagon loaded with boxes pulled up to the dock. Councilman Garrity stepped off the wagon. He was sweating profusely. A loud cheer arose from the uniformed men. The rifles had arrived. Barry gave the order, and the men carried the boxes up the gangplank. Willie carried a box, thrilled to be included. Garrity and Barry shook hands, following which Garrity, with great effort, climbed the gangplank. Barry was last to board. As he stood at the rail, he sensed that someone or something was missing. Then it came to him. It was Lugh. Lugh Finnegan was not among the returning soldiers.

It was 10:30 pm. The floating hotel berthed at Clark and LaSalle was crawling with people, many of whom were not passengers. The *Lady Elgin* couldn't sail with such an overload. Captain Wilson had dispersed crew members to shout:, "All people not ticketed passengers must leave immediately." How so many people got on board without tickets he didn't know, but he'd certainly look into it. To emphasize the imminent departure, he blasted the whistle. The din of the celebrants was so loud, they barely heard the whistle.

The weather did not look good. The wind was blowing from the northeast. The water on Lake Michigan was gray and choppy, and squalls were predicted. Wilson had already delayed departure, but the weather was not bad enough to delay much longer, and if he waited too long they would be way off schedule. They definitely would not set sail until they got rid of the nonpassengers.

The term "set sail" was hardly accurate, there being no sails on the *Lady Elgin*. Wilson had started his career as a deckhand on schooners. Later, he'd served on steamers, including the *Montezuma, Lady of the Lakes, Monticello, Baltimore, Algonquin, Southern Michigan, Illinois,* and *North America.*

One of the drawbacks of the paddlewheel was that it was crafted for travel on rivers. The great Mississippi, wide and slow, was a perfect waterway for the wheel. The Great Lakes, well, that was another story. In the open water, the swell of the waves aided by the wind could cause a ship to list. If the list was too far, it could lift the wheel out of the water, causing it to spin in the air, damaging the mechanism and causing irregularity in the motion of the ship.

Jack Wilson loved the paddlewheel steamers, and no one could sail them better than he. As long as they continued to build them, he would continue to command them. No one could fault his ability to command. He rarely left the ship. This morning he'd taken a rest, but he had the ability to survive without much sleep. As a younger man, he could go twenty-four hours without blinking an eye, but then it would catch up to him. He'd learned to pace himself—a few hours here and there, an occasional catnap.

This morning he'd supervised the loading of fifty head of cattle bound for farms in Wisconsin and had been present for the arrival of freight and the loading of mail. He'd overseen a minor repair in the boiler room. He'd spent time with Cummings discussing the disposition of the passenger Flaherty. Cummings had wanted Flaherty handcuffed to the bunk in the makeshift brig, but Wilson disapproved. The cuffing was unnecessary and inhumane. Locking him in the cabin was enough. Cummings was a good security man but inclined to get carried away.

Late in the afternoon, the captain had dined aboard with Louis Ferrier, a representative of the Chicago, Milwaukee, Lake Superior Line, owners of the *Lady Elgin*. Wilson didn't like Ferrier, who was a pompous ass, but one of the qualities that made Jack Wilson so well liked was his ability to get along with almost anyone. Wilson liked people, finding commonality even with people he disliked.

The two men exchanged small talk. Ferrier owned a yacht and wanted to discuss sailing. It was apparent that Ferrier didn't know a thing about sailing and didn't sail his own yacht. A "country gentleman of the sea," he'd acquired a few sailing terms to impress his non-nautical friends. Like Mrs. Malaprop in Sheridan's play, he displayed his ignorance by misusing words, misspeaking with great authority.

Ferrier expressed concern about the weather. Wilson reassured him but had his own concerns. The captain offered to give his guest a tour of the ship, but the offer was declined. Ferrier nibbled effeminately at a plate of roast beef. Wilson noticed that his hands were smooth and unflustered.

"I understand that you have a celebrity on board." Ferrier dabbed at a spot of gravy on the corner of his lip. The comment puzzled Wilson. A number of passengers could fit into that category. There was Colonel Francis A. Lumsden, co-owner of the *New Orleans Picayune*; Cyrus H. Walruth, nephew of the president of the Marine Bank of Milwaukee; and, of course, Captain Garrett Barry, West Point graduate and classmate of Ulysses Grant.

"Celebrity?"

"I refer, of course, to the Honorable Herbert Ingram, member of the British Parliament and owner of the *London Daily News*."

"Oh yes, Ingram and his sixteen-year-old son have booked passage to Mackinac."

"I assume Ingram will be given the red-carpet treatment in accordance with the difference due to a gentleman of his station."

"Do you mean deference?"

"Yes, yes, of course. Deference due, to be sure."

"Count on it, Mr. Ferrier. The amenities of the *Lady Elgin* will be at his disposal."

"Splendid. I knew we could count on you. Excellent meal. Now, sir, I must be off. Off and running, as they say at the races." Laughing at his own tired joke, Ferrier rose and pumped Wilson's hand. "No, no, don't get up. I can find my way to the gangplank. Bon voyage."

Ferrier left, and Wilson suppressed a belch. Condescending twerp. Why did so many privileged Americans imitate and admire the British? The Honorable Herbert Ingram would be treated like any other passenger. If he wanted special treatment, he'd have to pay for it. A worrisome thought entered his mind. A British parliamentarian would be on board with a shipload of drunken Irishmen, some of them rumored to be Fenians. A cloud of gloom hovered over him. He had bad feelings about this cruise.

In his nap this morning, he'd had a dream. He stood on the deck of the steamer *Algonquin*. He was alone and the wind was howling. He tried to move, but he couldn't. The ship was a giant icicle frozen into Lake Superior. His body was encased in ice and his vision blurred. Off in the distance, across the lake, he heard the happy voices of his family. Trying to call out to them, no sound would come from his throat. Suddenly there was a fearful cracking. A great split zigzagged across the ice. The *Algonquin* began to sink into the chasm, with Wilson frozen to the deck and screaming silently.

The dream recalled an actual event in the captain's life. The real *Algonquin* had nearly been stranded in the ice of Lake Superior. Wilson had been cited for heroism for his role in getting them out. The incident haunted him in this recurring dream, which saddened him, especially in the calling out to his family. His family was always out of reach. He thought of the farm in Michigan, which he hadn't visited in months.

Their wedding had been romantic—honeymoon on the sand dunes along the Michigan shore, running barefoot, hand-in-hand, making love on the dunes. They'd done it all. Caitlin now referred to herself as a widow. "I never see you," she complained. "I am jealous of your steamers. You like being a captain? Come home. Be my captain."

How he would have liked that. They both knew he couldn't quit. The medical bills to care for their crippled daughter, Alice, were a continual drain, and, on the rare moments when Wilson did get home, his wife was always tired and emotionally peaked. The romance had faded, but the love was ever present. To both, little Alice was the salt of the earth.

The forty-five crew members, some of whom had taken shore leave, were all back now. First Mate Davis reported to Wilson and saluted. Wilson did not require a salute, but the crew saluted voluntarily out of fondness and respect, for he was well liked. He treated them like professionals. He was firm but fair, maintaining absolute authority while encouraging independent thinking. He had never dismissed a crew member.

"Davis," he said jokingly, "I hope you haven't been on the sauce."

Davis, a teetotaler, was one of the few seafaring men he knew who did not take a nip now and then. Davis was momentarily offended. "The captain knows that I do not indulge."

"I know, I know. It was a joke. I do hope that you're well rested. This promises to be an arduous trip, with squalls predicted."

"There's always the Rush Street lifeboat, if you'll excuse my levity." In the Chicago area, the only facility for search and rescue was one unmanned lifeboat tied up at the Rush Street Bridge on the Chicago River.

"Thank God for our own lifeboat, and God help us if we had to depend upon Rush Street."

Darkness had set in, and the clamor of taxis, including an omnibus or two, continued to pour revelers onto the ship in alarming numbers. The band on the dance floor was being drowned by various bands on the pier and by musicians who had brought their instruments aboard. All seemed to be having a contest as to who could make the most noise. People filled the ship, and there were as many on the dock. Where had they all come from? The passenger list had changed. There were a number of new passengers booked for the return trip, some of whom were traveling with the ship all the way to Lake Superior.

"All people not ticketed passengers must leave immediately!"

"First Mate, give me your bos'n whistle and tell the engine room to stoke the engines." Wilson ran about blowing the shrill whistle and directing people to the gangplank, assisted by Cummings and other members of the crew. The sound of the furnace roar and the sight of black smoke belching out of the two smokestacks was enough to convey the message to those who had not heeded the other warnings.

Nonpassengers poured off the gangplank, shoving each other in their haste. "Raise the plank!" shouted Wilson, mildly enjoying their panic. "Wait!" shouted a little middle-aged bespectacled man still on the plank when the order was given. He managed to get off the plank, tripping and knocking two others off balance and causing them to fall in a heap to the amusement of onlookers observing the tangle of arms and legs.

"Cast off!" ordered Davis. The hawser lines were flung from the dock, and the *Lady Elgin* drifted into the channel, the mighty paddlewheel churning the water. With or without her original passengers, the *Lady Elgin* was underway. Captain Wilson stood on the bridge. In his pocket, he fingered a gift from his crippled daughter. It was a rabbit's foot she had given him for luck.

Chapter Eighteen

THE SCHOONER *AUGUSTA* DEPARTED THE lumber dock near Port Huron, Michigan, at 4:00 am, September 1, 1860, with a cargo of white pine bound for Chicago. A 138-foot, two-mast hooker with a tonnage of 332, the *Augusta* was owned by Bissell and Davidson of Detroit. Construction in the rapidly expanding cities of the Great Lakes was booming, and "sawdust" ports from which lumber ships sailed regularly blossomed all around the mitten of Michigan. Bissell and Davidson had purchased the *Augusta* as their first venture into the lumber trade, hiring Darius Nelson Malott to command.

At twenty-six, Malott was young for such a responsibility, but he had more experience than many men twice his age. Prior to this assignment, the company had commissioned him to sail the schooner *Caroline* from Lake Superior through the St. Lawrence and across the Atlantic to Liverpool.

Malott was a legend in his own time, an adventurer about whom tales were told, some true, some exaggerated, and some spread by Malott himself. There was the story, for example, of the voyage of the schooner *Gold Hunter* carrying a cargo of lumber from Montreal to London.

The *Gold Hunter* was dismasted and stranded just outside the Bay of St. Lawrence, where it lay on its side for forty-five days. According to the tale, the starving crew decided to eat one of their shipmates. Malott and one other were chosen to draw straws because they were the only unmarried men. The other man drew the short straw. By the time the rescue ship arrived, the loser had been partially eaten.

Born in Ontario and raised on a farm, Malott traded farming for sailing and had no regrets. He loved the waterways of the world and sailed to faraway places, including Van Diemen's Land and the Orient. At home on rivers, lakes, and the ocean, he had no desire to return to the land. He'd recently married a local schoolteacher, enjoying her company on rare visits home, not thinking about her much when he was gone.

The *Augusta* headed north, up the Lake Huron side of the thumb of mitten-shaped Michigan. The route would take them the length of Michigan's eastern shore to the Straits of Mackinac and south along the western shore. At some point, they would sail due west to Chicago. Strong wind filled the sails of the two-master, which pleased Malott greatly. The company encouraged speed. The sooner the ship could unload, the sooner she could return to Port Huron for another load. The builders of Chicago bought lumber as fast as it arrived.

The Detroit-based company was at a disadvantage being on the eastern side of the state. Companies on the western side could sail directly across Lake Michigan, making trips more often. Malott was sure that once Bissell and Davidson expanded, it would have ships on the western shore and would exploit the ports of Lake Erie as well.

This was Malott's first voyage on the *Augusta*. The company had assigned him to take charge of the lumber ship, replacing Captain Jenkins, the previous skipper. Malott was not enthused about commanding a lumber craft, routine work-a-day drudgery, but it was a good career move and would provide a period of stability in the young man's life.

Malott would have plenty to do to become acquainted with the ship. All schooners were similar, but each had its own quirks and each handled somewhat differently. Malott was uneasy about the *Augusta,* uncertain how she'd handle in rough weather. He would have preferred taking her on a short run first, especially since he didn't know the crew.

First Mate John Vorce and Second Mate George Budge had served under Captain Jenkins. Older than Malott, they did not respond to his authority, giving each other sly winks, which the captain was not meant to notice. Vorce and Budge argued continually, and Budge, in particular, was lazy, doing his chores with a grudging attitude. The other crew members did as they were told, but Malott wondered how they would work together under duress. He hoped he wouldn't have to find out on this journey.

One thing started out well. The wind was moving them along at a fast clip, which, if it continued, should get them to Chicago ahead of schedule. The load concerned him. They were top-heavy. Too much lumber was piled on deck. Whatever their problems, they were committed. As the *Augusta* sailed away from the thumb, the land disappeared. Next port of call: Chicago.

Barry stood at the bow of the *Lady Elgin,* staring into the darkness. Music wafted from the ballroom. The German band was playing Irish music, but they didn't have the knack. Real Irish music couldn't be captured by other nationalities. It had a lyrical quality, a lilt very much like Gaelic itself, requiring bohdrans, harps, fiddles, and tin whistles. The closest thing to it in America was the folk music of the South, where many Irish settled. A foot-stomping Virginia reel made many an Irishman homesick. Irish music had a soul borne of suffering and a tradition dating back to the ancient bards.

Barry himself was an accomplished bagpiper. In his mind, he heard the mournful, plaintive sound, which suited his present dark mood. The list of names Kelly had slipped him just a short while ago turned his world upside down. He glanced at the list for the hundredth time. The list was long, with names like Finnegan, Flaherty, O'Brian, Keane, Donahue, Buckley, Shay, McBride, Sullivan, Fitzgerald, and many more, including Kelly himself. All his boys, and all leading double lives. They were not his boys after all. They were Feeney's boys. Feeney—that manipulating, wretched, black-hearted Fenian.

Barry had known that some of the guardsmen were Fenians even before Kelly had come to him. When Feeney had tried to bribe Barry, Feeney had implied that Fenianism in the Guard was widespread. At the time Barry hadn't believed it. He imagined the list to include a few misfits, no more, but the list was long and some of the names stunned him. One name stood out like a slap in the face. Jack. Jack O'Mara, Barry's fair-haired boy, was underlined as a leader. After Jack's underlined name was scrawled "Cuchulain." Barry cursed under his breath. Jack O'Mara was the infamous Cuchulain.

Barry cherished his Irish roots and had no love for the British. He had relatives who perished in the so-called famine, "so-called" because there was food enough in Ireland but it was all being exported to England, and England did nothing to relieve the problem. He hoped for home rule and ultimate independence, but the Fenians were extremists who advocated violent overthrow.

Barry truly believed that a political solution could be found for tenant farming, including a negotiated end to absentee landlords and their agents. Armed conflict with England would only result in more Irish dead. He understood the romantic appeal, the revolutionary call to arms that Fenianism held for young Irish Americans.

He could see how Jack, so steeped in Celtic lore, would find the movement attractive. He couldn't condemn Jack, but he felt betrayed. The Brotherhood was using him, using training and equipment that he provided his men, to carry out criminal activities behind his back. The Union Guard did not exist to solve the problems of Ireland. If this were made public, he would be humiliated. Why hadn't he known? Why hadn't he perceived it sooner? Why hadn't he stopped it? That damned Feeney had won after all.

The mass confusion and wild enthusiasm attending the departure of the *Lady Elgin* waned after she was underway. Too much liquor and too little sleep had taken its toll. The weather was rough and passengers afflicted with *mal de mer* retired to their staterooms or clutched green-faced at the rails. Many were sprawled on sofas in the saloon and parlors or reclined on deck chairs, having brought the chairs inside because it had started to rain.

The German band, which had played with zest, if not quality, had quit, deferring to impromptu performers from the Irish audience. A little girl sang a heartrending version of "The Croppy Boy," accompanied by a fair colleen on the piano. Two guardsmen played a tin whistle and fiddle reel. Listeners stamped their feet.

Jack wondered why Maeve didn't volunteer to play the harp, but she sat quietly with Brian and Liam looking at Jack with deep, enigmatic eyes. Thinking of talent made Jack think of Kelly and his lilting tenor. Where was Kelly? For that matter, where was Lugh Finnegan? He hadn't seen either on the return trip. Of course, they might be somewhere in the crowd. After all, there were more than three hundred passengers.

A pianist played a sprightly rendition of a popular ballad. Onlookers sang along with gusto.

> I would climb the high hills of the land,
> I would swim to the depths of the sea,
> For one touch of her lily-white hand,
> *Ach ar Eirinn ni neosainn ce h-i.*

Two uniformed guardsmen, O'Reilly and Fagan, entertained the lads and lasses with bagpipes and bohdran, instruments that they had played in the parade. "Glory be, where did they come from? Would you listen to that?" laughed Maeve, pulling Jack out to the dance floor. Jack, needing no encouragement, swung Maeve in a whirl. Before long, the two were improvising variations of reels and high-steps that went beyond tradition.

The dance continued, the participants oblivious to the presence of an audience. The performers were in the grip of an enchantment, the puffy-cheeked trance of the red-faced O'Reilly, the fierce intensity of the drummer Fagan, and the dreamy-eyed Maeve and Jack. They were transported into a dark netherworld of Celtic fire dances, savage chariot battles, druids, harps, and mysticism.

The floating ballroom became the green field of Tara, ringed meeting place of the High Kings of Ireland. The drums conjured thunderous hoofbeats of majestic Connemara ponies. The melancholy bagpipes summoned Maeve, Queen of Connaught; Cuchulain, warrior of Conchober MacNessa's army of the Red Branch; the braying of bulls and the cawing of crows.

The spear, thought Maeve, *where is the spear of Cuchulain? I have captured the bull, but where is its shaft?* Giving a lusty, guttural cry, Maeve threw her body into wild, abandoned, erotic movements. Cuchulain leaped and kicked, chanting bardic odes from "The Tain." The mountains of Ulster sang in the heart of the Hound and echoed in the pass where he defeated Maeve's army.

Maeve, wearing a flowing white gown, stood atop the stump-shaped Ben Bulben near the village of Bundoran and the Bay of Donegal. It was not to the misty sea she gazed, but to a mound known in legend as the Mound of Maeve. A moonbeam illumined the mound. Sitting on the mound was a giant crow. The crow was singing:

The Banshee mournful wails
In the midst of the silent, lonely night.
Plaintive she sings the song of death.

Maeve felt sadness and release. She moaned and went into a swoon. As she plunged into darkness, a vision of her drowned fisherman husband floated after her. When she awoke, Jack was cradling her in his arms on a sofa in a parlor, and the boys were curled up at the far end of the sofa. She tried to sit up, but the pitching of the ship made her dizzy. "Leave me, my brave Cuchulain, for I am tired." She smiled and drifted back to sleep.

Jack rose and the boys stirred but did not awaken. His eyes were glazed. He had not yet come out of the enchantment. The beat of the Bohdran and the wail of the Uileann pipe echoed in his soul, and he could feel the white horse under his bare thighs and the spear in his hand. He was in a fever and had to cool down. He had never wanted Maeve as much as he wanted her now. What he needed was a cold blast of rainy wind in his face. Then he needed to find Flynn.

He stepped out onto the forward deck. The ship pitched, and he nearly lost his balance. After a moment, he found his sea legs. The wind and rain refreshed him, and he took deep gulps of it. Being out here was glorious. Jack was not a sailor, but he liked being on a ship.

Jack had not had a drink since he had left Chicago, but he felt intoxicated. The Celtic spell, the sensuous Maeve, and the wind and rain gave him a feeling of supernatural power. The lake was black. Staring at it was like staring into an abyss. Out there was the giant Finn McCool, the poet Ossian, the pirate Grania, and brown-haired Diarmuid. Jack had the urge to leap overboard, to go out into the darkness and do battle with the gods, but he would not abandon Maeve.

He thought he was alone on the deck, but he noticed a lone figure standing at the bow, impervious to the weather. The figure was standing very still, gripping the rail. The man had his back to Jack, but there was something familiar about him. Jack, with an inexplicable sense of foreboding, cleared his throat to get the man's attention. The man turned slowly to face Jack. It was Captain Garrett Barry. His eyes were burning with the intensity of glowing coal.

Something was holding Blevins afloat in the cold water of Lake Michigan. It was his father's strong arm. Blevins lay on the arm, keeping his head above water. "Now I'm going to let go," his father's voice said. "It's time for you to sink or swim."

Panic. Suddenly the arm was gone. Blevins sank. His father's voice came from a distance. "Kick, Blevins, kick." Blevins was paralyzed. He went down and down into darkness. He thought his lungs would burst, and he had a headache. Light penetrated the black void. He gradually became aware that he was in unfamiliar surroundings and that the throbbing in his head was not just in his head but all around him. The wail of a whistle brought him to consciousness abruptly. He was in a train and the train was moving. What was he doing on a train?

He looked out the window. Fields and farms sped past, giving no clue to location, other than they were not in Chicago. The pain in his head spread to his jaw, which he touched gingerly, wincing. What time was it? What day was it? He squinted to force reality into focus and took a deep breath, noticing the stench of stale whiskey in his clothes.

"It's 1:00 am," said the conductor, observing that Blevins was awake and confused. "It's September 8, year of our Lord one thousand eight hundred and sixty. You're on the Chicago–Milwaukee Line bound for Milwaukee. I'd say you had a night of it. Hair of the dog?" The conductor offered him a nip of whiskey, but Blevins waved him away.

He felt a small, shiny object in his pocket, which he took out and examined. It was a key, and its significance dawned on him. It was the key to the stateroom on the *Lady Elgin* where he was supposed to be now. He tried to reconstruct what happened prior to his passing out. He reeked of liquor, but he was sure he hadn't consumed more than a cup or two of punch at the press reception. He remembered Jack calling his name and clobbering him. There had been no warning.

The face of the conductor loomed above him. "Ticket, sir?"

"I don't have a ticket."

"Why, of course you have. There, in your hand, paid for by your good friend in Chicago. It's no wonder you don't remember. You were dead-to-the-world drunk."

"Who put me on the train?"

"Cabbie. Said a kind gent gave him money to put you on the train and purchase your fare."

Jack. It had to be Jack. This was a horrible misunderstanding. Brother of the bride who didn't know he was brother of the bride. Or did he know? What had he seen, and what conclusion had he drawn?

"Conductor, what is the first stop?"

"Winnetka. There will be a layover, and it may even be necessary to change trains."

Blevins could get a train from Winnetka back to Chicago, but there would be no point. The *Lady Elgin* was already underway and Flynn would be on board, unless she had come looking for him, which seemed unlikely. In spite of the delay, the train would reach Milwaukee ahead of the ship. Blevins would be waiting at the dock. In the meantime, Flynn would be crazy wondering what happened.

There would be much to resolve. Poor Flynn. Her words at their prenuptial shipboard dinner rang in his ears. "I don't want to think about problems. I want to wrap us in a warm cocoon of now."

The conductor's voice filled the train. "Winnetka! We are now arriving in Winnetka!"

Chapter Nineteen

GOING THROUGH THE STRAITS WAS always a memorable experience, thought Vorce, awed to be passing from one vast body of water into another. No matter how many times he'd done it, he still got goose bumps even though he was a veteran of the lakes. For some reason, he had a sense of foreboding about this voyage. He wished Captain Jenkins were still in charge. Malott may have sailed the seven seas, but he'd been in a number of disasters. He was young and reckless and lacking in judgment.

"Three days out and he spends most of his time in his cabin," grumbled Budge. "It's a good thing for him that he has a couple of salts like us to run the ship."

"In the first place, we ain't salts. I don't see no salt water, do you? How much sea duty have you done?"

"I was only speakin' figuratively. I don't think Malott knows a hawser from a bowline."

Vorce had his own doubts about Malott, but he wasn't going to share them with Budge. The second mate was not trustworthy, a two-faced troublemaker who wouldn't think twice about betraying a confidence if it were to his advantage. Vorce had been burned by Budge before and now kept his own counsel when he had to work with the man. He didn't want a pal. He was superior to Budge in more than rank.

"Cap'n Malott may be a young pup, but he knows a hawser from a bowline. His seamanship is renowned. Surely you've heard the tale of the *Edward Hyman*."

"The *Edward Hyman* burned at sea somewhere between Hong

Kong and Peru. A big clipper, she was, with two small boats. The crew abandoned ship. Way out in the mid-Pacific, they were."

"You do know the story."

"Was Malott involved?"

"Malott was in charge of the second quarter boat. With a crew of seven, he brought the lifeboat two thousand miles across the Pacific to Peru, not a man lost."

"That ain't what I heard. I heard the men were lost at sea. I never heard Malott's name in connection with it."

"There were two quarter boats. The first boat, with the captain and seven others, was lost at sea. Malott made it to Peru. Does that sound like someone who doesn't know what he's doing? Tell me now, does it?"

"A clipper on the Pacific ain't the same as a lumber hooker on the lakes. We've hardly seen the captain since we reached the straits. He's been sleepin' in his cabin."

"How do you know what he's doing? There's nothing here we can't handle ourselves. Everything's shipshape and we're on course under full sail. John Terrett's on the wheel, and John's brought many a craft through the straits. Why do we need Malott?"

"That's my point, Vorce. Why do we need Malott? I'll say no more."

The lake was getting choppy, and the stars and moon were hidden by clouds. A storm was brewing. Budge felt it in his bones. They really would need Malott soon enough, and they'd learn what kind of sea legs he really had.

"Let [any man] place himself in my situation—without home or friends—without money or credit—wanting shelter, and no one to give it—wanting bread, and no money to buy it—and, at the same time, let him feel that he is pursued by merciless men-hunters, and in total darkness as to what to do, where to go, or where to stay ... then, and not till then, will he fully appreciate the hardships of, and know how to sympathize with, the toil-worn and whip-scarred fugitive slave."

The words of Frederick Douglass from his autobiography, words that Mary Barry had read aloud to Ned, were remembered now, for this was the situation in which he found himself. Never had he felt so alone and vulnerable. Not only was he a fugitive slave, he had killed a white man who was an officer of the law. Sooner or later, investigators would link the disappearance of Deputy Marshal Doughty with Doughty's hunt for Ned, and they would link Ned to Mary Barry. He doubted they would ever locate Doughty's remains.

The only thing to do was to get to Canada. He could head north, but he was a domestic slave, unskilled in outdoor survival and unable to cope with the wilderness of northern Wisconsin and Michigan's Upper Peninsula. His best chance was to stow away on a ship out of Chicago with the help of the Underground Railroad.

His first thought had been to head for Racine, but he'd had second thoughts. Racine was a center of Underground activity. It had been via Racine that Ned had been placed with the Barry family. He was too well known in Racine. It was the first place they would look for him.

It would make more sense to go to Winnetka. It was close to Chicago, and he knew a family there who might help. If he used Mary Barry's name, he would be safe. He'd keep the horse, avoiding the well-traveled planked stagecoach road. When he was close to his destination, he'd let the horse go. It wouldn't do for a black man on a white horse to be seen riding the streets of Winnetka.

Flynn stretched in the luxurious, soft down of the opulent quilt, half awaking from a dream. In the dream, she was being rocked in a cradle and her mother was crooning an Irish lullaby. She tried to tell her mother that she was really grown up, but the words wouldn't come. The cradle started to move, floating on a gentle stream away from her mother. The warm feeling of security vanished. The lullaby faded. Ahead something terrible awaited in the darkness. Aware that she was dreaming, she tried to awaken. The struggle was too much. She returned to a deep, dreamless sleep.

A few of the boys were gathered at the forward hold near the cow pens on the *Lady Elgin*. They were discussing what had become of Lugh Finnegan, deciding that he must have been waylaid by a lady of the evening.

"Quite the lady's man, Lugh," said McNeill. "Did anyone see him after the rally?"

None of them had. Stories were swapped about the lads' exploits in Chicago. Fitzgerald, sporting a black eye, spun an elaborate yarn about a brawl with a German. As he embellished the story, he emphasized the action by pantomiming the punches he had given and received. To hear him tell the tale, the German had fared much worse.

The ship pitched, disturbing the lowing cattle in the pen.

"Mooo," said Monohan, and several cows responded. The boys laughed. "Mooo."

"Sweet Jaysus, Monohan," chuckled Fitzgerald, "next it'll be milk you'll be producing, and you not even a farmer."

"You sound just like one of them four-legged beasts," said McNeill. "Don't he, Keane? Don't Monohan sound like a cow?"

There was no response. Keane, a tall, gaunt lad somewhat older than the others, was silently absorbed in his own dark thoughts. Keane was a loner. Although a dedicated Fenian, he was not a disciplined guardsman, even now on probation, placed there by Captain Barry himself. Within the Brotherhood, Feeney had a liking for Keane, so the others left him alone. Keane had a violent temper that intimidated his companions.

"Keane?"

"What?"

"Don't Monohan sound like one of them cows?"

"I've no time for such effing foolishness. It's a two-legged beast that occupies my thoughts."

"What two-legged beast?"

"That English bastard. I refer to the Honorable Herbert Ingram, Esquire, Parliamentarian."

"What's Ingram done to you?"

"To me, personally? Why nothing, McNeill. Don't you see? It's not what he's done; it's what he is and what he represents. He's a parliamentarian, for Christ's sake, a member of the British ruling class."

Mooo. This time it was a cow, and no one laughed.

"Here's a chance to make a statement much stronger than burning a ship."

"Make that point to Feeney."

Keane spat. "Feeney! Feeney'd never approve. Burning property says nothing. Killing a symbol of the British Empire, now that's something else. Anyway, Feeney's not here. The time is now."

"So it's killing, then?"

"Killing's part of war. Why do you think we've been training all these months?"

"Ingram has a son. Would you be killing him, too?"

"Didn't Cromwell murder man, woman, and child in his bloody purge of Ireland?"

"How would you go about it?" asked Monohan.

"Are you with me?"

"I am not with you, by God."

"Then it's better you not know. McNeill?"

"The Fenian oath didn't include murder."

"Not murder, execution. Fitzgerald?"

"Such an act would burden my immortal soul."

"Then we never had this conversation. If you repeat it, I will get you, and your immortal soul is all you'll have left." Keane stalked away from the others. Contemptuous cowards. He would do the deed himself.

Captain Barry's icy stare stopped Jack in his tracks. For an eternity they stood staring at each other. *He knows*, thought Jack. The cold silence continued, and the old familiar guilt welled inside Jack. He grinned sheepishly and tried to break the ice with a half-hearted salute that came off as insolence.

"I trusted you." Barry's wet hair was plastered on his scalp and water poured off his chin, making him look like a demented gargoyle. He spoke with a controlled fury. "How dare you betray me?"

"Betray, Captain?"

"Don't deny it. You're a damned Fenian."

"If that's so, and I'm not saying it is, how would that be a betrayal?"

"You are using the training and facilities of the Union Guard in the commission of criminal activities, and you are sneaking behind my back to do it."

"Criminal activities? And what would they be?"

"The high mischief engineered by that cunning antichrist Feeney and implemented by that lawless gang, Feeney's Boys, of which you are a member. Did I say member? I should have said leader."

"What if I am? What horrible crime has been committed by this sinister gang, and how is the Guard being hurt?"

"What crime? Arson. You set fire to the *Lynne*, but that wasn't the only crime. How about vandalism, destruction of cargo, assault? The act has international implications, the *Lynne* being a British ship. God knows what other mischief you are into, but just this one black deed is enough to send you to prison—Cuchulain."

"What did you call me?"

"Cuchulain, rider of the white horse and igniter of the torch. Don't play the innocent. I know you. Jack O'Mara … Cuchulain … traitor."

"Traitor, is it? You are the traitor Captain Garrett Barry of Barry's Irish Brigade. Erin go bragh. Some Irishman you are. Where are your loyalties, boyo?"

"I'm not an Irish citizen, and neither are you. So your da was born in Ireland. Is Dan O'Mara a Fenian? We both know he isn't. And your sister, married last night to the newspaperman, what would your sister think?"

"What did you say about my sister?"

"I said, 'What would your sister think?'"

"No, before that. What about my sister and the newspaperman?"

"Why, that they were married last night."

Jack grabbed Barry by the collar and shouted into his face. "What do you mean, married? Married! Tell me about that."

The unexpected reaction put Barry on the defensive. "I … I assumed you knew. Blevins told me in confidence, but I thought you were part of it. Captain Wilson married them last night on shipboard."

Jack loosened his grip on Barry's collar. Barry pushed him away. The ship pitched. Jack lost his balance and fell. "You're finished," said Barry, "expelled from the Guard. What the civil authorities do when they learn your identity is no concern of mine."

Jack did not seem to hear. His wide eyes looked through Barry. "Fer Diad! I challenge you. Fer Diad!" He scrambled to his feet and ran toward the ladder leading up to the bridge. Barry stood in thought. Fer Diad—who or what was Fer Diad? Then he remembered the myth.

Fer Diad had been Cuchulain's best friend. The friends had parted and fought each other in mortal combat. Barry shuddered. Cuchulain had slaughtered Fer Diad. Would it come to that? If so, he was ready.

Captain Wilson gripped the rail of the hurricane deck and watched his fear come true. Sixteen miles north of Chicago and ten miles east of Winnetka the storm struck in full force. The *Lady Elgin* sailed against the wind, which churned the lake into a watery mountain range and blew clouds of hard rain across the ship. The night sky was illumined by violent streaks of lightning followed by claps of thunder.

The *Lady* was a well-constructed vessel with strong horizontal supports and the finest quality wood. She had weathered many a storm, which is not to say that she had never been damaged. Two years ago, she'd been stranded on the Au Sable Reef near Munising, and later that year she'd sustained $8,000 damage while stranded off Copper Harbor during a Lake Superior gale.

He didn't mind the wind and the rain in his face. The roiling elements heightened his senses, carrying him to a dimension of increased awareness. Lake Michigan was a giant bathtub. The wind raced back and forth causing majestic whitecaps and waves that were not regular but traveled in threes, the second wave smashing a ship before the ship could recover from the impact of the first. This wave action was called "three sisters" by Great Lakes mariners. Three sisters caused ships to toss and turn, battering them and flipping them over during severe storms.

The captain returned to the wheelhouse. The second mate was on the wheel, while the first mate, Davis, stood by. Neither man wore a worried expression. The captain smiled. The *Lady* was in good hands. They'd been through worse. He wondered how many other ships were out in this gale, and what direction they were heading.

Malott awoke to a hard pounding on the cabin door. *My God*, he thought, *how long have I slept?* The pounding continued.

"Captain Malott!" the voice of Budge shouted. "It's getting squally, sir. The others sent me to fetch you. It looks like a bad 'un."

"Tell them I'm on my way."

There was a clap of thunder and the wind hit the *Augusta* hard on the starboard, causing her to list steeply to the port. Malott, in the process of rising from bed, lost his balance and fell on the cabin deck. Loose objects slid off his desk and bounced across the room. A compass came close to braining him. He cursed and struggled to his feet.

Malott was fully dressed, having fallen asleep in his clothes, intending only to take a short nap. He could hear banging and crashing up on deck and a lot of yelling. He rushed to the door, flung it open, and raced up the ladder to the main deck. He thought he heard someone shout something about spotting another ship's light, but the severity of the storm swept all other thoughts from his mind after he stepped out on deck.

Rain pelted the ship like hailstones, and visibility was zero. The *Augusta* continued to list, shipping water on the port side. The banging and crashing was the lumber, which had shifted. Crewmen struggled to lower the sails. Vorce and Budge secured the canvas. John Terrett struggled at the wheel. Steering was nearly impossible. The ship was always sluggish with a heavy load, a fact known by Vorce and Budge but not shared with the captain.

The *Augusta* was on course, Malott believed, but visibility, poor enough without a shipboard light, was marred by the height of the lumber and the position into which it had shifted. He climbed to the top of the lumber. When he reached a vantage point, he saw a sight which filled him with the fear of God. The lights of a great paddlewheel steamer were bearing down on him. They were headed for a collision.

"Hard up! Hard up! For God's sake, man, hard up!" It was too late. He flung himself onto the lumber and hung on for dear life. Just before impact, an unrelated thought entered Malott's mind. Today was his twenty-seventh birthday.

Chapter Twenty

Flaherty sat on the brig bunk smoking the last long nine. He inhaled the smoke deeply into his lungs and exhaled slowly, savoring the moment. Cigar stubs littered the cabin floor. The fetid air stank of urine and tobacco, causing him to reflect that the secondary smoke might tide him over.

Lieutenant Hogan, who always had a cigar in his big mouth, had warned Flaherty of the dangers of inhaling. Flaherty had thought a lot about his boss since luck had turned against him. The lieutenant hated scandal within the department and would be furious when he learned of his subordinate's escapades. Flaherty would rather have faced a Chicago jail than return to face the boss. Hogan would kill him. The man's fists were lethal. Flaherty's battered corpse would be found on the waterfront, his death attributed to the denizens of the boarding house. He had seen Hogan kill with his fists. Others had seen it, but who would be fool enough to testify to it?

Flaherty would escape somehow when the ship reached Milwaukee. He'd call in his markers. There were people on the waterfront who would hide him until he could get far away from Hogan. Unfortunately he was flat broke. He should have known enough not to trust that kid and those two chippies. Feeney ... Feeney would stake him. Flaherty had a few things on Feeney, not the least of which involved the money in the safe. Also, Feeney didn't care much for Hogan.

He dropped the stub of the final long nine, which he ground into the carpet with the heel of his brogan. Then he yawned and reclined on the cot, tired of thinking, tired of pacing the cramped floor. His eyelids drooped.

Without warning, a jolt flung him from the cot with a brutal impact. His head struck something hard, causing a concussion that stunned him. Confused, he lay on his back for a moment. There was something above him he couldn't discern because his vision was blurred.

What was up there? Whatever it was, it wasn't the ceiling. It had come from outside, letting in wind and water. His body ached all over, but vision returned. What he saw horrified him. The bowsprit of another ship had penetrated the hull like a shaft. The tip had crashed through the cabin and hung above him.

Before there was time to react, the bowsprit slid back out, leaving a gaping hole through which he saw the swell of the lake. He rolled over on his belly, struggled onto all fours, and crawled to the locked cabin door. He managed to stand, leaning against the door to avoid falling down the listing cabin deck and out the hole into the abyss.

"Help!" he screamed. "Get me out of here!" He pounded on the door and shouted. Mercifully, Flaherty never saw the bowsprit crash through the cabin a second time, slamming into him and impaling him on the door like an insect.

Captain Malott, who had fallen from the lumber onto the slippery deck, managed to crawl to the bow near the point where it had penetrated the steamship. "Ahoy, the *Lady Elgin*!" he shouted "Get your captain. I must speak to your captain." Passengers were scurrying about, but no one took notice.

"They're dragging us along with them," cried Vorce. "We're jammed into them. Their engine's steaming full forward and we're stuck together."

Budge stood on the stern. The crew of the *Augusta* was helpless, rooted to the spot. The only one doing anything was Malott, who continued to try to get the attention of the other ship. It was an exercise in futility. Budge tore off the sign of the *Augusta* and threw it over the side. Someone would find it and know that the ship had gone down. The sign floated away, disappearing into the darkness over the crest of a wave.

Terrett, on the wheel, was terrified. If the *Augusta* were dragged, she would be irreparably damaged, and if she parted violently she would capsize. The bowsprit slid out of the hull of the steamer for a moment, but the force of the wind and water slammed it in again.

"Turn, damn you, turn."

As if on cue, the *Lady Elgin* negotiated a turn, heading west toward the Illinois coastline. The movement shook the *Augusta* loose. The schooner listed so sharply Terrett was sure they would capsize. Lumber broke loose and washed overboard, but the hooker righted herself. No man aboard could take credit for that. It was an act of providence, but there was no time for thanksgiving. They were free, but not safe. It was impossible to know how much the other ship had been damaged.

Captain Malott burst into the pilot house. "Terrett! Get this ship back on course, southwest to Chicago." He clapped Terrett on the back. "Good man, Terrett. I thought we were goners."

"How much damage have we sustained?"

"Hard to tell. The bow is in bad shape. I don't think we're in much danger."

"What about the *Lady Elgin*?"

The *Lady Elgin* was steaming toward the coastline. Malott couldn't see the gap in her hull because the damaged side was no longer visible, but he knew they had struck above the water line.

"Do we contact her, offer assistance?"

They could easily catch up, but the storm and accident had caused a delay, and the cargo was shifting. Besides, the actual extent of the damage to the *Augusta* hadn't been determined. Malott had to make a decision, so he made one.

"The *Lady Elgin* will survive. Get us to Chicago."

Vorce and Budge were below deck. Ankle deep in water. The water was not rising, which meant it had not been caused by a leak. "We haven't heard the end of this," said Vorce. "There will be an inquiry. The *Lady Elgin*'s the most popular craft afloat. Her captain, Jack Wilson, has a lot of clout. Darius Malott's going to be in deep trouble."

Budge was silent. If an inquiry were held, he'd bite his tongue. He wasn't clever. Every time he opened his mouth, he incriminated himself. In this case, it could mean dishonor, even prison. He had seen the *Lady Elgin*. He had seen the steamer's lights twenty minutes before they collided. If he had spoken up, the accident might have been avoided. He had said nothing.

"For God's sake, Davis, get a boat overboard and outside to try to stop the leak."

The order was a last-resort measure to stuff the gaping hole with canvas in hope that the outside pressure of the water against the hull would hold. It was a stopgap that would gain crucial time, if it worked.

Davis and three crewmen were lowered from the stern in a small boat. Using ropes held by the small boat crew and by passengers on the steamship, the small boat was pulled along the side of the hull to the damaged area. By the time the boat reached the breach, the water in the boat was ankle deep and the men had to bail feverishly. They had to let go of the ropes to bail, causing them to drift away from the steamer. Davis manned the oars in an attempt to get back, but the closest they could get was about one hundred feet.

They lowered a second small boat with more success. The crew of the second boat made it to the gap. With help from the crew inside the steamer, they worked at stuffing the hole. The strategy didn't work. The canvas didn't hold. A wave slammed the boat, causing a crew member to fall into the lake. "Man overboard!"

Efforts to save the man were unsuccessful. In the meantime, the boat drifted—the ropes forgotten. It was only after they were separated from the umbilical cords that joined them to the *Lady* that a crew member discovered the oars had been inexplicably left on the steamship.

"Oh God, the oars! The oars!"

On the ship, people heard the cries and the oars were found. The oars were flung over the side in the direction of the boat, but they fell short of their mark. The boat drifted into the turbulent darkness.

Inside the *Lady,* crewmen continued filling the gap using mattresses, canvas, and any material they could find. The effort held back water for a time. Then the water exploded into the hold and the mattresses knocked over crew members, who found themselves waist-deep and scrambling out of the hold as fast as they could. If the *Lady Elgin* was going down, they weren't going to be at the bottom of it.

Nothing is more unstoppable than a stampede of crazed cattle, thought Jake Mudd, cattle driver for Armour to whom the penned herd had been entrusted. *Thing is, how do I make this herd crazed?* Captain Wilson had convinced Mudd that the herd had to be deep-sixed. It was a matter of ballast, as Wilson put it. The *Lady* was shipping water. Mudd had been reluctant.

"Fifty head is a sizable piece of change."

"The shipping company will make good on it. If they don't, I will."

"Well, fifty head …"

"Let me put it this way. If we sink, you, the passengers, the cattle, and I will all go to the same place, and there'll be no piece of change in that."

So Mudd had agreed, hoping the decision wouldn't cost him his job. It was the thing to do, but how to do it? He wished it were a herd of sheep. Cattle were dumb enough, but nothing surpassed sheep for dumbness. Sheep were real followers. Well, first things first. He opened the pen, hoping the animals would take the hint and jump into the lake. It came as no surprise when they didn't oblige.

The ship listed. Several cows skidded to the edge and toppled into the water with a loud splash. Instead of following, the other cows backed away, crowding into the far end of the pen. "Well, it's crazy time. I sure as hell don't want to be on the deck. There may be no good way to die, but bein' trampled by cows has got to be one of the worst."

He'd never mounted a cow, but he supposed it would be the same as mounting a horse. It would be no picnic without a saddle. He chose one of the tamer-looking animals—a bull. He mounted the beast but was mistaken about the tameness. The bull started to buck.

"Yahoo!"

Drawing two pistols, he shot into the air, screaming while he shot. Bullets ricocheted around the pen. Several cows were hit. Mudd narrowly missed being hit by a bullet on the rebound. The deafening din had done the trick. The cows stampeded. Mudd continued to shoot and yell. The bizarre spectacle of cows committing suicide fascinated him so much that he barely noticed the bull he was riding had reached the front of the line. By then it was too late. "Yahoo!" He fired two more shots as he and the bull sailed through the blackness into the cold lake.

"Awesome," said Brian to Liam, standing above the pen and watching the whole spectacle. Cows were floating all over Lake Michigan.

———————————

Wilson knew the ship wasn't going to make it when the water quenched the fire in the engine and the paddlewheel ground to a stop, causing the *Lady Elgin* to drift helplessly. The only hope had been to maintain sufficient power and speed to reach the shore before sinking, which was why he hadn't given the order to stop engines after the collision, even if it meant dragging the lumber schooner with them. He could not be concerned with the safety of the schooner. His priority was the safety of the three hundred souls on the *Lady*.

Damn that schooner. Crewmen who had witnessed the collision informed him that the name of the schooner was the *Augusta*, but no one knew the name of the captain. The hooker had come from nowhere and had no lights. He wondered why the craft hadn't sighted the bright lights of the *Lady Elgin*.

He'd ordered the *Lady* to right full rudder, which separated the two vessels and nearly capsized the lumber craft. The *Augusta* recovered and then, incredibly, sailed off, disappearing as suddenly as she had appeared. How could she? Lives would be lost that could have been saved by the *Augusta*, which may have been damaged but was seaworthy. Maybe the two-master was unaware of how badly the *Lady* was hurt, but there was no excuse for not staying to find out. If Wilson survived, he would track the captain of the damned hooker and see justice done.

No time to think of that now. Crew members were rounding up women and children and getting them into the remaining lifeboats. Passengers who had just arrived from staterooms were struggling with life jackets. Until now an atmosphere of cooperation had existed. Hadn't the captain assured them everything would be all right?

This facade was crumbling in the face of stark reality. Everything was not all right. Wilson saw panic setting in and knew that soon he would lose control of the situation. Things would fall apart. He was more than a little afraid himself, but he couldn't let it show.

The lifeboat was ready to lower and could not accommodate more passengers. Only a fraction of the people on board would be on the boat, and most of them were women.

"Second Mate Snyder."

"Aye, aye, Captain."

"Board the small boat and go with them."

"With the women and children, sir?"

"Would you cast them off without a mate? Take charge. Do it, man. Get them safely to shore, and God be with you."

Snyder boarded the lifeboat and gave the sign to lower. "Lower the boat," ordered Wilson. Tearful farewells were called across the water as the lowered boat embarked upon its perilous voyage.

Garrett Barry, who made certain that his son, Willie, was in the boat, had helped with the lowering. Barry and his guardsmen had been of enormous assistance during the crisis. Barry's calm authority helped keep things on an even keel as much as Wilson's. Now Wilson would ask a final favor.

"Captain Barry, may I have a word with you?"

"Captain to captain?" Barry grinned. Wilson didn't smile.

"Barry, we're going down. There is no doubt. Hundreds are on board and the last lifeboat is gone. Straightaway, it will be every man for himself. One last measure can be taken that may increase the chance for survival. Your men can help."

"Tell me how."

"I want you to know how much I appreciate—"

"Yes, yes, do go on."

"Round up the lads and give them axes. I will show you where the axes are. Then start chopping down the superstructure. When we go down, the pieces of the ship will give survivors something to hold on to—a life raft, if you will. Chop doors, pieces of bulkhead, anything that floats. The entire ship is wooden, so that means anything, really. While you and your men are chopping, the crew and I will inform the passengers of their options."

"What a waste of timber, if we don't go down."

"Oh, we're going down, Barry. Have no doubt of that. We're going down."

The guardsmen were summoned, and axes were distributed. As the men began their grim work, a familiar voice froze Barry in his tracks. He spun around. It was his son.

"Willie! For God's sake, son, why aren't you in the lifeboat? I saw you get in."

"I'm not a child, Da. I want to be with you and the lads."

Barry stared for a long moment. "No, you are not a child, my brave young man." He handed his son an ax.

O'Reilly stood alone on the dance floor playing the bagpipes. Occasionally, someone rushing past would stop to urge him out on deck, but he waved them on. He wore full clan regalia, kilts and a tam-o'-shanter. He knew his time had come, and he was dressed for the occasion. This was the way to go, his moment. Tears streaming, O'Reilly played the stirring strains of "The Minstrel Boy," with the words, "in the ranks of death you will find him." He hoped the strains would comfort the souls who would join him on the last voyage.

Someone was pounding on the door and wouldn't stop. "Flynn! Open the door. For Christ's sake, open the door!" It was Blevins, and she'd promised him that she would stay awake. How long had she slept? As she walked barefoot across the plush carpet, it dawned on her that the ship was moving. Blevins must have misplaced the key. When she flung open the door, she'd give her husband a wicked kiss.

The man at the door was not her husband. "Jack? Jack! What are you doing here? I thought —where's Blevins?" Then she gasped, remembering that her brother didn't know, and here she was in her nightgown. "Wait. Oh God, let me get dressed." Jack averted his head while she donned a skirt and blouse. "Jack, I know how this must look to you. I can explain. Blevins and I are married."

"There's no time. You must get on your shoes and jacket. There's been a terrible accident. The ship is sinking."

"If this is one of your stupid jokes, it's not amusing."

"You must have heard the commotion."

"I heard nothing. You don't act surprised that I'm married. You know something. What do you know? How did you find this room? Where's Blevins? Something's happened to him. If he were on the ship, he'd be here with me. Where is he?"

"We can't talk. There's not a second to spare. Come."

"No. Where's Blevins?"

"Flynn, for the love of God—"

The ship shuddered and tipped to one side. There was loud shouting everywhere, which brought a lump of awareness to her throat. Flynn's heart beat rapidly, but she stood fast.

"Jack O'Mara, I won't move until you tell me where Blevins is. You know."

"Blevins is on a train to Milwaukee. Now hurry."

"On a train! Tell me everything."

"Sister, we're sinking. Let's go. Now!"

"I will stand here and sink, and you with me, until you explain. I will know if you are lying. I always know. What did you do to my husband?"

Jack told her the whole story, talking as fast as he could. He opened the door. People jammed the passageway. He tried to pull her to the door, but she resisted, so he talked faster and faster. Flynn's fear was overcome by rage. When Jack finished, she slapped his face. They stared at each other. Then she collapsed into his arms and passed out.

He carried her into the teeming passageway, as he had carried her when they were children. Now the old game returned. He was Cuchulain, rescuing a maiden in distress. The maiden was his sister, no longer a maiden. The list of the *Lady* increased, making the headway slow. People were screaming.

When he reached the deck, a grim vision stunned him. The last small craft had been lowered, filled with women and children. People at the rail stared at the boat as it vanished over the hill of a wave. Maeve was at the rail. Eyes brimming with tears, she came to Jack.

"I hope they'll be all right. They must be saved, my boys. They must get ashore safely."

"Maeve. Oh God, Maeve. Why did you not board the lifeboat yourself?"

"There wasn't a choice. It was a mad scrambling. Brian and Liam made it. There was no more space. They were the last. You know, it's queer. I came to America to escape the sea. I didn't want my boys to suffer the fate of their father. Maybe they won't. They have a chance. This will be the death of me."

"You will survive, too."

"I will not. I had a dream about it. I am going to die, Jack, and so are you."

Flynn came out of her swoon. "Let me down, please. I'm all right."

Jack helped her to her feet and assisted her with a life jacket. She was dazed, disoriented, unable to comprehend the chaos of the world around her. A bagpipe was wailing, and the bell on the pilot house was ringing over and over. People were yelling and crying, and the tilting ship drifted with no power, floundering out of control. The strangest sight was that of men wielding axes and hacking the superstructure. They were chopping down the ship. Why were they doing that?

She started to tell Jack to stop the men, when there was a horrendous cracking sound like the earth opening during a quake. Her stomach dived, as it did when she was in a high place looking down. At that point, the engine crashed through the belly and sank to the bottom of the lake. People grasped anything they could find. Then suddenly it happened.

With a final, shuddering gasp, the *Lady Elgin* went down. The pressure of the water rushing into the cavernous air trap inside caused the steamship to explode, spewing debris everywhere.

Chapter Twenty-One

THE SHORE OF LAKE MICHIGAN north of Chicago was dangerous, uncharted water under which sand bars extended, some as far as ninety feet. The beaches were bordered by high bluffs. Ned decided to follow the shore to reach his destination. In an area north of Winnetka, he abandoned the horse. He hated to let the horse go, but someone would find the handsome steed and care for it.

"Goodbye, old boy, I free you. I wish someone would free me. You're on your own." The horse tried to follow, but Ned climbed down the steep bluff to the beach. The horse stared down at him from atop the cliff. "Shoo! Shoo!" The horse turned and disappeared from view.

Ned turned his attention to the task at hand. A mile was not too far to walk, but the jagged coastline was intimidating. There were natural obstacles, such as boulders and stumps, and some areas with no beach, which required wading or swimming.

The sky was darkening. This morning's violence seemed a lifetime ago. His world was upside down. If he could reach the Artemas Carter estate, things would be all right, at least for a while. The estate was located on a high bluff. Mary Barry had told him about it, and told him to go there if he were ever in trouble. It wasn't much farther, but he had to find it before dark. The wind was blowing and the lake was acting up. If he didn't get there within the next half hour, he'd have to spend the night on the beach, a prospect that filled him with fear.

Then he saw it, across a cove. He could see a flag flying and the top of a roof, all that was visible from his perspective. Walking around the cove would take too long. Straight across would be faster. Taking a deep breath, he plunged into the black, icy water and swam to the other side of the cove, using all the strength of his arms and legs. The surf was building, and he felt the pull of the current. Thunder rumbled and rain started sprinkling.

When he reached the other side of the cove, he was directly below the Artemas Carter estate. Climbing the steep bluff was all that remained. Wet and cold, he began the ascent. In spite of a narrow path, the climb was arduous. Several times he fell, slid back, and scraped himself on the rocks. He arrived at the top on his hands and knees. As he was about to rise, he heard a clicking noise like a gun being cocked. He looked up into the grizzled face of an old man and into the muzzle of a pistol.

"My name is Artemas Carter. Who the hell are you, and what are you doing on my property?"

"My name is Ned. I am known to my people as Moses."

"Moses. Yes, I've heard of you. Federal marshal's been makin' inquiries. Fellow named Doughty. Reprehensible man. I wouldn't give him the time of day." Carter kept the pistol pointed at Ned. "Get up. Get up slowly with your hands above your head." The wet clothes stuck to Ned's body as he rose. Cold penetrated his skin and he stood there shivering. Carter stepped back, still holding the slave at gunpoint.

"You answered the first question. Now answer the second. What are you doing on my property? What do you want?"

"I want to escape to Canada. I think you may help. I have a letter from Mary Barry, the missus I've been serving."

Ned slowly reached into his pocket. The letter, which Mrs. Barry had given him, was inside *The Narrative of the Life of Fredrick Douglass*. He yanked the book out of his pocket. The book was dripping wet and the letter, too, which he handed to Carter.

"Mary Barry, eh?" Carter relaxed, shoving the pistol under his belt. The ink on the letter was so blurred that it was impossible to read. Carter smiled. "Did you swim here, Moses?" The signature was legible. He recognized Mary's handwriting. They corresponded on matters regarding the abolitionist movement. Spunky lady, Mary. If she weren't hitched to Captain Garrett Barry, and if Carter were younger, he'd have a hankering for her. "What's the book?"

Ned handed him the soaking book, which was the same edition Carter had in his bookcase. He noticed the blurry inscription on the inside cover: "To Ned from Mary." He returned the book to Ned and studied him with a sharp, appraising look. Carter prided himself on his judgment of character, and character was etched into the lined face of this old Negro. He made a decision.

"Come into my home, Moses. We'll get you into dry clothes and pour hot broth into you. You'll be safe here. We'll discuss your future later."

Poor Richard's Almanac was Jared Gage's bible. Gage memorized Ben Franklin's homilies and did his best to live by them. Gage's late wife, God rest her soul, would chide him about it. Didn't he know that Franklin had been a reprobate, an old lech who never followed his own advice? Mrs. Gage's skepticism never fazed Jared, who raised three sons on Poor Richard. One of Gage's favorite maxims was "Early to bed, early to rise, makes a man healthy, wealthy, and wise." Therefore, a loud pounding on the door in the wee hours of the morning filled his sleepy head with moral outrage.

He ignored the pounding. Whoever it was at this hour could only mean trouble. "Go away!" he shouted, but the pounding continued. The Gage home was situated on a bluff, not far from the Artemas Carter estate. Visitors rarely came during the day, never mind at night. He rolled over in his bed and covered his head with a goose-down pillow. The pounding continued. He groaned.

"Caleb! Seth! Answer the door. Confound those boys, they'd sleep through anything. Jonathan, answer the door, damn it!" The noise intensified, and he heard yelling. "All right, all right, I'm coming," he grumbled. Couldn't really fault the boys. All three had put in a hard day's work at the Chicago–Milwaukee Railroad and had earned an uninterrupted night of sleep.

He stumbled down the stairs in the dark, without lighting a candle. Whatever this was, he would dispose of it quickly. When he opened the door, a gust of wind and rain blew into the house. A flash of lightning illumined three bedraggled figures huddled on the steps.

"Who are you and what do you want at this hellish hour?"

"George Davis," said the man in the center, "First mate of the *Lady Elgin*. The *Lady's* down. We were in a small boat trying to repair the ship when she went down. The small boat was broken to pieces in the surf. Two of our number were killed."

"God's mercy, come in, come in. You look to be drowned."

Caleb, Seth, and Jonathan had awakened and lighted the house. Jonathan fetched blankets to warm the men, who stripped and wrapped the blankets around themselves. Davis's lips were blue. He rubbed his hands to get the circulation going.

"The *Lady* was rammed by a lumber schooner. Tonight and for the next few days bodies and wreckage will be floating in. God willing, there may be survivors. The accident occurred just a few miles offshore."

"Jonathan, run to the Stagecoach Inn and spread the news. Caleb, ride south to the Patterson Inn, and Seth, ride to the Chicago–Milwaukee Railroad station in Winnetka and tell them to telegraph the two cities. Get help and get back here as fast as you can. I'll head over to Artemas Carter's and arouse the other neighbors. We'll head down to the bluffs and try to get fires going along the shore."

"And we will join you," said Davis, whose teeth were chattering.

"Yes, eventually, but you need a rest. What happened to the lumber schooner?"

"She took off. Left the scene."

"What was her name?"

"The *Augusta*."

One o'clock in the morning was no hour to ride horseback on the bluffs of Winnetka, but Edward Spencer rode, ignoring the storm clouds brooding in a moonless September sky when he'd left the campus of Northwestern University. Edward's ritual midnight ride caused tongues to wag on campus. Where would a divinity student go in the middle of the night? Was he involved with a married woman, or, since he was not a lady's man, with another man? One rumor involved clandestine meetings with smugglers. There were dark whispers of covens and doing the work of the devil, whatever that may have entailed.

Edward's refusal to explain the matter added fuel to the fire. Truth disappoints. All Edward sought was inner peace. An insomniac, he couldn't sleep because he was consumed with doubt about his choice of vocation, worrying that his heart wasn't in it, that he couldn't live up to people's expectations. He kept it to himself because he was sure others wouldn't give weight to his concerns. He'd broached the subject to a few classmates, who dismissed him. "This is a problem? If you don't want to be a preacher, don't. We should have such problems."

It wasn't that simple. Unlike his peers, some of whom were poor as church mice, Edward was privileged. His parents were influential. He would move into an affluent parish right after ordination. They wanted him to become a preacher and were not interested in what he wanted. The faculty considered him a fair-haired boy, so capable that he assisted teaching underclassmen.

Senior students gave sermons at the campus church. The rhetoric of Edward's sermons was delivered with conventional oratorical style garnished with impressive theological words and phrases. He cultivated a soft-spoken manner and patronizing smile, not forgetting to say "praise God" and bow his head.

He didn't drink or smoke cigars, but he managed to seem a regular fellow by telling an occasional mildly risqué joke, never quite crossing the borders of propriety. A token listener, he nodded and responded in platitudes. He knew a prayer for every occasion.

But it was all surface. Deep within was a vacuum, an empty chamber where God rarely made an appearance. Strict parents provided abundantly for material needs, but measured love in proportion to achievement. "Don't ever be satisfied, son. However well you may do, there is always room for improvement."

The pressure to continue down a life path others had chosen for him was strong. He liked to please. He was not a rebel. The nagging feeling that he was on the wrong life path was what drove him out here at night, where he could be alone to think.

"Whoa! Whoa, there!"

Horse and rider were familiar with the bluffs at night, but the moon was hidden. The sheen of the lake and open sky provided limited visibility, but he kept the horse away from the edge. Aware of the danger of night cliff-riding, the danger was part of the appeal. He'd been protected all his life and usually chose the safe path, rarely encountering life-threatening situations or having his courage tested.

No matter what he did, it was never enough. What would be considered more than enough in the eyes of the world was not enough. Perfection itself was not enough. He came out here to ask himself soul-searching questions. He didn't know what he believed or even if he believed in God. How could he help others believe, if he didn't believe himself? Was he living a charade? He had to answer that within himself. He hadn't found the answer.

Perhaps he took himself too seriously. Getting away from others, riding out here, gave him time to reflect. Also, it made him tired, helping to cure the insomnia. He liked to empty his mind by staring across the lake, a stunning vision on a clear night. Tonight was not clear. He'd been unwise to venture out.

"Well, boy, it's time to go." Edward didn't know if he was talking to himself or the horse. The horse, having its own opinion, snorted. The rain was steady. Edward was soaked.

The moment the horse turned, a streak of lightning illumined the sky, revealing a sight that nearly stopped his heart. Floating in from the blackness was the debris of a wreck, such an amount of flotsam and jetsam that it could only have been made from a large ship. Heads were bobbing in the water and people were clinging to rafts created from broken pieces of ship. Surf pounded the beach. It wasn't hard to imagine what would happen when the rafts reached the breakers.

Help was needed as was equipment, such as ropes, torches, and stretchers, medical assistance, and a place to take survivors. If he rode the horse hard, he could make it to Northwestern in fifteen minutes. This was too big a disaster for him to handle alone. The faster he could ride, the more lives could be saved.

Horse and rider flew toward the campus. He didn't know the horse was capable of such speed, hooves barely touching the ground all the way. He rode right up to doors, banging, shouting, and spreading the alarm. Word got around that it was the *Lady Elgin*, the only ship of any size scheduled to pass by at that hour. Two underclassmen broke into the church and rang the bell. The clamor brought people to doors and windows. Led by Edward Spencer, students swarmed to the bluffs on foot and horseback.

Chapter Twenty-Two

THE SHIP WAS GONE. ONE moment it was there, and the next it was not. One moment they were on deck, and the next they were cast into a turbulent lake. It had happened so fast. Twenty people were huddled on a giant raft, formed by a section of superstructure that had remained intact. Lightning flashed, revealing a maelstrom that might have served as a backdrop for someone's worst nightmare. Other people were scattered over a wide area. It was impossible to see the full extent of it because of the waves. The raft riders couldn't see beyond the wave in front of them and the wave behind them.

Within range of what they could see were bits of wreckage, some large enough to serve as rafts for several people. Individuals clung to small pieces of debris. Others bobbed in the water, nothing holding them afloat but life jackets. Some distance ahead, near the crest of a wave, floated a piece of hurricane deck carrying five passengers. How many souls had already gone down with the *Lady Elgin*?

"Jack!" Flynn shouted into the abyss, over and over. "He was beside us when the ship sank. He was standing right there. Where is he now? Oh God. Jack! Jack!"

They crested a wave. As the big raft descended, several women screamed. Captain Wilson lay on the edge of the raft, reaching out to assist a swimmer. After an attempt that nearly resulted in Wilson being pulled into the lake, the man struggled aboard.

A middle-aged man who had occupied a stateroom gripped a wet prayer book and prayed intensely. Another man sat still on the big raft staring unseeing into space. The man had arrived on deck with his wife and baby too late to put them on the lifeboat. When the ship exploded, the baby disappeared from the wife's arms. Then the wife disappeared. The man knew he would never see either of them again.

The rafters saw a sight that cheered them momentarily. A man floated past clinging to an object not part of the ship. The object was a piano.

"Good luck, mister!"

"Play us a tune!"

"Know any sea chanteys?"

"See you on shore."

The man wouldn't make it to shore, Wilson thought. The piano was already partly submerged.

Jack was a strong swimmer and did not panic. He'd gotten a life jacket onto Flynn but not on himself. He removed his shirt and shoes. The cold water was exhilarating as he sliced through it, occasionally turning on his back and floating. Screams and calls for help filled the night air. Pieces of ship were drifting in the same direction, toward the shore. He couldn't swim that far, but he would find a piece of debris to hug. Maybe he'd find Maeve.

A large object, which appeared to be a section of the hull, floated toward him. He treaded water. The object was upon him. He reached for it. Suddenly a creature's head emerged and emitted a loud inhuman bellow. This was no debris. It was a bull, one of the animals destined for the Plankinton-Armour slaughterhouse.

It was too late to get out of the way. When they collided, a horn gored Jack's leg and became entangled in the material of his belt and trousers. Why hadn't he removed his trousers? The bull started to sink. Panic set in. Jack took a deep breath before they submerged. He struggled under water to free himself to no avail.

Bull and man rode down, down to the bottom of Lake Michigan, following the ghostly herd that had leaped from the *Lady Elgin*. As he met his destiny, Jack thought of Maeve, imagined he heard the harp and her musical laughter. Was this Maeve's magic bull of Coolie dragging him to his doom? The last thought he had was, *What happened to the spear—the spear of the warrior Cuchulain?*

Then he took a deep breath and the lake rushed into his body, turning all to blackness.

––––––––––––––––––

Keane's raft, a piece of the hurricane deck large enough for several people, was occupied by Keane alone. In spite of wind and wave, Keane stood upright. Let others cling, not he. He prided himself on his sense of balance. A blacksmith by trade, he was a landlubber who avoided ships but was not daunted by them. If anything, he lacked the proper respect an old salt would have under similar circumstances. He boasted of his sea legs and scorned people afflicted with *mal de mer*.

As the raft began its downward plunge into the valley of a wave, he slipped but caught himself, feeling a rush of adrenaline. Elated, he laughed deliriously as the raft began its upward climb. He loved danger. This was the way to live, on the edge.

Caution was an attribute his Fenian cohorts Fitzgerald, Monohan, and McNeill had to a fault. They didn't have his daring. Keane wanted to kill that English lord. He'd set out to Ingram's stateroom, gun in pocket. The plan was to knock on the door and shoot point-blank when the man answered. The collapse of the steamship thwarted him. He still felt the bulge of the pistol, where he had put it.

Carnage floated all around him, drifting landward. If he kept his head and his balance, he'd make it. The raft vibrated and listed. He fell and started to slide. Someone in the water was clutching the raft, trying to climb aboard. The top of a man's torso was on the raft, but the rest of him was in the water. The swimmer was unable to gain leverage.

"Please give me your hand. Help me."

"There's no room. Get off."

"Yes, there is. There's room for three or four. Please."

Keane was on the edge on all fours, a grim smile on his face. The man reached toward him, imploring. He stared back coldly. The man slipped off without a word and disappeared. "Sorry," Keane said, feeling a brief twinge of remorse. The word was carried off by the wind, so he shrugged. He remained on all fours until he regained his bravado. Then he struggled to his feet.

He was distracted by a floating object he couldn't identify. "Help!" a man shouted. The man was barely staying afloat. What was the object? It was a drum, the man a musician in the ship's band, a German. The man would drown, surely. That wasn't Keane's problem.

He drifted for a long time, finally tiring and sitting on the raft. Others were behind or ahead of him, but within the scope of his vision, he was alone. What seemed like hours passed. Lightning streaked the sky as he crested a wave. He saw lights blazing on a distant beach. He traversed three more waves. The beach was closer and crowded with rescuers holding torches. Bonfires were burning along the shore. Saved, he thought.

Then he noticed the surf and his momentary sense of well-being vanished. For the first time, he felt fear. Had he come this far only to be battered by surf? No, by God, he had not. He crouched, body leaned forward, ready to spring from his perch. He didn't need to be rescued. He would rescue himself. Before the raft crashed, he would leap. His superior sense of balance, his own equilibrium, would land him on his feet. Keane spread his arms and soared in like a bird in flight. Only three or four waves to go—

Suddenly he saw a man on the beach, a man he knew. It was the Englishman. The image drove all else from his mind. "Ingram! Ingram, you English bastard, this is for you!" He fumbled for the pistol and squeezed the trigger, producing a wet click. The raft hit the beach, and Keane flew off, whacking his head against the raft and slamming into shallow water, which pulled him back out. He floated back in before they noticed him. By the time they got to him, he was dead.

"Put it right there," the conductor was telling a passenger. The words triggered a rush of memories. Blevins had come home from school one day bloodied. Ma had said to Bill, "It's time to take your son in hand. Teach him how to defend himself." Trouble was, Bill wasn't skilled in the manly art, his sole experience being a barroom brawl from which he had to be carried home.

They went out behind the print shop for the lesson. Bill bobbed and weaved, jabbing his fists in the air, in the manner of a pugilist. Blevins stood still, scrawny arms dangling at his side, staring at his prancing dad.

"Hit me, son. Hit me as hard as you can. I dare you." He jutted out his face and lowered his guard. "Put it right there."

Blevins complied. His bare fist connected with the soft flesh of his father's nose. Bill stared in disbelief. Then he howled and covered his nose. Ma ran outside. When she saw Bill, she burst into laughter. The laughter was too much for Bill, who charged into the house. The lesson was over.

They hadn't seen Bill until at least one pint later, when he stumbled into the parlor full of contrition and corn liquor. "Good lad," he said, and clapped Blevins on the back. "You really put it over on your old man."

"Sorry, Dad."

"No, no. I told you to hit me, and you did. I didn't know you had it in you."

"I guess I'm my father's son." Everyone laughed.

The train was at the Winnetka station. It would be hours before the journey would resume. Blevins was bored, so he stepped out for a stretch. It was raining, so he stepped into the station house. He was stiff. The pain in his jaw reminded him of the boxing match with his father. That had been the one and only lesson. Nothing was mentioned again about Blevins not being able to defend himself.

After that, they always seemed to be in competition. As a child, Blevins worshiped his dad, a handsome, kind bear of a man who could do no wrong and was invulnerable. The boxing match had revealed a crack in the armor. Dad was discovered to be mortal, a revelation that all sons must learn about their fathers.

Blevins went into the station's water closet. Something about water closets on trains made him ill at ease. For one thing they were too small. For another, he didn't like urinating in motion. He was afraid the train would lurch, causing the door to fly open. It never occurred to him to lock the door. He returned from the water closet to a station bustling with activity. A telegrapher was frantically at work in the office, which was hardly normal at this hour. Blevins sensed a news story, so he entered the office.

"What's going on?" The white-haired telegrapher ignored Blevins and continued working. "I'm a reporter on my way to Milwaukee. Can you tell me what's going on?"

"Reporter, eh? Well, here's a story, son. You've heard of the *Lady Elgin*, luxury paddlewheel steamer. The *Lady*'s down. They're searching for survivors along the shores of Winnetka."

The giant raft plowed through the waves slowly, making poor headway. The storm had abated, but the sea was high. The rafters were silent, fear and despair in their faces. The man who had lost his wife and baby let out a sudden cry. Without warning, he leaped from the raft. In a moment, he was out of reach. "Isn't anyone going to do anything?" asked Flynn. The question was rhetorical. There was nothing anyone could do. They were forced to watch the man float away. The man with the prayer book crossed himself. "We are helpless," a woman cried. "Helpless."

They would never make it in that frame of mind. Captain Wilson had to do something to boost morale. In a way, it was fortunate that a large section of ship remained in one piece, thus saving more lives. The down side was that they were not saved yet, and a large group was more difficult to control. Control was vital at this point. The worst was yet to come when they tried to beach this juggernaut in high surf with twenty rafters aboard.

That is, if they reached the beach intact. The raft had taken a beating. It was some consolation that they hadn't gone down with the ship, He wondered how many had been killed in the explosion and guessed the number was high. A surge of anger consumed him when he thought of the *Augusta* and the inexplicable behavior of its captain. He thought about himself. It bothered him that he was alive and so many souls under his care were dead. Perhaps the reason was right here on this raft.

If they made faster headway, they would stand a better chance. The longer the raft took this punishment, the more likely it was to fall apart. He had a plan. It would give people hope, and it might even work.

"Listen to me. If we tear apart some of the raft's material, I, with your help and support, can rig a makeshift sail. We can take turns holding it against the wind. That will increase our speed. We may be able to fashion a rudder of sorts. The wind is blowing us toward shore. A sail and a rudder would put us in control. What do you say? Who will help?"

Flynn was the first to volunteer. Others came forward. Following Wilson's directions, they removed a door that dangled from the end of the raft. They stood the door upright against the wind. The captain,

Flynn, and two others held the makeshift sail and the raft picked up speed. Everyone cheered. A few even joked, their spirits revived.

Thank God, Wilson thought. "What about a rudder, Captain?" someone shouted. The question went unanswered. Just then, they sighted land.

Maeve and Captain Garrett Barry stayed afloat on the roof of the pilot house. Barry was silent for a long time, wishing that it was his son and not he who was there. Willie was gone, of that he was sure. *Brave lad*, he thought, his eyes clouded. *I wasn't the father that you deserved.* The raft was only a section of the roof, and the combined weight of the two rafters was sinking it. They weren't going to make it, not both of them.

"Do me a favor, if you reach the shore. Tell Mary that I love her dearly, that she was the one love of my life. Tell her Willie died trying to save the lives of others." It was not in Barry's nature to cry, but there was a catch in his voice. "You're a courageous woman. Hang on to this miserable block of wood. Remember, you're not alone. Hundreds are out here. Someone will find you. Help will arrive."

"I'm not alone, Garrett, if you're with me. You are with me, aren't you? What are you saying?"

"Together we'll sink for sure. One of us may have a chance. God be with you, Maeve. Take care of those two boys." Barry dived off the roof.

"Garrett! Garrett!" No voice answered. She was alone—never so alone. She thought of Jack. She knew in her heart that he was dead. Soon she would join him. Hadn't she dreamed it? In the distance, she imagined she saw the small boat with Brian and Liam aboard. She called their names. The boat was too far away and they didn't hear. Was it a vision? They were safe. They had to be safe.

Where was her harp? Then she remembered it was at the bottom of the lake. She imagined she could hear it and yearned to stroke it. The music was in her soul, the music of Moore's plaintive ballad.

> The harp that once through Tara's hall
> The soul of music shed,
> Now hangs as mute on Tara's walls
> As if that soul were fled.

She didn't see the wave—the third sister—that overturned the roof and flung her into eternity. Her last thought was of running barefoot along the strands of Dublin Bay.

———————————————

It happened just as rescue was in sight, fifty yards from the shore. The giant raft fell apart in front of the horrified eyes of rescuers. People fell into the water and disappeared, pulled back out by the undertow. Flynn fell between two of the pieces of raft and desperately clung to both. "Help … oh God, help." Captain Wilson, still on a piece of wood, leaped into the water to help Flynn. He swam a short distance and grasped one of her hands when he was struck by a piece of debris and vanished beneath it. Flynn let go of one piece and gripped the other, which hurtled toward the breakers. She closed her eyes, held on, and prayed.

She braced herself, waiting for a swift drop and massive shock, hoping it would be over with quickly. The shock did not come. Instead, her body floated upward, suspended in air. There was only one explanation. She was dead and had risen. Recalling no pain, she kept her eyes tightly shut until she realized she had been lifted and was being carried. Then she opened her eyes and looked up. An angel smiled down at her. The angel had a black face and a halo of white hair.

———————————————

Rescuers worked tirelessly through the night. Help continued to arrive, so much so that helpers were in each other's way. Not all came to help. Scavengers robbed bodies and made off with valuables that drifted ashore. One popular item was liquor, which would have grieved bartender Lacy, had he survived. The effort that began in a cove beneath the Gage and Carter estates spread over a five-mile area. Beach bonfires roared, turning night into day. Survivors were given warm food and taken into local homes. The closets of Gage and Carter were emptied to provide warm, dry clothes.

Linked by ropes to people on the beach, rescuers waded into the roiling surf, which hurled sharp, splintered shards of wood and heavy sections of broken ship at them. It was an unlikely community. Bible students, railroad workers, inn dwellers, rich old men, professors, old maids, and young wives worked together. When it was over, they would return to their own lives. The experience would change each of them.

Certain individuals stood out and would be remembered. The Gage brothers, returning home from spreading the news, organized volunteers. Each brother took a position at the far end of a rope. Artemas Carter, old as he was, entered the cold water, which came as no surprise to those who knew of his legendary bravado. What did come as a surprise was a mysterious black man accompanying Carter. None of the locals knew who he was. In stories told about that night, he is the Black Angel. He was everywhere at once, and when it was over, he disappeared.

The hero of the rescue was Edward Spencer, who leaped into the surf over and over, refusing relief. He retrieved eighteen bodies, some alive, some not. On his last trip, bloody from the battering of wreckage and delirious from a blow to the head, he was unable to reach a man and his wife who were on a piece of canvas and wood. Letting go of his rope, he swam to the couple, defying the surf and undertow, and dragged them ashore.

Once on shore, Spencer turned again toward the surf. He would have plunged back in, but he was restrained by classmates. "Edward, Edward, no. You must stop. You must." Spencer collapsed on the beach, sobbing, repeating the words that would become famous in local history. "Did I do my best? Did I do enough?"

Blevins arrived in a rockaway drawn by long-tailed bays that had been loaned by a local middle-class family to transport volunteers to the rescue area. The carriage, built to hold six to eight passengers, was crammed with twelve. The coach unloaded and headed back to town to pick up more volunteers.

Heart in mouth, he raced to the edge of a bluff and stared down into a corner of hell. Fire cast an eerie glow, revealing a row of bodies stretching the length of the beach. Debris filled the lake and the rescue work had slowed down.

"Flynn! Flynn!" The tortured voice came from a place deep within him that he did not recognize and no one seemed to notice.

"If she's down there, she won't be answering," said a man quietly. "Why don't you go down?"

Blevins ran down the path, falling twice before reaching the beach. The bodies had been positioned face up. There must have been twenty-five. It didn't take long for him to check because only three were women. Flynn was not among them.

"Up there," someone said, pointing to a steep path leading to the Carter estate. Just before he reached the path, he noticed an object gleaming in the sand, an object that looked familiar. He scooped it out of the sand and examined it closely. It was a gold locket, similar to the one he had given Flynn. That didn't mean anything. Gold lockets were common. He made the sign of the cross, as she had taught him to do. Hands shaking, he pried it open, letting out a cry when he saw his own face staring at him from inside.

St. Anthony was the patron saint of lost things. Flynn had lost her locket and now it was found. Blevins didn't know if he believed in saints. There was a time when he would have said that he did not. He said an intense prayer now to St. Anthony, and, just in case, to all the other saints whose names he hadn't learned.

Was she alive and safe? If the locket had reached shore, there was good chance that she had, too. Infused with hope, he didn't even notice the scrapes from rocks and bushes that bloodied him as he scrambled up the bluff. He was unprepared for the sight that confronted him at the top.

The vast lawn of Artemas Carter was littered with bodies. Hope fled when he saw the extent of it. Could she have survived this? There were so many—so many. He had to know, but he couldn't move, couldn't breathe.

"Blevins—"

Someone was speaking to him. Block it out. Block out the painful reality.

"Blevins."

Hearing her voice, he turned. In a second she was in his arms sobbing. He started to tell her about Jack. "Jack's gone," she said. "I know he's gone. Please don't talk. Just hold me." They clung together for a long time. There would be time to speak of Jack later. Jack. In an ironic way, he may have saved Blevins's life.

The Third Ward was deserted. Although it was Saturday, all places of business were closed. People who had not departed for Winnetka were in church praying or staying quietly at home. What was to have been a glorious homecoming celebration for the new volunteer Union Guard had become a day of anxiety and tragedy, as the dead and missing were identified. It was a day of disbelief. It seemed impossible that the *Lady Elgin* had gone down.

Dan O'Mara was among the first to arrive in Winnetka. Marion would not, could not, come. "I can't go, Dan. I can't face it. It's all turning out like my dream. Go. Find them, Dan. Bring home my little boy and girl. Maggie and I will stay here and pray. There is nothing more for us to do."

Dan had found Flynn right away. Blevins stayed in the background. They had decided to keep their marital status a secret for now. The family would have enough to do in dealing with the death of Jack O'Mara. Dan proceeded immediately to search the dead.

"Da, there is no need. Jack isn't there. I checked. I checked them all."

"I'll find him, darlin', I'll find him." Flynn tried to restrain him, but he brushed her away and continued to search.

"If it will make you feel better, do it."

"I promised your mother that I would bring both of you home." He stared blankly at several more uniformed bodies, then crossed to a bench and slumped onto it, controlling his grief as he had been taught a man must do. Flynn sat next to him and hugged him. Only then did his shoulders start to shake. He was unable to stifle a sob.

Mary did not expect to find Garrett alive. Her husband was a hero, self-sacrificing to a fault. There was no bitterness in the thought. That was the way he was. In a crisis, he would put others above himself. If he was there, she hoped to find him, to see him one last time. He wasn't there. She spent the most painful hour of her life looking into the young eyes of soldiers and closing some eyes that were open and staring.

There were no children on the lawn. The first thing she had done upon arrival was to search for Willie. A few children had come in on the lifeboat, including Brian and Liam, now orphans. They told Mary that Willie had not been in the boat with them. "Lost. My dear Willie. Oh God, it's my fault. If Garrett and I hadn't argued. If I hadn't insisted upon Willie's going. I killed him. I killed my son. I sent him to his death." Someone tapped her shoulder, and she turned.

"Mrs. Barry?"

"Yes."

"I am Sister Katherine, in charge of the nuns who are administering to the bereaved. Your husband, I believe, is among the missing."

"Yes, Sister. My husband and my son."

"I am so sorry, Mrs. Barry. This is a terrible tragedy. So many lives. I have something to ask you. It is asking a lot. If you can't do it, I will understand." Mary was silent, so the nun continued. "The bodies of these poor young men will be transported by train to Milwaukee within hours. Relatives will meet the train to take them home. It is so sad."

"How can I help?"

"There is a group of unidentified bodies over there." She indicated a meadow behind the estate. "All are uniformed guardsmen in your husband's brigade, men you know. If they remain unidentified, they will never get to Milwaukee. They will remain here in unmarked graves."

"You want me to help identify them."

"Yes."

"As you said, that is asking a lot."

"I understand." Sister Katherine moved away. "I am sorry for your trouble."

"But I will do it."

"Bless you. Are you sure?"

"Of course. Garrett would expect me to do it."

With a heavy heart, Mary went to the meadow. As she looked at each man, she saw Garrett's face. She forced herself to continue, unaware of the tears streaming down her face. In the distance, she noticed Father Delaney talking to Brian and Liam. The poor dears, where was their mother? By the time she had looked at the last soldier, she couldn't have looked at another. Altogether, she'd been able to identify only five.

"I'm sorry."

The nun put an arm around Mary's waist and led her to the steps of the Carter home, where she collapsed. She sat a while, head spinning, emotions churning. She thought she was going to be sick. Then she heard a voice above her, a gentle voice.

"I'm sorry for your trouble, Missus Mary."

Only one person in the world called her Missus Mary. "Ned. Oh, Ned, Ned." Without regard for appearances, she let him enfold her in his strong, old arms.

Chapter Twenty-Three

"HELLO, JIM," SAID FRANKLIN HARTE, manager of the Milwaukee Depot where the trainload of bodies arrived. "Sad business, eh?"

"What's the count?"

"I don't know. One hundred bodies on the train, tagged and ready for delivery. Nearly that many unclaimed dead buried at Winnetka. Who knows how many went down with the *Lady* or will wash up during the next few weeks?"

"That the best you can do?"

"Complete passenger list was never found, so anyone's guess is as good as anyone else's."

Jim didn't like that. He didn't like guesswork. Jim Trapper was agent for the fledgling Northwestern Mutual Life, headquartered in Milwaukee. News of the disaster had caused panic in the downtown office. Northwestern Mutual was an up-and-coming firm, but a huge mass payoff would sink the company as fast as the *Augusta* sank the *Lady Elgin*.

"Could I ask a favor, Franklin? Could I see a roster of the dead on the train?"

Franklin hesitated. The favor was against regulations, but Jim Trapper was a good sort and well liked. He'd give you the shirt off his back, Jim would, and was a supporter of the community. Wherever folks needed help, you'd find Jim. His wife, Joan, was the daughter of a local horse dealer. A respected midwife, she had delivered many of the young soldiers whose bodies were on the train.

"I guess there'd be no harm. Only for a moment, mind you."

As relatives began the grim task of claiming the dead, Jim compared the roster with his own list of policy holders. To his utmost relief, only a few were insured by his company. It was unlikely that the bodies now buried at Winnetka would ever be identified. Others might surface during the weeks to come, but it wouldn't amount to anything the company couldn't handle. Franklin was scrutinizing him, sensing what Jim was thinking.

"Any of them yours?"

"Only a few. Although I'm relieved, to be sure, I take no pleasure in the fact. I know these people and have several close friends among them. I do hope they are insured. If not, there will be much hardship with the grief."

"Will you attend the wakes?"

"There are so many families."

"Ah, indeed. Due to the number, several group wakes will be held, at different times. You'd be welcome, you know, you and the missus, God bless her. We Irish are noted for hospitality, even in troublesome times. Especially in troublesome times. Only one fella wouldn't be welcome."

"And who might that be?"

"Captain Darius Malott, damn his soul to hell."

The truth of it was, Malott was exonerated by his peers. The hearing found him blameless. If Captain Wilson had survived to carry out his threat to track Malott and seek justice, things might have turned out differently. Wilson's body was found three days after the sinking of the ship. It floated to shore on the coast of Indiana and was returned to its final resting place near his farm in Coldwater, Michigan. The *Chicago Daily Press Tribune* printed the obituary:

> In all these years there has lived no man who could declare that he ever betrayed a trust, or deserted a friend, or proved faithless to duty. With a great, generous heart, a clear, warm hand, thorough sailor and all in all a man.

In the eyes of maritime law, Darius Malott had broken no rule. The case resulted in the forming of a study group that eventually changed the rules of night navigation regarding the amount of lights a ship must display, but in the year 1860 the *Augusta* was legal. The question was never raised as to how the *Augusta* could have missed seeing the lights of the *Lady Elgin.* The hearing accepted Malott's explanation of why he left the scene. He thought the *Augusta* was seriously damaged and his first duty was to his own ship and crew. There was disagreement within the hearing committee regarding the latter. Some wanted to hold Malott responsible, but they were persuaded that this was a moral and not a legal issue.

Not so, in the eyes of the public. The Irish called Malott a murderer. In the Third Ward he was a pariah. He was relieved of his command. The *Augusta* was painted black and renamed. One day the ship pulled in to Milwaukee under its assumed name. The ruse was discovered and a gang of Irishmen marched toward the ship with murder in their minds and arson in their hearts. The new captain hauled anchor and was underway before the gang arrived. The ship never again scheduled Milwaukee as a port of call.

Malott was haunted by the *Lady Elgin.* Bad luck followed him. He continued to work for Bissell and Davidson. In 1864 he was given command of the company's flagship, the *Major.* On September 8, the *Major* disappeared on Lake Michigan. That day was the last day anyone ever saw the *Major* or Captain Darius Malott. It was four years to the day from the sinking of the *Lady Elgin.* It was also Malott's thirty-first birthday.

In May 1861, after Lincoln's inauguration, Stephen Douglas addressed the Illinois legislature.

"That the present danger is imminent no man can conceal. If war must come—if the bayonet must be used to maintain the Constitution—I can say before God my conscience is clear. I have struggled long for a peaceful solution of the difficulty. I have not only tendered those states what was theirs of right, but I have gone to the very extreme of magnanimity. The return we receive is war, armies marched upon our capitol, obstructions and dangers to our navigation, letters of marque to invite pirates to prey upon our commerce, a concerted movement to blot out the United States from the map of the globe.

"The question is, are we able to maintain the country of our fathers, or allow it to be stricken down by those who, when they can no longer govern, threaten to destroy?"

Stephen Arnold Douglas died a month later, on June 3, 1861. The last words he spoke to Adele were instructions to his children. "Tell them to support the Constitution and the laws. A man cannot be a true Democrat unless he is a loyal patriot."

London: 1861

HE STOOD ON THE EMBANKMENT, puffing on a calabash he had purchased for a modest sum at a tobacco shop in Soho. The tobacco was sweet. Contentedly, he watched the boats sailing up and down the Thames. Above the river loomed the Tower Bridge, symbol of that bastion of horror, the Tower of London, with its menacing, ever-present ravens. How many heads had rolled? What malevolent instruments had been used over the years to torture prisoners? Bloody lot, the British. He should know. They paid him well enough.

He reached into his pocket for a scone, which he crumbled and scattered to the pigeons. Killing Feeney had been necessary. Murder had not been part of his assignment, but Feeney had learned that he was a British agent. It had been easy enough, after all. The spear of Cuchulain, left behind by Jack O'Mara, was standing in the corner of the room.

He had driven the spear through Feeney's back. It was all so easy. Feeney, who sat peering out the window with his telescope, hadn't even seen him coming. The money had been a bonus, sitting there on the table where Feeney had been counting it before something outside had caught his eye. The money had made Lugh a rich man. Now, here he was in London, hiding from the Brotherhood and living like a lord.

"Mr. Finnegan," a voice said, "Mr. Lugh Finnegan." The soft voice had a Gaelic lilt. He turned. The man wore a trench coat and a felt hat. "This is for Feeney," he said.

They were the last words Lugh Finnegan heard before the bullet ripped through his brain and knocked his body into the Thames. The pigeons on the embankment continued to nibble on the crumbs he had left for them.

Donegal: 1867

IT WAS THE YEAR OF the Fenian Rising. Fenians attacked police barracks in rural Irish towns in a doomed attempt to drive out the British. Much of the rising was concentrated in Cork and Kerry, and one of its leaders was a defrocked priest who had returned after fifteen years in Milwaukee.

The same year, in County Donegal, two young men stood atop Ben Bulben.

"That's it, then?"

"Yes. That's what we came so far to see."

There it was, the Mound of Maeve, which their mother had described to them so many times. The mountain was shrouded in mist, yet the area surrounding the mound was clear, illumined by a mysterious source of light.

"She's there."

"Yes."

They stood there for a long time, Brian and Liam, the moisture in their eyes more than mist. One laid flowers on the mound. Then the brothers walked hand in hand down the mountain. Somewhere behind them came the voice of Cuchulain, echoing across Donegal and out to sea.

Caw! Caw!

A Historical Perspective

This is a work of fiction, based on actual events. Most of the details involving the *Lady Elgin* tragedy are factual. Captain Wilson of the *Lady Elgin* and Captain Malott of the *Augusta* were real persons whose fates were as depicted. Edward Spencer, the Northwestern University divinity student, did save eighteen people and utter the words, "Did I do enough?" There is a statue of him in Winnetka and a plaque honoring him hangs in the gymnasium at Northwestern University. Spencer's injuries suffered in the rescue left him confined to a wheelchair. In 1924, Ensign Edwin Young penned a hymn inspired by Spencer's heroism. He titled it, "Have I Done My Best for Jesus." Spencer died in California in 1917. His obituary in the *Los Angeles Times* attributed his death "directly due to the hardships of that wild day." Artemas Carter may or may not have been an abolitionist, but he did play a part in the rescue. Bodies were buried on his property, and reinterred later in Milwaukee.

Captain Garrett Barry, a West Point classmate of Ulysses S. Grant and several Civil War generals for both the Union and Confederacy, perished on the *Lady Elgin,* as did his son Willie and most of the soldiers in the Union Guard. There have been numerous estimates regarding the number of casualties, anywhere from three hundred to five hundred total. It is generally considered to be the worst disaster, in terms of lives lost, on open water in the maritime history of the Great Lakes.

Mary Barry was pregnant when the *Lady Elgin* went down. She gave birth to another girl, naming her Garritta, presumably after Garrett. The bodies of Garrett and Willie were eventually recovered and are buried in Milwaukee.

The tragedy decimated the Irish population of Milwaukee. More than one thousand children were made orphans. There were political ramifications. Stephen A. Douglas lost the election. The loss of the Third Ward certainly contributed to that. Eventually, the German population outnumbered the Irish and became a stronger force in Milwaukee politics.

That Fenians may have infiltrated the Union Guard is conjecture on my part, but not without foundation. The IRB was alive and well in the late 1850s, founded by James Stephens, who appointed John O'Mahony leader of the Brotherhood in America. The main activity was raising money for guns for a rising in Ireland that did take place in 1867. The IRB was a precursor to the IRA and the Irish Revolution.

As to Feeney's plan to invade Canada, outrageous though it may seem, there was a real plan, proposed by Fenian William R. Roberts in a power struggle with John O'Mahony. In May 1866, Fenians, using American guns and ammunition, invaded Canada with a force of six hundred men, skirmishing with Canadian volunteers and retreating before the main Canadian forces arrived. The Fenians escaped back across the border, and nothing more came of the incident.

In Celtic lore, Cuchulain of Ulster single-handedly defeated the army of Maeve, Queen of Connaught. An account of this may be found in the epic poem "The Cattle Raid of Coolie." Unlike Jack and Maeve in my novel, there was no love lost between the two. There really is a mound on top of Ben Bulben called the Mound of Maeve, where the ancient queen is said to be buried.

There is a statue of Cuchulain in the General Post Office in Dublin, site of the 1916 Easter Rebellion. A large crow is perched on his shoulder, a crow said to have accompanied him whenever he went into battle.

In recent years, public interest in the *Lady Elgin* has been rekindled, and parts of the ship have resurfaced, thanks to the efforts of Harry Zych, a diver who spent much time and money finding the exact location of the wreck. A prolonged court battle with the state of Illinois finally resulted in Mr. Zych receiving salvage rights. Many artifacts resurfaced, including the rifles. As of this writing, a group in Milwaukee is raising money to erect a monument to commemorate the sinking of the *Lady Elgin*.